André Jute was  the United State racing driver, act tions consultant a to artist Rosalind Pain-Hayman and they have a son, Charles, who travels with them in search of locations. They live in Adelaide, Australia and County Cork, Eire.

By the same author

Reverse Negative
Festival
Eight Days in Washington
The Zaharoff Commission
Sinkhole

ANDRÉ JUTE

Iditarod

GRAFTON BOOKS

A Division of the Collins Publishing Group

LONDON GLASGOW
TORONTO SYDNEY AUCKLAND

Grafton Books
A Division of the Collins Publishing Group
8 Grafton Street, London W1X 3LA

A Grafton Paperback Original 1990

ISBN 0-586-20619-1

Printed and bound in Great Britain by
Collins, Glasgow

Set in Times

For
LINDA

Should I be allowed
to coin only one word,
it would be

lindavan (lin'-da-van'), n, *Lit. sl.,* a
writer's friend-at-court [name of person]

Contents

5
Countdown

Out of the dreaming past, with its legends of steaming seas and gleaming glaciers, mountains that moved and suns that glared, emerges this creature, man – the latest phase in a continuing process that stretches back to the beginning of life. He is the heritage of all that has lived; he still carries the vestiges of snout and fangs and claws of species long since vanished; he is the ancestor of all that is yet to come.

Do not regard him lightly – he is you.

Don Fabun: The Dynamics of Change

4

Skull Mountain

Though she was too close to the mountains to look up at them, Rhodes was very much aware of their massive presence. Once, at college in California, a roommate told her, 'You're lucky to live in the shadow of the Rockies.' But she never thought of them as the Rocky Mountains or even as the constituent parts locally of the range that bisects Colorado: the Park Range in the north, the Sawatch Range and the Sangre de Christo Mountains running alongside the Rio Grande, and, on the other side of the river in the southeastern part of Colorado, the San Juan Mountains. Mount Elbert and Pike's Peak were grand enough for her, and the thousand-and-one trails to unnamed peaks, along gullies where the snow did not melt from one year to the next, in valleys and on slopes where a hundred hikers could pass without crowding each other, out of sight or shout. The year she was twelve, she and her father had ridden horseback all the way to Albuquerque, following a trail her great-grandfather had opened with a drive – legend now had it – of thirty thousand cattle. As she rode the runners of her sled, driving her dogs flat out around the base of Skull Mountain for Atlas Gap, she tried to imagine controlling thirty thousand cattle.

When the whirring sound of skis sliding very quickly over deep but not very hard snow interrupted her thoughts, she looked up towards the high snowdrift to her right to see the skier already irretrievably in the air, heading straight for her head, his mouth open to shout at her as her own opened to shout at him. Her foot hovered over the snowbrake but, if she slowed the sled, he would crash into the two large concrete blocks she carried in the basket of the sled for ballast or, worse, into her dogs. There was no time left for her to jump.

The skier flung his arms wide as he threw his lethal poles away, spread his legs to carry his skis past her sides, and crashed into her with his trunk, ripping her from the sled and into the loose downside snow, where they rolled in flailing embrace, pushing a wave of snow before them against which they finally came to rest. All this took long enough for the dog team to swing around and catch up with them. The two humans lay for a moment, panting, then the skier raised his arm to disentangle himself from Rhodes. Toots, her team leader, thinking he was renewing what the dog must have seen as an attack on her mistress, bit his wrist, let go momentarily and, as the hand swung, grabbed it and dug in for good purchase to hang on through blows and shouts from the skier until Rhodes took hold of the dog's harness and prised her jaws apart to give the stranger back his wrist. He backed hastily away from the barking, snarling pack of dogs straining towards him.

'Sorry!' Rhodes shouted up from where she held the gangline down near the trampled snow. And 'Sorry!' again, raising her voice over the dogs' hubbub.

He looked up from tying his scarf around his bloodied wrist. 'If my wrist doesn't heal in six weeks flat, sports lovers in every State will vote you Most Unpopular Woman.'

Rhodes very nearly ordered him off their land but the Delaneys had always allowed free access to anyone who did not carry firearms, left no litter, and put out campfires properly. Before she could frame another answer, he bent to feel the fixings of his skis, zigzagged to pick up his poles without any break in his gathering momentum, and

11

sped down the hill. Rhodes shook her head and led her dogs back onto the trail to continue practice.

By that evening Rhodes had forgotten the incident. It was Dona Ana's birthday; the widow of a long-dead chargehand, she was Harvey Mannesman's housekeeper. Harvey owned the big ranch next to the small one operated by Rhodes's father, he was her father's best friend and his daughter Margery had been Rhodes's best friend since she could remember: the Mannesmans were almost family. It was one of the comforting, immutable rituals of their lives that on Dona Ana's birthday both families took the housekeeper to dinner at the country club. Dona Ana was the only mother Margery had ever known (her own had died in childbirth) and a surrogate for Rhodes, who had lost her mother when she was seven and who was in and out of the Mannesman home like her own. The ritual birthday dinners had started when she and Margery were little girls, sent home from the country club at six o'clock: Dona Ana's birthday was the one day in the year they were allowed to stay. Only Dona Ana's tightly drawn gray bun rose much above five feet but at seventy she still stood ramrod-straight and radiated, as always, the indomitable dignity with which she had controlled two unruly girls from the time Rhodes outgrew her at twelve – even the petite Margery at fourteen was taller than Dona Ana – until they left for college. These affairs had a routine and an order by now grown ironbound: Rhodes's father would drop them and, while he parked the car, Harvey would see the women to their table in the diningroom and leave them there while he reserved a billiard table on which he and Paul Delaney could play before dinner. Once upon a time, Dona Ana had used this breather to warn the girls not to become 'es-juberant' and to allow them each a half-glass of sherry; now Margery and Rhodes would press a second aperitif on the

12

old lady they held dear. It was at this point that Lorette Tremayne stopped at their table.

'Dona Ana, Margery, Rhodes,' she greeted them politely. 'I'd like you to meet James Whitbury, who's staying with us for a couple of weeks.'

Rhodes saw Margery suppress a flash of irritation at this intrusion into an intimate family affair. But Lorette couldn't know, Rhodes thought and rose smiling. Her eye fell on the man's lace cuffs ruffling halfway down his hands from the sleeves of his dinner jacket. That's funny, she thought, Lorette usually prefers the brawny sporting types. As she offered her hand, she saw the rugged face, incongruous above the effeminate shirt.

'How'd you do, Mr Whitbury.'

Recognition illuminated his smile. 'Why, it's Dog Woman!'

Surprised, Rhodes squeezed his hand harder than she intended, at the same time as Margery murmured, 'How dull. "Bitch Goddess" is so much more distinguished.'

At this, Rhodes laughed and simultaneously James Whitbury jerked his hand back so that the ruffles flew up and framed the bandage on his hand and wrist they were obviously intended to cover. He also howled in pain, 'Eeehowww!' and grabbed his hurt hand in the other one to stem the pain – and he danced on the spot, oblivious to the other diners who stared, then looked away, embarrassed.

Before Rhodes could apologize, James said furiously, 'Do me a favor and stick to cooking or mending or something, just until after the Winter Olympics, will you. After that you can conquer the world all you want.'

'He's a skier,' said Lorette, 'he's going to win a gold medal.'

Rhodes clamped her lips shut and sat down.

Everyone ignored Lorette. They had been friends at

13

school, the 'three girls most likely to . . .', Lorette, Margery and Rhodes. Then Rhodes had gone West to college on her scholarship, Margery to New York to make her name as a writer, Lorette to finishing school in Switzerland. Rhodes had returned to work on Fairplay, the ranch she would one day inherit, and to race sled dogs. Margery published a book of acerbic short stories to ecstatic reviews and sales just large enough for her publishers to commission the 'big novel' she was now writing in a small whitewashed room on her father's ranch. Lorette, suitably 'finished', returned to work at inheriting her mother's place as the arbiter of the Blue Book, Denver society's form sheet. Lorette, though too well bred for her essential lack of intelligence ever to be manifest, naturally assumed her friends would help. But Margery recognized only one natural order of superiority, that of the intellect, and Rhodes was hard put to hide her distaste for the frantic round of false gaiety in which Lorette tried to involve her. Sometimes Rhodes felt sorry for Lorette.

Margery said, in the same casual tone she had used for her remark about grades of dogs, 'Rhodes may be too superior to respond to your gratuitous slurs, Mr Whitbury, but I'm not. Anything you can do, Rhodes can do better.'

'Margery!' Rhodes knew her friend too well to be deceived by Margery's light smile.

James Whitbury, rubbing his sore hand, missed the sudden tension. 'Yes, I'm sure she's a demon downhill racer.'

'Are you challenging her?'

'Hey, this is childish!' At last he looked up to see Margery's sweetest smile. 'I only pick on people my own size.'

Rhodes, fair to a fault, thought, Margery's sitting down

14

and he can't see she's not too tall and there's no way he can know how sensitive she is about it. (Margery had once told a glassy-eyed chat show host: 'Napoleon revenged himself for being small by firing cannon. I don't have cannon but I do have my brain and I can type with two fingers. If you're lost for words, you could call me the bitch-Napoleon of the word processor.')

But Margery thought fairness weak. Her smile dripped saccharine. 'Don't worry, nobody will call you a big bad bully.'

'Margery, that's enough,' Rhodes said.

James sighed. 'If she skis that well, why haven't I met her before?'

'Ah, but the *challenged* chooses the weapons, not so, Mr Whitbury?' Before he could protest that he had been trapped, Margery returned to the attack. 'Don't worry. I'm sure Rhodes will choose something you can relate to, say another winter sport, won't you, Rhodes?'

'Well – ' Rhodes was about to say they would let him off as a courtesy to a visitor but then she saw James Whitbury raise an eyebrow at her and thought, He expects me to chicken out. Impulsively, she said, 'All right. The Iditarod.'

Rhodes saw the shock on Margery's face. Margery didn't race dogs herself but her father did and she was constantly in the company of dog sled racers: she knew the Iditarod is the musher's ultimate dream, as tantalizingly unattainable as Mecca.

'The Iditarod,' Margery breathed. 'Twelve hundred miles running behind your dog sled across barren Alaska and into the Arctic shadow – through the life-sapping storms, howling blizzards, thirty- and forty- and fifty-below zero temperatures, over treacherous slippery mountain passes where the sun never reaches, on frozen rivers where a moment's exhausted mind-wandering can drop you forever into the freezing torrent under the ice, past the enraged bull moose and the ravenous bears and the world's largest, hungriest wolf packs.' Margery positively glowed with her recital of the dangers of the Iditarod.

(Later, she would tell Rhodes she had expected her to challenge James Whitbury to a twenty-five-mile sprint right there in Colorado the next day or week, a race he could not possibly train for, and for which his hand would not have healed – a race he would stand no chance of finishing, never mind winning. 'This time,' Margery would tell Rhodes, 'your sense of fair play will be *fatal*. The Iditarod, Jesu Christu!')

Lorette's mouth opened with an audible pop.

'Quite,' James said. 'The Iditarod is a big jump from racing sled dogs in Colorado,' he added judiciously.

His unruffled tone infuriated Margery all the more. 'Frightened by Nature except in small, manicured doses, Mr Whitbury?'

'No,' he replied shortly, understanding at last that Margery's perfect smile glistened stilettos. He ignored Lorette's restraining hand on his elbow and turned to address Rhodes directly. 'A rookie stands no chance of winning the Iditarod, so let's make it first home between the two of us.'

Rhodes had thrown in the Iditarod in the hope that everyone should immediately see this whole business as too ludicrous for words and burst out laughing. Instead she too was now trapped. She would never tell anyone, not even her father or Margery, that only in that moment had even the *possibility* of competing in the Iditarod ever entered her mind. To her vast amazement, she heard herself say, 'All right. First of us into Nome wins.'

'Done,' he said briskly. 'I bet ten thousand dollars I beat you.'

16

'Oh no, you don't,' Rhodes said hotly. 'You can't push me out just because I don't have that kind of money. No bets!' That, she thought in a cooler part of her mind, will be the first problem: finding the money the race itself will cost; I have only a year to raise a huge amount – less really, because I must set aside several months for training.

He was taken aback. His hands rose, the incongruous lace ruffles falling away from the bandage. 'I'm sorry. I –'

Rhodes saw Margery's lower lip tense in anticipation: she too expected James Whitbury to commit the further gaffe of saying that he had assumed any friend of the Mannesmans and Tremaynes was also wealthy. But –

'I'll take the bet,' Harvey Mannesman boomed behind him. 'How much?'

'Ten thousand,' Margery said, adding dutifully, 'My father, Harvey Mannesman. Dad, this is James Whitbury.'

Harvey stood over six feet, as tall as the younger man, and weighed over three hundred pounds, very little of it middle-age spread. He put out his huge muscled paw but James jerked his injured hand behind his back and retreated a step. Harvey mistook the gesture. 'My word not good enough for you?' he asked in his most danger-ous, softest voice. Harvey Mannesman exuded good cheer – until he lowered his voice, then he frightened the hell even out of bankers he owed.

'Maybe he wants your marker,' Margery added fuel to her father's temper.

Harvey was already reaching for his wallet.

'Of course your word is good, Mr Mannesman,' James said hurriedly. 'My hand got cut up by the hounds of hell of Wolf Woman here.' He gestured at Rhodes and the lace once again fell away from the bandages. To Lorette

17

he said, 'No wonder your father never once wore this bloody shirt.' He made a slight bow of the head to Dona Ana and said, 'Con permisso, Dona Ana,' and, nodding at the others, turned towards his own table to hold Lorette's chair.

Lorette hesitated but, unable to frame a suitable reproach, merely shook her head at Margery, said 'Tch, tch!' and followed James.

Dona Ana said, 'A man who is courteous to older women always turns out well in the end.'

'It's all a bit beyond Lorette,' Margery said unrepentantly as Rhodes's father came in from the car park.

'What's beyond Lorette?' Paul Delaney asked. He was a tall, slender man and, though just over fifty, he had been whitehaired since his wife's death sixteen years before. He always spoke quietly but people listened when he spoke. Rhodes had inherited her reserve, taste for privacy, and dignified bearing from him, and her spectacular Irish beauty from her mother.

'Those lumberjacks she insists on going with,' Harvey told him. 'The latest has more money than sense. He just bet me ten thousand dollars he beats Rhodes next Saturday. Our drinks are waiting in the billiard room.'

'Not Saturday's race,' Rhodes put the record straight. 'The Iditarod. I'm racing him in the Iditarod.'

Both men sat down heavily, their billiards forgotten.

3
Isle Royale

In 1974, two years before Rhodes put aside her dolls in favor of sled dogs, rangers on Isle Royale in Lake Superior were worried. The island was then, as now, a big tourist attraction for Americans and Canadians who came for periods ranging from day-trips to fortnight-long camping and hiking tours. Isle Royale was highly regarded not only by the visitors, but by tour operators, the managers of other tourist attractions and even, unusually, by conservationists. For visitors the island geography of the site combined with intelligent management of the flora and fauna to make both uniquely accessible. None went away without seeing some animal and many glimpsed animals that anywhere else were seldom seen in their natural habitat. Word of mouth spread the fame of Isle Royale and tour operators and travel agents understood the commercial sense of giving customers what they wanted. The managements of other tourist attractions were keen to discover how a facility becomes so popular that it is necessary to ration visitors to it . . . Conservationists were impressed with both the range and the tameness of the animals on Isle Royale: that the animals bred was proof of intelligent management, that the animals were tame was a clear signal of close control by the rangers and the total exclusion of human predators.

What worried the rangers on Isle Royale in 1974 was their very success, in particular their success with their wolves. Originally, years before, there had been no wolves on Isle Royale. Then a pair swam ashore, seeking refuge from mainland hunters. Opinion differs as to whether they came from Canada or Michigan; if from Michigan, they must have been the last wolves from that State, very probably the last wolves outside a reserve in the lower forty-eight. No other animal had ever been hunted with such brutal persistence. The result was predictable: extinction.

Men cannot mollycoddle wolves driven by other men to the limits of their endurance, and the rangers of the time were too wise in the ways of the wild to overdo care and attention to their new charges, but they did everything possible to make them welcome and to protect their growing yet fragile sense of security. Their success was soon manifest: the pair of wolves bred! As wolves will invariably choose not to breed unless they can confidently expect to provide their offspring with both food and security, the rangers considered the cubs a vote of confidence. Over a couple of decades the nuclear family of wolves grew into a pack, hunting deer and being killed by deer, dying of natural causes, breeding, raising cubs, learning and adapting to their environment. The rangers were part of the environment, but an unobtrusive background part.

In the foreground, from Spring through Fall, were other humans, the campers and hikers and day-trippers, walking, sleeping, eating at the picnic tables, putting leftovers into the dustbins provided . . .

At first the wolves dug into the dustbins when the people had gone. Humans were wasteful animals and there was much to eat, new tastes the wolves came to prefer.

Soon enough the bolder wolves, the alpha leader and his two beta lieutenants, found that people would throw them scraps of food. They would grab the food and retreat to eat it at a safe distance. Of course the warier members of the pack, the mass of omegas, wanted a share

20

of the booty brought back and would fight for it. People offered no fight, so the alpha and the betas took to eating scraps where they caught them. In time the omegas learned there was no threat from the humans and came closer. To be certain of the choicest bites the alphas and betas had to approach even closer, still without threat from the humans. By small steps the final two generations of wolves on Isle Royale arrived next to the picnic tables, eating from the hands of tourists.

The visitors were delighted, but the rangers saw the wolves beg ever more aggressively and wondered how long it would be before the pack picnicked on a visitor. It was not a risk they could long entertain and, when a family from Atlantic City was driven into a tree, abandoning their midday meal to the wolves, the rangers had to act. Certainly neither the Michigan nor Canadian farmers wanted the wolves back and two attempts at netting them for zoos failed. With the July 4th peak of the tourist season approaching, in late June the rangers reluctantly started shooting the wolves. The youngest wolves fell on the first day, most of the rest on the second and third days. After that the wolves hid from the rangers. One ranger, Bob Deal, thought that – since none of the wolves alive in 1974 had ever been shot at – even the highly intelligent wolves could not adapt almost overnight to such a novel circumstance without the guidance of a genetic memory of men hunting their ancestors. The other rangers laughed uneasily, practical men unhappy with mumbo-jumbo but unable to offer an alternative explanation.

By July 1st the rangers had accounted for every wolf but one, a male in his prime named Big Jim. A concerted drive by every ranger on the island finally cornered Big Jim but he could swim – and was last seem swimming strongly northwards, tail contemptuously high above the water. The last shot from the shore severed the tip of his tail. Then he disappeared into the gathering dusk.

Over a period of years, a lone wolf missing the tip to his tail was sighted running northwestwards across Ontario, Saskatchewan, Alberta and a corner of the Northwest Territory, until he found a single female in the Yukon Territory and started a pack of his own. Pressed by existing packs already on the territory, Big Jim, his mate, and their first litter travelled on into Alaska. By the time Big Jim died of blood poisoning from a beaver bite, the troupe had increased by two more litters; there were several couples of mating age – and they *would* mate, because they had established a rich territory of their own, contested by no other wolves, and could offer their offspring both security and food. In addition to a secure territory Big Jim left his descendants a confused jumble of genetic memories – among others, of humans hunting them mercilessly, of humans being harmless providers of food – which would, in time and when prompted by exterior circumstances, inexorably lead them to intersect critically with racers on the Iditarod Trail.

2
Celebrity

Rhodes doubted she could ever account logically for what
happened next: true, there was a clear sequence of events,
but the motivational links were missing and what was left
was base and irrational, offensive to her intelligence and
distasteful to her sense of propriety and privacy. First
reporters reminded James, in the press conference immediately after he won his Olympic gold medal, that he had
almost not passed the necessary medical. He told the
reporters 'a lady called Toots who lives below Skull
Mountain in Colorado' had almost wrecked his chance of
even making the team, never mind triumphing over strong
opposition. He held up his wrist for the television cameras; the scars were still red and angry, hardly healed.
Carelessly (Margery was certain he did it on purpose) he
neglected to explain Toots was a dog. James Alderston
Whitbury III was wealthy, of impeccable standing in the
Social Register, the latest hero of a sports-mad nation,
and it no doubt helped that he was young and personable
and single. That a woman had gnawed his wrist so
savagely to keep him to herself, to keep him from his
destiny of an Olympic Gold, to keep him from providing
the thrill two hundred and fifty million Americans
expected, was almost a bigger media event than his victory
on the slopes and certainly promised a more lasting thrill,
more column-miles. All this Rhodes could understand
rationally as that excess which is the price of free speech,
of democracy. But emotionally she considered it the kind
of misfortune that befell others, unfortunates and exhi-
bitionists. The reporters and their supporting photographers and cameramen arrived at the ranch in a crowd and

immediately started jostling each other and Rhodes, importuning her, flashing lights in her eyes, thrusting microphones aggressively at her face. Rhodes stood stunned until a recognizable sentence emerged from the braying:

'Hey, Tootsie, show us the teeth you gnawed James Whitbury with, huh.'

Then she lost her temper, though none of the reporters were sensitive enough to notice. 'Wait,' said Rhodes, 'and I will send Toots to you.' She turned on her heel and disappeared into the house.

Margery remained on the porch. She held up her hands for silence. 'You really are scum,' she said pleasantly to the reporters. 'But I'll put you straight all the same. *Rhodes* did not bite James Whitbury. Her *dog* Toots did. And now you're about to meet Toots face to face. Enjoy yourselves.' And Margery too slipped into the house as the dogs, released from their kennels at the back of the house by Rhodes, came racing around the corner.

They were working dogs rather than lapdogs, certainly not pets, but they were used to people (Rhodes drove them into town once a week in winter for groceries) and would never bite anyone who was not attacking their mistress – or them. But the reporters, photographers and cameramen were conditioned that these were savage dogs and the dogs, trying to jump up and lick faces, were met with a barrage of kicks and blows from microphones, swinging nicad battery cases, even cameras. Of course they bit back. A number of reporters were savaged and several vehicles damaged when they all tried to leave at once with the greatest possible speed. On the porch Margery and Rhodes hugged each other and danced gleefully up and down.

After that, it was not surprising that the more sensational newsmongers kept to their story that Rhodes

24

'Toots' Delaney had jealously bitten Olympic hopeful James Whitbury so badly that he needed stitches. Others had a good story about a ravishing beauty who valued her privacy so much that she set her dogs even on a hero like James Whitbury when he came calling: they would stick with that, milk it for all it was worth – plenty! – and they promptly dubbed her Wolf Woman. ('And where do you think they heard that cute appellation?' Margery asked Rhodes, who said, 'Margery, you're all brains and beauty and no compassion. Maybe he can't help being awkward and clumsy. Some people are like that.') One underground sheet hailed her and Margery as heroines of the lesbian movement, which amused Margery not at all. The rest of the reporters somehow found their way to Lorette Tremayne ('Guess who guided their twee little slip-on Guccis,' Margery asked), who, in the innocence of one whose acquaintance with the press was limited to the society pages, told them of the meeting at the club, of Rhodes challenging James to a grudge race in the Iditarod, of Harvey Mannesman's casual acceptance of the ten-thousand-dollar bet. Lorette, herself very beautiful, in the hands of the cheap media instantly became the wronged woman in 'The Battle of the Blue Book', which made her parents intensely angry with the Mannesmans and the Delaneys, adding spice to the melange of bad tastes the affair left in every mouth.

Of course, all these decent, quiet, hardworking Coloradans were naïve in expecting anything less once the snowball of misrepresentations and outright fabrications gathered momentum. A rich attractive young sportsman and a beautiful young woman of spirit racing each other in the Iditarod for a large bet – it was the stuff every editor dreams of; all this surefire recipe lacked was a romance between Rhodes and James, and that the reporters promptly erected with building blocks of thin air cemented together by throwaway remarks from James who seemed, to Rhodes at least, to be enjoying the whole affair. 'We're just good friends,' was the least inflammatory of his statements to the press. He told reporters who trekked to his training camp at Frontier Construction's Prudhoe Bay base inside the Arctic Circle, 'The Colorado Rose blushes only in private,' – and added that the reporters could find Rhodes at Emmonak on the Bering Strait, where they turned up next and ruined her Sunday, the only day of rest she had from laboring in the fish factory there to earn the $20,000 she would need to run the Iditarod. The nickname infuriated Rhodes . . . and stuck.

Only once did Rhodes strike back and that was before she left Colorado for Alaska. Margery persuaded her father to send a ranch hand to sit at the gate of the Delaney ranch with a shotgun to turn away reporters; Rhodes told a reporter who caught her at the vet that James had used his Mafia connections to hire a bodyguard for her.

The whole affair could have been conducted in a much lower key, or might have faded altogether once they both removed themselves to the desolate reaches of Alaska – except for James Whitbury's sleds. Born rich, and with a selfmade fortune from skis and other winter-sport gear he designed and manufactured, he now developed a light-weight and unbreakable alloy dog-sled and took an order for several thousand from a pipeline construction and maintenance corporation under pressure from conservationists. Frontier Construction's publicity machine made a big deal of preserving the tundra by using the Whitbury sleds rather than tracked or wheeled vehicles; it was Frontier who flew a score of reporters to Prudhoe. It would stretch faith in human kindness for the reporters not to ask James about Rhodes as well. But he need not

have answered, thought Rhodes, who was no longer
inclined to give him the benefit of doubt but convinced he
generated the unwelcome publicity to torment her, as
psychological warfare on a competitor. But soon she
would be running the Iditarod, where no-one could reach
her to ask asinine and impertinent questions and then,
whatever she replied, fabricate the answers they wanted
to hear.

1

Salvage

What set Big Jim's descendants on their way to their fateful meeting with the Iditarod sled dog racers nearly a year later was killing and eating a survivor at a crashed plane. Even so, the wolves would have stayed put and the racers would have passed safely except for the coincidence of the salvage team arriving simultaneously with a group of Indians being resettled by the government in a purpose-built village on the pack's territory. Normally the salvage mushers would have coexisted with the wolves, rarely sighting one and probably, if a rifle were handy, shooting 'on principle' at those they did see. The salvage experts, experienced and sensible, had no trouble reading the legend in the snow at the crashed plane: one survivor ate two bodies and was in turn eaten by wolves. (Because cannibalism is an all but unmentionable subject in societies that live so close to extinction, they reported to Juneau that the wolves had eaten two corpses and one live survivor. No one asked how the survivor had survived so long without food. People are collusively polite in such matters.) But they had a job to do in dismantling the mechanical parts of the plane and would not deliberately have hunted these particular wolves merely because they were man-eaters. In the opinion of most professional outdoorsmen of Caucasian origin, all wolves are, if not actual man-eaters, merely awaiting their opportunity: therefore, despite heavy fines and even jail sentences if caught, they shoot wolves 'on principle'.

The wives and mothers among the Indians in the new settlement were not so sanguine. The moment they heard there were forty-plus man-eating wolves in the strange

28

new forest surrounding them, there was an outcry and, when a new mother mistook a shadow for a wolf hungrily eyeing her baby, an anguished demand for extinction of the wolves. The women were deaf to arguments that wolves are shy of people, that thirty construction workers had toiled three seasons building the village without ever seeing a single wolf, that killing the wolves would anger the government officials who had given them this magnificent village. A concerted and persistent demand by their women soon drove the men to action and, since the youngest salvage musher, son of the foreman, was courting a nubile girl from the new village, the salvagemen brought their own rifles and experience to the hunt. The Indians in the new village were lumbermen and, without the tracking expertise of the salvagemen, who between air crashes earned their living hunting and trapping fur-bearing animals, would probably never have sighted a single wolf. But, given backbone by the salvagemen, in three weeks of concentrated hunting they tracked and killed four wolves and wounded five so severely that they were destroyed by the other wolves in pack-euthanasia or died of their wounds. One wolf gnawed off a foot caught in a snare but survived and learned to keep up with the pack and therefore could not be counted as even seriously disabled.

Towards the end of the third week the hunters became frantic. The mushers knew they had to dismantle the plane and sled the salvageable mechanics out before the spring thaws or leave them exposed until next winter, when many of the delicate electronics would have corroded and become useless for salvage. The salvage season was running out. The Indians knew that, without the expert tracking of the mushers, they would never finish the wolves off. Desperation bred vicious measures. A moose was shot, the carcass poisoned and laid out for the wolves who, late in winter, should have been hungry

29

enough to eat anything. A number of foxes, a plague of rats, and an armada of crows died from eating poisoned elk but the wolves were seen to urinate contemptuously on it.

The men were ragged with chasing wolves over the four hundred square miles the pack had made its own, in which it knew every tree and animal, every path passable and impossible, every fold in the ground, every horizon to avoid, every piece of thin ice through which pursuers could fall into the freezing water beneath. In the minds of the men, whose women refused to understand the elusive nature of an enemy aided by this tortuous landscape, the wolves took on the image of malicious demons bent on destroying their hunters. In fact, the wolves were hard-pressed and daily becoming more nervous. Genetic memories of relentless persecution and killing by men were re-awakened and the less stable members of the pack were already becoming neurotic, snapping at their younger rela-tives. A free range had inexplicably become a network of snares, and familiar, safe trees would blur to reveal a man firing painful or fatal bullets. The dogs associated with the men were particularly relentless because they commanded a sense stunted in men, smell, and did not need to see the wolves or their tracks in order to be dangerous. The wolves killed many more of the settlers' dogs than vice versa (wolves 11, dogs 1) but each time the dogs came near enough to attack, the men were close behind with rifles and shotguns.

The wolves could not win. The settlement was smack in the middle of their hunting ground and, even when they took to hugging the borders of their territory, the men started out every morning from only ten miles away, just far enough to digest their breakfast and start their blood circulating. Inevitably it would be only a matter of time before the wolves were exterminated.

0
Go!

We are the children of the earth
and removed from her
our spirit withers.

George Macauley Trevelyan (1876–1962)

Tell me, Father, what is the white man's heaven? Is it like
the land of the little trees when the ice has left the lake?
Are the great muskoxen there? Are the hills covered with
flowers? There, will I see the caribou everywhere I look?
Are the lakes blue with the sky of summer? Is every net
full of great, fat white-fish? Is there room for me in this
land, like our land, the Barrens? Can I camp anywhere
and not find that someone else has camped? Can I feel
the wind and be like the wind? Father, if your Heaven is
not like all these, leave me alone in my land, the land of
the little sticks.

Dogrib Indian to Oblate Priest
Richard Perry: Polar Worlds

1
Number One

At 10 A.M., Saturday February 28, the announcer called Number One to the starting line but no one came. Instead a two-minute silence descended over the crowd inside the stadium; over the racers mustering their teams in the parking lot outside; even, as they were gradually influenced by the humans' mood of hallowed contemplation, over the eight hundred hypercharged, barking, yipping, howling sled dogs. For at Number One would run no present-day musher, at Number One would run the spirit of the race, even of Alaska: Leonhard Seppala, dead these four decades but even in his lifetime a legendary sled dog racer and the hero of the 1925 relay which, in a superhuman feat of endurance by men and their dogs, carried diphtheria-serum from Nenana across Alaska to save the children of Nome.

Rhodes felt a stirring in her stomach and heart, and tears on her cheeks, as in the silence her imagination carried her back sixty years: the epidemic diagnosed, the panic when it was discovered not enough serum was available to save everyone, the frantic appeals over primitive radios and precarious telegraph lines; the precious serum despatched against all hope that it could arrive in time, the train puffing strongly into the railhead at Nenana where the first of a relay of mushers awaited arrival of the fur-wrapped parcel; the race against death, until 170 hours later and 1000 icy trail miles away, the last of the nineteen men in the tenuous chain of hope staggered behind his sled into Nome with the life-giving package.

Of such exploits are legends and myths born and

standards of achievement established for others to measure themselves against. Leonhard Seppala's ashes were scattered over part of the course of the contest instituted to commemorate the feat and preserve the legend – the Iditarod Trail Sled Dog Race from Anchorage to Nome, the most gruelling test in the world, the last great race. As Marathon beckoned Athenian youth, so beckons Nome the heart of the twentieth-century athlete.

Race distance was officially pegged as 1049 miles – because the organizers knew it was more than 1000 miles and because Alaska was the 49th State admitted to the Union – but Rhodes had meticulously calculated with the aid of such large-scale maps as existed that it was at least 1200 miles. Yet, at the start of such a venture, determined to finish the race though by no means cocksure about outlasting the distance, the weather and the other manifest dangers of the race, Rhodes was aware that the achievement of Seppala and his fellow-mushers in the diphtheria-serum relay humbled even her grand ambition: they had been alone, each against the elements, on an unmade trail. As a rookie in the toughest race on earth, she was under no illusion that she would ever lead the Iditarod, ever have to break trail for others to follow. Her aloneness would be, by the test of the serum-relay mushers, severely qualified in that others of the sixty-odd mushers in the race would always be within a few miles of her. And checkpoints: if she were too late, and the weather permitted, planes would be sent to search for her. All these advantages Seppala and his fellow-mushers lacked but neither, Rhodes had been warned, should they make her less careful. It was a widely-shared opinion of Joe May, a veteran of the race and the winner in 1980, that it was only a matter of time before someone died on the Iditarod, that it was a miracle it had not happened already. Some had come very near. There were stories told at the mushers' pre-race banquet. . . She had spent more than a year of saving and scraping and backaching work and training and heartbreak and injury to arrive at the start line today: she would finish the race even if she had to take such care that she finished second-last. Or even last, as long as James Whitbury dropped out first.

Fifteen yards from her he stood explaining to reporters that his light alloy sled would revolutionize transport for pipeline servicing crews, with consequent benefit to the environment. She had heard that his sponsors, Frontier Construction, had a thousand of his toboggans on test. So he'll make another fortune out of the Iditarod, she thought but did not stay with it. Money by itself failed to impress or excite Rhodes who by nature was competitive rather than envious. What concerned her much more deeply were reports that his alloy toboggan weighed only twenty pounds while her medium-weight ash-framed sled, handcarved by her father, scaled in excess of sixty.

'I hope that newfangled sled lasts the course,' Rhodes said to Harvey Mannesman. Two of her dogs were expensive gifts from Harvey. Next to her father, Harvey had always been her most important mentor and adviser as a sled dog racer. If her father and Harvey and Margery had not arrived to cheer her to the start, she might have chickened out in fright at the immensity of her undertaking to cross Alaska. Now she was at Mulcahy Stadium, ready to go. Harvey stood by to lend a hand if, in the excitement surrounding the start of the race, the unaccustomed rest they enjoyed in the couple of weeks before the race, her dogs should become hyperactive. For the same reason her father sat on top of her gear in the sled; once out of town and away from the crowds, she would leave him behind. Other teams, in addition to the 'handler' sitting on the sled, dragged chains or a large tire on a towline behind the sled but Rhodes felt her father was no featherweight and Harvey, of course, was frankly huge – they would do.

'Why should you root for him after the way he's treated you?' Harvey demanded with a scowl.

'Because I don't want him to have any excuse for losing except that I outran and outlasted him.'

Harvey snorted derisively. 'That playboy will come out in the wind or lose the trail or run across an angry moose and scratch right there, long before that fancy sled breaks.'

Rhodes had doubts but kept her peace, listening to the announcer calling the drawn numbers of the early starters. Rick Swenson and Herbie Nayokpuk had gone already, legendary runners, Swenson a multiple winner; and now Emmitt Peters was called, another winner who for five years held the record for fastest finishing time. There were rookies called too, but many of the names were of men – and a woman, Susan Butcher – already in the lexicon of heroes, reserved places in the modern Alaskan pantheon. Twelve minutes after Emmitt Peters it would be her turn to leave the start line on the cleared 440-yard track inside the stadium.

'Never mind Whitbury,' her father said, smiling gently from atop the sled. 'In a race over 1200 miles you can't pace yourself against anyone else. Only yourself. You're the only one who knows the pace that will carry you into Nome. Don't let him fluster you, Rhodes. Stick to your plan.'

He had told her before, but Rhodes listened carefully: her father had many years experience of racing sled dogs and had never guided her wrong.

Rhodes nodded and bent compulsively to inspect the feet of her dogs: there was nothing wrong with their feet that her own several inspections or those by her father and Harvey could uncover. But a dog with sore feet would have to be carried in the sled: one less to pull the weight, more weight for the remaining dogs to pull. Already she was at a weight disadvantage to James Whitbury because his alloy sled scaled only a third as much as her traditional one.

Harvey could have been reading her mind. 'Just you forget about him. All you have to do is aim to finish and you'll get there before him. Let me tell you, by just finishing, you'll do us all proud.'

A truck backfired and startled the Whitbury dogs. Immediately they started fighting nervously among themselves. Earlier, James and his professional dog trainer, Dave Cohen, had harnessed them only with difficulty and much help from experienced bystanders. Now they failed to restore order. They had trained at Frontier Construction's Prudhoe Bay base, the northernmost human habitation in the world, and the dogs were not used to people, never mind crowds. Finally Harvey generously walked over, stood on the edge of the melee, and bellowed at the top of his voice. In awe of this fearsome noise the dogs stopped fighting to stare at its source. As soon as Harvey turned his back, they started fighting again but their heart was not in it and trainer and owner quickly sorted them out.

'Thanks,' James, breathing quickly with his exertions, called to Harvey. Behind him Dave Cohen stuck an Elastoplast from the first-aid box in the sled onto the hand of a swearing journalist. 'Hey, there are ladies present,' James added to the journalist. 'Watch your language.'

The reporter was spurred to greater obscenity. Rhodes hid a smile. James Whitbury's outstanding characteristic was his total lack of comprehension of people – that was essentially what had brought him and her here today.

The announcer called the second number ahead of hers; her father looked at his watch. Four minutes from her

36

drawn start. For the first time she heard the howling of the dogs all around her – she must have tuned them out earlier.

The Tannoy reached over the hubbub for her. 'At Number! Twenty! One! Rhodes! Delaney! from Fairplay! Colorado!, running for the first! time! in the Iditarod! Trail! Sled! Dog! Race! THE COLORADO! ROSE! AT NUMBER! TWENTY! ONE!'

She had missed the announcement of the musher before her. Time had just gone.

Her dogs were moving already, perhaps having recognized her name, but Rhodes nevertheless shook the drivebow and called softly, 'Hike!' The dogs surged ahead. Rhodes looked around to find Harvey trotting at her shoulder with that speed which in one of his bulk always amazed strangers.

Rhodes talked softly to her dogs, calling each one by name, gentling them so that they would not run away with her before the start. Toots's mother, now no longer racing, had led the team when six years ago her father and Harvey Mannesman had gone into a blizzard which grounded search helicopters and rescued a pair of snowed-in campers who otherwise would have died of exposure. She was very proud of her dogs. They were working dogs, rescue dogs, shop-for-groceries dogs, and they were racing dogs she had bred or selected and trained herself, not sent a hired somebody else out to buy, like Mr Flaming Whitbury. 'Gee, gee,' Rhodes called to turn her dogs right through the wide gate, and 'Haw, haw,' to turn them left onto the cleared 440-yard track. 'Whoa!' She arrived at the line just as the starter raised his arm, her eyes not on the official but on the shrunken men who stood near him – and them she saw not as they were today but as they had been almost a lifetime ago, young, vital men, strong, large and exuding energy: Billy McCarthy

37

and Charlie Evans were survivors of that 1925 Nenana–Nome serum relay which inspired the race she was about to start, a living link with an heroic past. From them her eyes fell on Margery Mannesman, who had come from the shelter of the rented car into the cutting wind to hold up the banner hand-embroidered by Dona Ana: COLORADO LOVES RHODES.

'See you in McGrath,' Rhodes called to Margery, pitching her voice just high enough to carry over the cacophony of dogs and spectators.

'Wait for me if you get there first.' Margery's whole petite blonde body bounced up and down with excitement.

Rhodes laughed. Margery would fly to McGrath with Harvey and Paul.

James had brought his team up behind hers before he was called so as to be ready – wisely so, Rhodes thought, considering the over-excited state of his dogs and his lack of control over them. Moments later she would wish he had not.

'Go,' called the starter, dropping his arm. 'Go!' he added, perhaps feeling he had not sufficiently emphasized the command the first time. Only one third through the list of mushers to be sent off at two-minute intervals, his voice was hoarse.

At that moment the Whitbury dogs took it into their heads to break into a run. James Whitbury's outraged shout startled Rhodes's dogs and they too jerked into a furious run. For a second Rhodes was merely irritated: she had planned to start the race with the command 'Marchez', as used by the old-time mushers and from which the word 'musher' to describe a modern dog-sledder is derived. She could not afford another second for nostalgia: she had to act or there would be the most almighty accident on that narrow track as the two teams and their speeding sleds crashed into each other. As it was, in her moment of irritation she was nearly humiliated before the two thousand spectators standing on the berm raised by clearing two feet of snow from the 440 yard track, and the peering eyes of the television cameras, through being left behind at the starting line by her dogs. She jumped for the runners, with their treads of new bicycle tyre screwed on by her father for extra purchase. For another precious second she could only hang on for dear life. Her arms were nearly jerked out of their sockets as her hands closed around the drivebow. Nearby she heard James shout at his dogs in a voice almost as loud as Harvey's. *But almost misses by a mile*, she thought. Out of the corner of her eye she saw him stand on his brake, cutting a furrow in the track she knew baseball players would curse him for all summer and footballers would stumble over in the fall. But still his dogs, full of beans after their pre-race fortnight of rest, pulled as strongly as ever. His lead dog cut across her own team and she had milliseconds to react. 'Haw, haw!' she shouted the old muleskinner's command to turn left, knowing that above the roaring of the crowd she stood as little chance of being heard as James, who was level with her and only three feet from her shoulder. In that moment, fraught with risk of damage and injury and the ruination of a crack at the Iditarod they had both worked more than a year to achieve, he grinned quickly at her and she could swear she heard him shout, 'Attagirl!' She could not resist grinning back even as she tried to outshout the crowd.

Toots glanced right at the other team leader closing on her. Perhaps she heard Rhodes, perhaps she merely sensed what her mistress wanted, perhaps she reacted from her own innate intelligence: Toots veered left and almost halfway up the berm. The two swing dogs, immediately behind her, followed promptly, the team dogs turning with them, with the powerful wheel dogs just in front of the sled pulling strongly so that the sled ran up the berm, escaping the arc of uncontrollable swing of the Whitbury sled by fractions of an inch. Later Rhodes would be amazed that, while still in great peril, she found time to produce a small sigh of relief. The sled teetered at an angle it had never been designed to run at. Paul Delaney tucked his feet behind the downside stanchions and leaned out of the other end of the sled with his whole body, the back of his head inches from the packed, frozen snow, arms waving for balance; his action moved the center of gravity but not enough: the higher runner already rode a clear six inches above the top ridge of the berm – spectators scattered frantically – and rose by the second.

Rhodes jumped. Her boots scrabbled for purchase on the packed ice as she slammed her shoulder into the sled to keep it from turning over. But she could not hold it; the sled was, against every expectation, accelerating *up* the berm and tilting more precipitously with each increment of velocity. She had to find traction for the weight of the sled and also for her own forward momentum along the steep and treacherous berm. Out of the corner of her eye she saw Dave Cohen dive for General, leader of the Whitbury pack, and pull the dog's nose down by the simple expedient of throwing his own body full-length on the ice. *Lateral thinking!*

The track was now clear for Rhodes if only she could move her sled down onto it before it rose over the top of the berm and killed her father or fell back and crushed her and her dogs. *Lateral thinking!* Instantly she let the sled go, shouting, 'Gee, gee,' to turn the dogs to the right and back onto the track. As soon as it was released from the restraint of her weight the sled accelerated sideways at even greater speed. But Rhodes was ready, flinging herself across the back of the sled and onto the high, rising side just as it was about to slip over the berm. Here, where the spectators had tramped furrows, she found purchase to bring her strength to bear and slam the flying runner back to earth just as Toots obeyed the command. Now, with the sled on top of the berm, it was in danger of being pulled over the other way by the combined weight of Rhodes and her father; Toots obeyed instantly but the pair of swing dogs, the four pairs of team dogs and the pair of wheel dogs made up a line thirty feet long and Rhodes hung perilously underneath the sled on the berm, kicking and shoving as best she could to keep it from dropping on her, until at last all the dogs had turned. With a sickening lurch, the sled shot down the incline of the berm and onto the blessed smoothness of the track.

Rhodes, still hanging onto one end of the drivebow and surprised by the sudden reversal, was dragged along until she could recover her balance. At the bottom of the berm the sled swung viciously to and fro. Sensing that her dogs were away and running and would not stop to wait for her, Rhodes jumped desperately for the runners and flung her other hand over to smack into the far side of the drivebow. Then she just hung there, oblivious to the cheers of the crowd for her fine display of sledmanship, with barely enough breath to look up and see that her father was alright: he still sat on the sled, panting but smiling proudly at her. 'Wow!' he shouted and she managed a small grin.

In her peripheral vision she saw: Dave Cohen put his arms over his head as the Whitbury dogs piled onto him; James running beside the sled, trying to push it to one side so it would not run into Dave; officials jumping for their lives because there was only one other direction the sled could slide and that was straight at them; Harvey Mannesman flinging his three hundred pounds against the side of James Whitbury's sled to prevent it injuring Dave

Cohen; the space where her sled had been on the berm still clear of spectators because everything had happened so quickly they had not had time to step back – and then she was through the gate and *racing in the Iditarod!*

Outside the gate Toots turned right without command from her, following the trail laid down by the teams who had gone before. It was a small consolation that, unless she fell too far behind, she would always be following trail broken by someone else. Even so, foul weather could obscure the trail or the dogs could lose it at night, when she intended doing most of her travelling, or she could lose it herself. Theoretically the trail was blazed with pink ribbon. Theoretically. She had heard an experienced musher tell another rookie at the mushers' banquet that only a fool would expect a pink ribbon to stay up for three weeks. 'Or even a day, with forty- or fifty-mile winds already blowing,' her father had murmured beside her. (The organizers made the banquet compulsory precisely so that veterans should share last-minute advice with rookies. As added insurance against disaster, no rookie was allowed to enter unless recommended by two known, established mushers.) The wind was a serious hazard: one musher had lost several dogs and broken his arm when the truck bringing him to Mulcahy Stadium for the start blew over; incredibly, he calmed his dogs, had his arm set, and started at his drawn place – a musher who cannot start at his allocated number must wait until last and then has to start within sixty minutes of the last team or is automatically disqualified. She cautioned herself not to draw false confidence from knowing there were more than sixty other mushers on the trail with her: Remember the honeymoon campers who nearly froze to death in Colorado less than a mile from our own homestead and right next to a regularly cleared road, she told herself.

For the time being she allowed her dogs to set their

42

own pace to let them shake the excitement of the start, to become used to working again after doing nothing more strenuous than a daily fifteen-mile milkrun for three weeks now. Soon, but not too soon, she would have to settle them down: there was a psychologically right moment, before which the dogs would resent being slowed, and after which they would be burning more energy than they could afford if they were to manage the long haul she planned for today and all the other long hauls of the days and nights to follow, all 1200 miles across Alaska to Nome. She stood on the runners and grinned at her father as her dogs ran along sidewalks, roads and parks until they came into the open beyond the buildings of Anchorage.

Without any warning except a quick smile and thumbs-up, her father rolled off the sled and into the snow. They had not discussed it but she had assumed she would stop to drop him, receive his last-minute advice, kiss him goodbye. But now she knew Paul Delaney saw no need of that. She looked back to be certain he was not hurt; he stood upright, brushing snow from his clothes, looking after her. He raised a hand; she waved and turned her head so he should not see the tears suddenly in her eyes. Somehow she felt this break from her father was more final than when she had left home for college.

'Easy now, Toots,' she called, 'easy!' Toots perked up her ears but ran no slower. To Toots, Rhodes knew, twenty degrees Fahrenheit was just pleasant Colorado temperature. Toots had come from home with her, but all the other dogs were Alaskan-bred and until last week had been living and training in temperatures ten and twenty degrees *below* zero. For them this was hot weather and they could not shed their fur coats, the way she discarded her bright orange parka and flung it into the basket of the sled. Her two swing dogs, purebred malemutes bought in

43

the Arctic Circle where the temperature seldom rises above zero (still thirty-two below freezing), were working in what was for them a heatwave. These two swing dogs, whose function was to keep the team dogs behind them on the trail after the leader had turned, so that no short cuts across the rough caused accidents, had been a gift from Harvey Mannesman and in his honor she had named them Gin'n'Tonic and Seven'n'Seven, because all Harvey's dogs back in Colorado were named for drinks. The team dogs, running behind the swing dogs, made up the brawn if only because they outnumbered all of the other dogs: there were eight of them and they had only one function, to pull the sled. Both swing dogs could double as leaders if necessary but Rhodes, who had lived with these dogs for a year and knew them better than she knew Margery, with whom she had grown up, harbored no such hopes for any of the team dogs. The biggest dogs of all – at ninety pounds each, less than twenty pounds short of her own weight – worked directly in front of the sled: the wheel dogs had to start the sled moving, break it loose from ice, act as anchors for the sled over rough ground covered at speed, contribute simple brute strength. The Iditarod rules stated that she had to start with no fewer than seven dogs and no more than eighteen and had to finish the race with no fewer than five dogs pulling on the towline; dogs could not be added to the string after the start of the race, nor led behind the sled: the rules required them to be working on the towline or carried in the sled.

Rhodes had chosen her string of thirteen dogs from twenty-three she had bred or bought or been given. Her choice was based as much on whether the dogs could do what was expected – lead, keep trail, pull – as for the attributes the race would demand – stamina, speed and reserves of power at the end – plus an indefinable characteristic mushers call 'head' which describes, approximately, a dog's attitude. Dogs will work only while they remain interested, therefore the wise musher chooses dogs that do not easily become bored and then works hard to keep up their interest; the dog which scores high on this measure is easily spotted by the alert attitude of its head, its pointing ears and response to new stimuli. She had also paid attention to how well each dog worked with the others in the team. Now all that was behind her: she was away and running in the Iditarod, on her way to the Eagle River checkpoint fifteen miles away, the first of twenty-three checkpoints on the Iditarod Trail. 'Hey, Toots,' she called again, 'we're not sprinting in Colorado, you know. This is the long haul.' Toots looked quizzically over her shoulder at her mistress, decided she was talking to herself and went back to leading the team down that easy trail. Rhodes knew they were still on trails used over the weekend for the Fur Rendezvous World Championship Sled Dog Race, for short-haul racers, and the going would never again be that easy until she passed under the victory arch over Front Street in Nome, twelve-hundred-and-something miles thataway, forwards, but nevertheless her exuberance burst forth in a joyous shout, 'Eagle River, here we come!' She was passing another musher at the time and he shouted after her, 'Easy, Sister, it's a long way to Nome,' then joined in her wild laughter.

They left the Rondy Trail when Toots turned to follow a fresher track, cut by an Iditarod team only minutes ahead. Rhodes looked up at the Chugach Mountains as the trail passed through the Fort Richardson Military Reservation and down to the Eagle River Valley, reminded that this adventure started on another day when she was thinking about mountains. Near the town of Eagle River she noticed with surprise that the roads

45

running parallel to the trail were jammed with spectators braving the harsh winds. Even passing them quickly and at a hundred yards, she fancied she could see in their eyes the gleaming dream of someday, one day, soon, themselves riding out to high adventure behind a team of their own dogs. A girl with two half-grown husky pups on a lead ran beside Rhodes, hard going on the loose snow beside the trail. Rhodes thought the girl about sixteen and suddenly it struck her that in five or six years this same girl could be on the runners, heading for Nome. Rhodes raised her hand from the drivebow, thumb up.

'Are you Susan Butcher?'

'No. I'm sorry. She must've passed already.'

'Oh.' The girl's face puckered a little as she fought not to let her disappointment show.

Rhodes knew how she felt. She had missed her heroine, the dream personified: Susan Butcher was not only the first woman ever to finish the Iditarod in the top ten but a couple of years after that notable feat had come second to multiple winner Rick Swenson, winning $16,000, and this year could be *the* winner. 'Hey, cheer up! When I was your age I didn't have any pair of purebred Siberians, just the mother of my leader who was, believe it or not, an Irish setter.'

'Ripley?' the girl asked, delighting Rhodes, who nodded solemnly. The girl looked suitably horrified, then studied Toots. 'She looks good.'

'Thanks. You've a head start with those two. I'll see you running here in a few years.'

'Gee, thanks! You're Rhodes Delaney, aren't you?' Rhodes nodded again. 'The rookie from Colorado.' The girl smiled slyly and hunted around for something more to say, reluctant to break contact. 'I read in the paper where it said you're the most beautiful girl running the race but not to bet any money on you 'cos it's a sled-dog

46

race, not a beauty contest.' She stopped, aghast, her brain
catching up with her words. Rhodes smiled encouragingly;
she well remembered the awkwardness of being sixteen,
of forever wishing you could think before you spoke.
'You're so nice, I almost wish it *was* a beauty contest.'

Everybody has a bet except me. 'You put your money
on Susan?'

'Nothing like your bet, though. Twenty bucks.'

Now was not the time to explain she had refused James
Whitbury's huge bet. 'If I see her, I'll tell her you're
rooting for her.'

'Thanks. And good luck. I just know you're going to
beat that James Whitbury hollow.' The two Siberians
gambolled back to the road, dragging their glowing mistress with them.

At the Eagle River checkpoint, Rhodes stayed just long
enough to log in and have her compulsory gear checked:
cold-weather sleeping bag, hand axe, snowshoes and
bindings for her, plus eight booties for each dog. She also
carried, as a symbol of the fur-wrapped serum parcel of
the 1925 relief relay, a packet of envelopes post-stamped
in Anchorage; these would be franked again when she
reached Nome, then sold as souvenirs to those who only
dreamed, with the proceeds going towards the huge
organizing cost of the race. The checkers also confirmed
that she carried the mandatory food: two pounds minimum for each dog plus a day's rations for herself, which
the rules did not define as closely as the dog food. Within
six minutes she had logged out and was running again.

This year, despite the relatively warm weather today,
the Knik and Matanuska Rivers were frozen at the
northern end of the Cook Inlet and the mushers could
cross. Rhodes had been told that in other years, when the
warm jetstream melted the ice, teams and drivers were
trucked twenty-odd miles to Wasilla to restart the race on

Lake Lucille: the organizers knew dogs and mushers could not walk on water but they had perforce to start the race at Anchorage, Alaska's biggest city, to receive full value of the publicity which in turn helped them raise the $100,000 purse and the further $250,000 operating costs of the race.

Now that they had left the sightseers and wellwishers behind, the real race began in earnest. Already Rhodes felt the chill of winds howling down the Matanuska Valley at over thirty miles an hour. Back in Anchorage she had been warned, with the other mushers, that 'the wind will be a bastard (sorry Susan, sorry ladies)' holding at forty to fifty mph once they came right out into it, and gusting at times to eighty, ninety, maybe even a hundred miles an hour. Only two years ago the Governor had declared the Valley a disaster area after just such winds and this morning Margery had heard on the car radio that the authorities were bracing themselves to do the same today. Rhodes shrugged into her parka and closed all the zips and snaps to keep out the wind. Toots settled down to a good, steady pace but the wind, bringing with it a chill factor that intensified the cold rising from the ice and snow, invigorated the other dogs because this was nearer the climate they were accustomed to. From one minute to the next they lost the listlessness that had worried Rhodes at Anchorage just over two hours ago.

They had been assured that the ice on the rivers was firm enough to carry the teams but all the same Rhodes studied each river carefully as she came down to it, tilting her head to catch the striations in the ice where cracks would start. Once, in a sprint in Colorado, she had fallen through the ice on a river where Harvey Mannesman, all 300 pounds of him, plus his sled and his equally huge dogs, had just passed without any trouble; she lost a couple of good dogs and the doctor later said that after only a couple of minutes more in that freezing water she would have collected her trophy to the applause of harps being strummed by winged musicians. In Colorado the first rescuer had reached the hole less than half-a-minute after she fell through. . . Rhodes, understandably, therefore considered it no guarantee that other mushers could be seen crossing the frozen rivers or that a line of poles had been frozen into the ice to mark the best line, nor that behind the poles stood a row of pickup trucks and campers belonging to the hard core of race followers and probably to the organizers. She hoped the weight of the trucks had not weakened the ice to the point where it would crack the moment she went onto it. She would cross a lot of frozen-over water in this race and no help would be available.

The wind stunned her for a moment as she came out of the trees and squarely into it on the open ice. Suddenly she understood why Harvey Mannesman thought James Whitbury would scratch the moment he felt this wind: it was like no other she had encountered, not just cold – God, it was *cold*! – but so incisive, so pervasive that zips and clasps and velcro could not keep it out and the fur lining of her parka froze an instant white edging where it peeped out behind the windbreak nylon.

Toots staggered sideways. Immediately the swing dogs proved their worth, holding to the trail until Toots recovered her balance. Rhodes called out encouragement but her words were swept away in the wind. People ran towards her from the trucks and campers, holding onto each other in pairs. One pair fell and the wind blew them over and over and over before the inertia of their mass slowed them. Some of the helpers grabbed the gangline and others held onto those who had the gangline. Rhodes jumped from the runners and pushed behind the sled but the wind found enough purchase even on its modest elevation to drive it sideways towards the poles, so she jumped back on and kicked the brake into the ice, which paradoxically resulted in faster forward speed because the sideways drag so eliminated was greater than the forward drag of the brake.

'Hey, that's smart!' a man pushing at the side of the sled shouted in her ear.

Then, seconds later, an eternity of fear, she was across one river and her Alaskan dogs, invigorated by the same wind that left Rhodes gasping, pressed hard on Toots' heels and Toots sped up to keep the lead: a lead dog must be accepted as the leader by the other dogs and must *want* to be the leader. Toots was an unlikely choice for a sled dog, and setters unheard of as leaders, but her motivation beat the hereditary odds against her selection. Rhodes had taken a lot of schtick from the other mushers about her leader but against Toots's excitable temperament there remained her towering competence at finding and holding trail under all conditions and weathers plus the inescapable fact that *Toots had never once given up and refused to continue.*

She hit the next river too fast and was out in the barren windseared center of it, the wind driving the sled sideways behind the dogs, before she could touch the brake and dig in. Here there were only a few trucks and campers, and the people in them were surprised by her sudden appearance and her speed; they reacted quickly once they grasped the necessity but by then it was already too late. Rhodes stood on the brake with one foot to dig it in and dragged her other boot behind the sled. 'Whoa, whoa, whoa!' she shouted to slow the dogs so that their weight could act as an additional restraint to the wind-driven sideways drift of the sled. Then, suddenly, 'WHOA!' She sounded monstrously loud in her own ears in a small lull in the wind. She slid her foot off the brake to take advantage of the interlude and the dogs, leaning against a wind no longer there, jerked the sled, adding impetus to its hazardous arc. The sickening thud and splintering of cured wood as the sled slid into the poles was heartbreaking. She knew it was not the solid pitchpine of the poles shattering but her sled. She had spare stanchions but no main runners: if a runner had broken this was the end of her race.

The wind resumed full-force in the instant the helpers reached her. In one concerted heave they carried dogs, broken sled and her across the river and into the trees, which cut the wind a little.

A bearded man bent to inspect her sled – he apparently knew the race rules about outside help because he was careful to keep his hands well clear. 'Bad,' he shouted. 'Three stanchions broken. You got spares or can we radio in for you?'

He was surprised by her wide grin. But to Rhodes this was good news: she was still racing. She put her mouth close to his ear. 'I have spares, thanks.' The helpers returned to the warmth of their trucks for a few minutes before the next musher would need their assistance. She pulled her sled off the trail and bent to make repairs. Rhodes thought, This is the last place I can expect help; how the hell I'll get to Nome I just don't know. In Colorado I never even dreamed of such winds. Then she thought wryly, If I can't fix this, I'll probably be the first Iditarod musher who didn't even make it to the Alaska Mushers' Hall of Fame at Knik – or perhaps they have a special Infamy Section for mushers who scratch before Knik. She cut the frozen rawhide bindings from the broken stanchions: her sled had no screwed or glued joints, all parts being held together by wetted rawhide stretched on tightly in a design, hallowed by tradition, which allows members of the sled to flex rather than bend

51

and break. As she crouched to study the runners anxiously for splits, a shadow fell across her. When she looked up, there was James Whitbury.

'Buggered up already, have you then?' He bent to inspect the damage and shook his head. 'I offered you one of my special toboggans, free and clear and gratis, and you behaved like Little Miss Smartass.'

Rhodes glared up at him. It was true, he had offered her one of his sleds. A journalist had accused him of using his money to unfair advantage in building a hi-tech sled only a third the weight of Rhodes's wooden sled. He had responded smartly by offering her one of his sleds free of charge. But the first Rhodes heard of this gesture was when reporters interrupted her day of rest in Emmonak to put it to her: she was intensely irritated by their ill manners, their assumption that she would automatically accept, their continuing refusal to believe she and James Whitbury were not conducting a long-distance romance. 'Mr Whitbury's sled is not, repeat, not proven,' Rhodes had snapped, 'and Mr Whitbury has not shown the elementary courtesy of making his offer to me. Even if both conditions were met I would still use the traditional sled my father is handcarving for me – as a matter of principle, something I don't expect you to understand.' Now that last remark, Rhodes told herself as she slammed the front door of her lodgings, is almost worthy of Margery.

'I don't accept gifts offered through the media.'

'Yes, that was stupid and ill-mannered. But those reporters were hounding me. To get rid of them I said the first thing that came into my mind.'

So he too felt harassed by the gossip-mongers! She turned to say something friendly but saw his hand reach to test one of the broken stanchions. 'Oh no, you don't!' She whacked him smartly across his mittened knuckles with the bundle of hard-frozen rawhide she held in her hand.

'Eeeow!' He jumped away, rubbing his smarting hand furiously. He turned to check that he had not sent his team off by his shouting.

'Every time we meet you do your level best to cripple me,' he said. 'It's only a race, you know, not a war.'

'Oh yes? And if I let you touch my sled when it is broken, you'll report me and have me disqualified out of "only a race".'

He shook his head again. 'Oh, ye of little faith. I don't have to sink to such tactics to beat you to Nome.'

She wanted to believe him. But the rules were quite clear and there had been talk of Frontier hiring a lawyer to interpret them for James Whitbury ('Find the loopholes is what that means in plain English,' Margery said). No musher was allowed to accept help unless in mortal danger. One year Emmitt Peters lost the race when he led it, merely by accepting hot water when it was offered: a race official held him up as a penalty while the second-place runner slipped through and won.

Rhodes kept a wary eye on him while she beat the rawhide backwards and forwards across her palm to soften it.

'We're both victims of the democratic institution of a free press,' he said.

That rang a bell with Rhodes and she nodded.

'Let's start afresh, eh? For instance, where did you go to school?'

Rhodes almost laughed: this was ludicrous, here, beyond the end of the civilized world, making exploratory conversation that would embarrass even the most awkward of teenagers. Somewhere she had read that people falling in love have no time for explanations: that was rubbish; what people falling in love have no time for is apologies. She had never been in love but that much struck her as obvious. She wondered if James Whitbury was offering himself as a candidate for love, or if he merely intended by courtesy to make amends for the invasions of her privacy he had caused, or if he thought of her as a playboy's conquest to be notched up and forgotten. She would not have been a woman if she had not wondered. . . The urge to laugh fled; this was not only her race but her life. She bent to tie in a new stanchion as a makeshift until tonight, when she would warm the rawhide with the food and retie it. 'USC, on a scholarship,' she said, but what she thought was, While he stands talking to me, he can't gain on me; not that an hour so early in a race this long is worth much, but still. What an unworthy thought! She added, 'I learned there that the world isn't perfect, but I'm not enough of a crowd-person ever to change it.' The moment the words were out of her mouth she was aghast. True, it was what she spent her lonely months on the ranch and in Alaska considering, but she had not confided her conclusion to anyone, not her father, not Margery. Once more it was as if he invaded her innermost thoughts. *Oh, come on, Rhodes, you can't blame him if you blurt out your secrets.*

'Nothing worthwhile was ever created by a mob or by a committee,' he said with conviction.

That was too tempting to resist. 'You built that aluminum sled of yours all by yourself, did you?'

'No,' he retorted cheerfully, refusing to be baited. 'I hired a lot of metallurgists and smelter engineers and even an expert in sub-zero crystallization. But *I* conceived the ultra-lightweight sled and had the initiative to bring all these people together and build it. Incidentally, pure ali is weak, so my sled is made of six finely matched alloys. Absolutely unbreakable.'

His enthusiasm was contagious. 'I hope you're right. I

don't want you to have any excuse for trailing me into Nome or not making it at all.'

'That's right generous of you, Miss Delaney.'

Her head jerked up but his smile was friendly, not matching his sardonic words. She said, 'I read somewhere that you won your Olympic Gold by angering your opponents so much that they made mistakes.'

His smile disappeared. 'I was very surprised to read that. It's pure invention. It's also bullshit because it would be counterproductive. A man competing at Olympic level isn't put off his stroke by anger. He has learned to convert it to an extra spurt of adrenalin which he uses to win by a bigger margin.'

'And women?' She did not look up from her work. Working with part-frozen rawhide was like trying to make slip-knots in barbed wire.

'Women are even better at it than men. Oh, you mean that display by Mary Dekker in 1984.'

It was as if he had read her mind. He seemed quite unaware of how uncomfortable such perspicacity could make others. But it probably accounted for part of his awkwardness with people. For the first time she saw him as intelligent; until now she had taken him at the media's valuation of a rich sportsman who gave his famous name to sporting equipment designed and made by others.

He was saying, '. . . a publicity stunt. The press was already down on Zola Budd because she is a South African and Mary exploited that. But you'll never hear a winner whining about unfair treatment.'

She looked up at him. 'Where did you go to school?'

He grinned and she wondered if he too saw their conversation as tangential to their situation. 'MIT. Engineering,' he said. Then he just stood there, at ease, as if they were sharing the companionable quietude of old friends rather than the tense beginnings of a race across Alaska.

Rhodes, tying in the third replacement stanchion, made a mental note to find out if there was some way of having more stanchions sent ahead to one of the checkpoints. She now had only two spares left and, if the wind again blew her into something hard, a tree or a rock, more than two stanchions could break. She packed her tools and secured the net over the basket of her sled, then rose, pressing her hands into the small of her back.

'I'll see you.' James shook the leather-wrapped alloy drivebow of his sled. 'Hike!' His dogs carried him away.

'Hike!' Rhodes called and set off after him. The trail was wide enough to pass but Rhodes was not tempted. He was driving his dogs at a good speed, the same speed she would have chosen were he not there, and she had no intention of wearing her dogs out in a futile sprint that would prove nothing. His dogs, she noticed, were notably heavier than hers, which, except Toots, were in turn heavier than the dogs she raced in Colorado. Outright sprinters could be bought or bred, of course, and many very fast dogs were physically capable of covering long distances but when Harvey Mannesman had tried the experiment, he had found the bred-for-sprinting dogs psychologically unstable and very unreliable. The problem with temperamental dogs is that they are inconsistent, reliable only under ideal circumstances. If the weather turns foul, if there is a snowfall, if the temperature rises a few degrees and turns the trail mushy, temperamental dogs strike by lying down in their traces and refusing to rise. But your heavyweight, stolid, untemperamental dog, while undoubtedly reliable even in bad weather and heavy going, is invariably slower than his quirky but swift cousins. So Rhodes, who had selected her dogs for a fine balance of sustained speed and long-range stamina, was reasonably certain she could outrun the Whitbury pack despite the weight advantage of his sled. But she had to save the spurt of speed for the last few miles into Nome. She spared a moment to admire the common sense of Dave Cohen for choosing, against the temptation of unlimited funds, heavy, workmanlike dogs that would see their musher through the heaviest weather: it was an important compensation to balance James's relative lack of experience in dog sled racing.

They were running uphill now. She watched James closely as they approached the crest of the hill, saw him jump off and hold the sled down as the lead dog disappeared over the brow. Dave Cohen had taught him well. Beside the trail, the snow bore testimony that another musher had already crashed here. The lead dog would crest the hill and stop pulling, the swing dogs and team dogs would in turn cross the brow of the hill and, feeling the towline slacken, slow down; then the biggest and strongest dogs, the wheel dogs, bearing the whole weight of the sled and therefore pulling so much harder, would come over the top and, suddenly relieved of the weight of the sled, would accelerate downhill right over the relaxing dogs in front of them. And *then* the sled would pile onto the tangled dogs . . . Rhodes shuddered. Once, just over the brow of a hill much like this one, she had lost a lead dog she had spent three years training.

Over the hill the geography changed: they were now in a forested valley, the trail crossing its width from ridge to ridge. The trail was cut and marked and excellent going with the wind, softened by the trees, now behind them. Rhodes prepared to check her dogs if they looked like running into the back of James's team but he gave his dogs their head and she had no need to brake or pass; if she misjudged a passing maneuver here, the trees would damage her, her dogs and sled more than the poles stuck

57

into the frozen river did. Down that slope she and her dogs reached eighteen, perhaps even twenty miles per hour, a third as fast as automobiles on the highway, but she had no protective metal around her. She passed two teams, one off the trail from an accident over that sharp brow, one still racing that pulled over promptly when James shouted, 'Trail!' Rhodes was exhilarated; this was almost like sprinting in Colorado! Up the incline on the far side James with his bigger, stronger dogs pulling his lighter sled much more easily, drew away from her. Rhodes had to resist the devil whispering in her ear: *Shake the drivebow for a little more speed. Your dogs have what it takes. You can beat him!* That earwig was in James's pay, cajoling her to tire her dogs unnecessarily. Forty yards ahead of Toots's nose, the Whitbury team turned to the left of the trail as they approached the crest of the hill. This was her opportunity. Almost involuntarily Rhodes shook the drivebow gently. Toots raised her head and put on extra pace: the lead dog had felt the tremor and it was enough: between her and Rhodes there were no reins, no physical connection except the towline tied to the sled but Rhodes marvelled, even now, at how sensitive Toots was to her every wish, sometimes anticipating the thought no less than the command. As they passed James's slowing team, Rhodes jumped off to push and so missed her chance of throwing him a triumphant glance which, she decided after the opportunity passed, would have been childish. She closed her hands on the drivebow, ready to fling her weight on the rear of the sled as it crested the hill. But her swing dogs veered right. Toots looked right while plowing straight on for a moment, then she too veered right, half-dragged by the weight of the swing dogs. Before Rhodes could respond the team dogs followed the swing dogs, the wheel dogs behind them. Toots and the swing dogs were already scrabbling in the loose snow for something Rhodes saw only as a flash of red. *Am I snowcrazy already? Is that really a large T-bone?* The team dogs joined in the fight for the meat and the wheel dogs, trying to reach the food, jerked the sled right out of her hands and – *crack!* – into a tree. Rhodes felt like crying and –

Out of the corner of her eye she saw James run by to grab the gangline at the front of his team to keep them from joining the fighting tangle of Rhodes's team. He shouted something at her that she missed, then was gone over the crest, doing the only thing he could, dragging his dogs away and downhill by main force, shouting commands and curses.

She had no time to indulge self-pity: if her dogs damaged each other, her race would be over right here; if her dogs fought much longer, they would drain themselves of energy and be listless for days and then her race might drag on for a while but be as surely lost. She flicked her mittens right and left to clear the tears of rage from her cheeks, then waded into the snapping, snarling dogpack to grab the T-bone from under the nose of one of her malemutes which, before he recognized his mistress, snapped at her, diverting his crushing jaws at the very last moment as he realized it was not another dog gaining the prize, biting right through the plastic sheath and stainless steel shank of the substantial zipper tag dangling close to her wrist. Rhodes held the T-bone, now the worse for wear, above her head and briefly fondled the dog's ears to reassure him she was not angry with him. One of the team dogs growled at her and strained to jump at the meat but Toots snarled softly and the obstreperous dog subsided. Rhodes took firm hold of the gangline, then threw the steak as far into the trees as she could. At the same time she shouted, 'Come on, Toots,' and started running downhill with the gangline in her hand. Toots of course followed immediately. Some of the team dogs pulled in the direction of the meat but Rhodes held the gangline taut and kept pulling, tugging at her dogs by their necklines tied into the gangline. It was not easy. Even through thick mittens, her hands smarted under the contrary pulls on the line, and her pride was pained to have fallen for the oldest dirty trick/practical joke in the book, meat buried beside the trail where a racing competitor would pass.

After a quarter-mile, she let go the gangline and swung herself onto the runners as the sled swept by. The dogs ran raggedly but they *were* running and quite briskly: her quick action had saved the moment – if not the day and the race, about which she would not know until later. She leaned over to each side and studied what she could see of her sled but it was impossible to see what had caused the loud, frightening *crack* when the sled hit the tree. One of her temporary stanchion bindings had a loose end of rawhide flapping but that would not be serious unless it came undone. Anyway, even parting rawhide, as long as it is wet and stretched, sounds *pffft*. If one of the runners was cracked, she was out, O-U-T. A cold fury possessed her: for the first time in her life she felt she could kill. And she knew with whom she would start her life of homicide. 'Hike!' she shouted at Toots and jerked the drivebow.

She rose over the crest of the next hill holding onto the drivebow, running behind her sled with her head down, casting her eyes from side to side along the runners: the sled ran level and true, which proved no more than that any break was not serious enough to cut through the plastic sheet under the runners – there could be a serious crack or even a complete break which would ride this smooth trail perfectly but destroy the sled over the first bump. There was nothing she could do about it except to stop and spend half an hour on an inch-by-inch inspection. But it would be stupid to stop the dogs before they had run the fight out of their system; in their present mood they would not need the full half hour to chew up each other seriously.

Three miles further she crested a hill just in time to see James disappear over the next one. But she did not ask her dogs for more speed; they would catch him soon enough for the simple reason that her team was faster than his. She whistled to herself to relieve the tension and studied her dogs minutely for signs of injury sustained during the fight. Soon, coming out of a sharp lefthander, she found herself at the top of a two-mile-long curving slope with James no more than four hundred yards ahead, looking over his shoulder at her, shouting up at the plane circling very low overhead, vigorously shaking the drive-bow of his sled as the plane's engine drowned his shouted instructions to his dogs. But his leader felt the toboggan shaking behind and put on a turn of speed.

She saw James grin up at the pilot and throw a fist aloft in a victory salute at Dave Cohen sitting next to the pilot. Then, suddenly, from the end of a tight little circle, the plane dived straight at Rhodes.

There was no time to watch in horror or scream in fear. The plane was almost upon her and her dogs. The pilot wore orange glasses – orange, not the yellow shooter's type – and affected a thin mustache with the ends turned up. *He's coming down to kiss me*. And then, *My brain's being Lycomingized. If I live, I must remember to tell Margery my fine new word for the way machinery brutalizes civilized – Pull yourself together!* Toots, whining piteously in her fear, reared up, turned left, led the dogs over the snowdrift the wind had blown on the downside of the hill. Rhodes felt the fur edging of her parka flutter icily in the propwash as the plane passed so close she

61

could almost touch it. She could certainly see Dave Cohen's molars as he shouted at the pilot. Her sled was on its side and her dogs in a tangle and she flat on her back in the soft snow, one hand still on the drivebow, and they were all sliding with gathering speed to the bottom of the drift. She did not know how it had happened.

The plane was gone from the sky, though not its sound.

Rhodes, her sled and her dogs came to a gentle halt at the bottom of the snowdrift.

Before her mind could explode in rage, she blocked it and jumped up. No broken bones. None of the dogs seemed hurt but Toots still whined, as did some of the other dogs, and the rest barked aggressively or snapped nervously at each other. She talked softly to her dogs as she disentangled them; almost miraculously, the necklines to the gangline and the tuglines to the towline straightened as she pulled the gangline and the dogs jumped erect. Still she talked soothingly to her dogs as she ran her hands lightly along the flanks and legs of each to calm them and feel for the hurt dog: it would always shy away from the reaching hand. Seconds counted now. She heaved at the sled to right it: it was heavy but, upside down, the weight was on top because her father had built her sled with hand tools and love to keep the center of gravity low, so that a determined push was helped by the weight distribution seeking its own gravity-assisted equilibrium.

As her hands rose towards the drivebow she nearly called, 'Hike!' but instead –

She stepped away from the sled and folded her arms and calmed her mind. She would convert the adrenalin of anger into Winner's Pep Juice. If she allowed these mishaps and incidents, however unfair, to upset her she might as well give the race to James Whitbury right now. No matter what happened she would run the race the way she and her father had planned. She turned and inspected her dogs limb by limb and then her sled inch by inch. The dogs were fine and the sled runners were not cracked, nor any additional stanchions: that loudly demoralizing crack must have been made by a twig explosively crushed by the weight of the sled.

Before starting she breathed deeply and resolved again to let nothing upset her rhythm.

But, when they started again, her dogs ran raggedly, without that well-oiled rhythm which marks a happy team moving at optimum speed, wholly out of sync now with each other and with her.

Rhodes pursed her lips. This way they would be lucky to see James again, even if her dogs did not lie down mutinously long before she reached Nome.

Suddenly she laughed aloud. *The hell with James Whitbury! I'll run this race the way I run all my races, against myself.* In the long run – and there is no longer run than across Alaska – she would beat him because she was a better dog-sledder. The dogs heard her laughing and she saw their ears peaking and heads rising from dejected plodding to alert interest as they sensed her change of mood, making it their own. Then the dogs were off, sprinting as they sometimes do after horses while on training runs. Rhodes could only hold on desperately until their new-found excitement subsided. On this curving downhill run she also had to hope that the heavy sled would not overturn on her and the dogs. And yet, knowing the danger, she laughed exultantly into the wind whipping at her face, pinching her cheeks around her glasses, threatening to disintegrate her cap if it failed to rip it off. She even shook the drivebow and shouted, 'Come on!'

She had never ridden a dog sled faster in her life and doubted she ever would but made no attempt to slow the dogs. When they came to Knik and the dogs slowed of their own accord, she was saddened, as she had been on the day she had to choose between her dolls and sled dogs, as she had been at each of the divides of her life. She had never been to Knik before, though she had intended coming as a tourist with her father and Harvey and Margery. But a couple of her dogs developed diarrhoea – as did dogs from several other teams – so they had all stayed to help her care for the dogs and to share her worry over whether they would recover in time for the start. Now there was time for no more than a glance at Knik, home of Joe Redington, Sr, who had earned the title Father of the Iditarod by mortgaging his homestead to put up the prize money for the first race; he had run in every race since. Rhodes knew little more about Knik: it had been the big town in these parts until construction of the Alaska Railroad, with its railhead at Nenana from where the relay of mushers in 1925 had carried the serum forward to Nome. The railroad had required a construction camp at Anchorage, from which grew Alaska's largest city while Knik died. There was not much of Knik, even now that it was the center of much Iditarod activity, the site of the Mushers' Hall of Fame, and once more supported a few families. Rhodes passed through Knik too quickly to retain any flavor of its history. With a faint sense of loss she headed into the trees on the far side of Lake Knik.

Then her spirits lifted. There had been no spectators at Knik! She was now into the race proper, too far into the wilderness for outside spectators to make the trek. Those who lived here were away taking part in the race or organizing the Anchorage end or helping at the first dangerous big river crossings. At last she was into the land of doers and achievers.

And she had caught James Whitbury, running through

the trees only a hundred and fifty paces ahead of her. Now she was calm again, icily composed, with no intention of passing him merely to prove the mishaps of the day had not unsettled her. She followed at the pace he set, a comfortable speed of perhaps nine miles per hour, which suited the routine she and her father had planned. She was travelling, and intended to continue so, on what she thought of as Joe May's schedule because it had first been propounded by that great musher; she would travel for five-and-a-half hours, stop for four, run for another five-and-a-half, then rest for nine hours. May admitted that at nine miles per hour on this schedule he had no chance of winning – except if foul weather slowed down the really fast teams. Other mushers had chosen their dogs to average eleven or twelve miles an hour and trained towards that target; Rhodes had considered carefully whether she should follow the example of this majority of experienced mushers but decided against it: if the weather turned foul – as it did every year without fail somewhere along the Iditarod Trail – she did not want to be out there in the middle of nowhere with sprinters lacking the gumption for tough going. Joe May had won in 1980. . . Rhodes had noticed with interest that most of the rookies followed May's example. James Whitbury's dogs in particular were much heavier than her own. Yet, while not having the fastest dogs in the race, she had passed several teams among the birch and alder which here and there broke the ubiquitous spruce and been passed by only three other teams. Rhodes recognized one of the passing mushers as Dick Mackey who, in 1978, after a thousand miles, had won by only one second from Rick Swenson.

'Hey-hey, hey!' she called to her dogs. 'We're still up there with the leaders. What d'you know!' She had talked to her dogs since she first started racing at fourteen and had never been embarrassed at being overheard.

'Got a map to Nome I can borrow?' one of the mushers they passed shouted good-naturedly at her.

'Lent mine to Swenson,' she called back. Many of the rookies and even some of those who had run the race several times regarded the whole affair as one long, dangerous, ultra-testing, superbly challenging camping trip. That was fine by her but she had to reach Nome before James Whitbury and he would not camp longer than was necessary to rest his dogs. Besides the 'campers' (a misleading appellation for men and women engaged in such strenuous and dangerous enterprise), there were those running this year's race as an apprenticeship, learning the skills needed to compete seriously in a later Iditarod; Rhodes hoped to keep well up with this group, reaching Nome a few days, at most a week, behind the winner of the race. The 'campers' would be straggling into Nome up to three weeks after the winners were back home and planning strategy for next year's race.

Night fell and she switched on her headlamp. She despised the puny thing, throwing its thin light always not far enough ahead, too weak to reveal important detail of the terrain, flickering with every swing of her head: it was the best she could find and she was certain other mushers suffered equally but that was no consolation.

Time for one of her scheduled breaks. The dogs ran strongly, without sign of fatigue. They were only now hitting their stride, recovering from their first-mile-miseries, the phenomenon known to every musher of the first mile of every journey being always the most frustrating because the dogs would stop to relieve themselves, dip into the snow for a drink, find distraction in moving branches, start fights. Rhodes had noticed that, as training encompassed longer and longer stints on the trail, so that first miserable mile stretched. There was no remedy but patience: the musher who lost his temper with the dogs before they settled down would merely ensure that his team remained unsettled for the rest of the day. Today the dogs seemed to know how long the total journey would be and to stretch the first mile proportionately, helped by the upsets of pranksters and pilots. Now, just as the dogs were running easily, relieved at being out of the towns, away from crowds and automobiles, it was time for a scheduled break. Rhodes was reluctant to stop; not only were the dogs running well but, if she stopped, she would lose sight of James Whitbury. On the other hand, she had already resolved not to let him dictate the pace of her race. Besides, it was unwise to break her schedule so early in the contest: Nome was a long way ahead.

'Whoa!' she called when she saw a clearing big enough for her and her dogs to camp well off the trail. She was too tense to relax. I will sleep tomorrow during the long mid-day break, she decided. She fed the dogs and inspected their feet and harness, then warmed rawhide thongs gently but thoroughly on the stove and made a permanent job of tying in the replacement stanchions. *Just a few broken stanchions and they could have put me right out of the race.* But she recognized that she was fortunate not to have been injured in one of the mishaps of the day and not to have lost any of her dogs. When the sled had slammed into those posts she had not given a thought to injury to herself, only to moving her sled out of the crushing wind, more concerned for her dogs. She had already seen several teams off the trail with damaged sleds or hurt dogs and spotted at least two dogs being carried in sleds, sick or too badly injured to run. Yes, she had been lucky: all her dogs were pulling on the towline, she was unscathed and her sled had been repairable.

Down the trail there was the steady light of another

musher camping just out of earshot. She felt reassured and worried not at all about James Whitbury gaining on her in this scheduled break.

When she hit the trail again, shortly after midnight, she found he had gained nothing on her. He had pulled off the track to camp as soon as he saw her stopping. She drove her team past his campsite and noticed that he had cleared up meticulously. He was waiting behind his toboggan, ready to follow the minute she passed. Toots, always a competitive dog, picked up speed for a while, then settled down to a steady nine miles an hour as Rhodes had taught her to do.

So Master Whitbury is pacing himself to *me*, she thought incredulously. Her father and Harvey Mannesman had agreed that pacing yourself to anyone else in a race this long was stupid; many of the experienced mushers were of the same opinion, though it was true that the leading mushers, potential prizewinners, tended to stick closely together, watching each other, not letting any serious competitor get too far ahead. But that was different – the veterans knew from experience their own abilities and limits in the Iditarod, something the rookies were still learning. *On the other hand, James and I are having a race within a race, so why shouldn't we think like the leaders?* But she was determined not to change her schedule.

They ran in the dark across the musk-smelling swampland towards Susitna Station, crossing many little lakes, detouring around others, racing up the Susitna River Valley at angle to the lie of the land. Rhodes knew they were passing Flathorn Lake and longed to see and experience it. *Will I ever come back this way, will I have another chance to see Flathorn Lake?* She turned her head into the darkness but her light picked out only confusing shapes of grey-green shadowed in purple. And yet, despite her sadness at missing the grandeur of it all, a strange exhilaration took hold of her: THIS IS RACING! She could feel the combined spirit of the other mushers straining towards Nome. And, even when she was not aware of these modern-day competitors . . .

Number One ran ephemerally just in front of her, Toots's nose almost down between the booted feet on the runners of the sled in front; beyond the burly figure of the musher, Rhodes could see the fur-wrapped parcel of serum on its way to deliver the children of Nome from a killer disease. The ghost of Leonhard Seppala broke trail for her . . .

Before she would have thought it possible she reached the Susitna River checkpoint.

'Rhodes Delaney,' the checker repeated her name. Then, voice rising in surprise, 'Rhodes Delaney! You're fourteenth through here, do you know that?'

Rhodes smiled happily. The first twenty places pay prize money. It was flattering to be up with the potential winners, though she would not fool herself she could stay with them all the way to Nome.

'You gained on seven teams already. Okay! Now, the next fifty miles to the Skwentna checkpoint is good trail. Just follow the Yentna River to where the Skwentna joins it. You can't go wrong. You're only a couple of hours behind the leaders,' he added, as if still unable to believe the evidence of his eyes. 'Okay, I checked off everything you're supposed to have, except the post. Where do you keep that?'

A sudden exam-room knot formed in her stomach as she started digging into the gear on her sled. If she failed to show the parcel of envelopes, she would be disqualified. Frantically she tore equipment from the sled and threw it down on the trampled and refrozen ice. She had packed the post packet, she *knew*; anyway, she had shown it to the checker at Eagle River checkpoint. 'I had it at Eagle River!'

'Yes, I know. Otherwise they wouldna let you leave.'

'I know it's somewhere in there,' she said with all the confidence she could muster and once more piled into the untidy stack of gear. 'Everything on the compulsory list was right on top to make it quick at the checkpoints.'

'Maybe you dropped it along the way.'

'No! I tied the net down myself. It was still fastened until you undid it.'

The checker wriggled a finger underneath the rim of his cap to scratch his head. 'Yah, it was properly fastened. But I can't let you leave without your post packet. Pull off the trail over there while you look.' He started throwing her gear back in the basket. 'You can repack the sled as you look, okay?'

'Yes, all right,' Rhodes agreed dejectedly and then, with a little more spirit, added: 'I'm sorry to confirm your suspicion that a rookie ought not to be so far up.'

He laughed. 'Hey, don't take it like that. Anybody can lose something along the trail. Do you want to declare your compulsory twenty-four-hour layover here so you can get a new post packet?'

Every musher has to lay over for twenty-four hours at one of the checkpoints along the trail to rest the dogs; during this compulsory stop the difference in starting times is equalized so that all competitors are in the same position as if they partook of a simultaneous mass start at Mulcahy Stadium.

'I was going to call it after Rainy Pass,' Rhodes said.

'Yeah, right, that's where everybody is rushing to before the weather closes in. But your other choice is to backtrack on the trail, looking for it. What if you can't find such a small parcel in the dark?'

She looked up into his kindly red face: he was genuinely concerned for her. 'I'll declare my twenty-four-hour lay-over here if I can't find it in the basket.'

Carefully, she re-packed her sled, marvelling again at how little gear she had brought to cross one of the largest expanses of snow and ice on God's earth; she had spent many evenings agonizing over the weight of this or that, especially after she heard that James Whitbury's alloy sled weighed no more than twenty pounds and that most of his gear too was made from the same featherweight material.

The post packet was not there.

She was being punished for her pride in how well she had done, running near the leaders. She rose, pressing her hands into the small of her back, to watch two teams pass through in quick succession. She wondered where James Whitbury was: had he run into trouble, like one of the mushers coming through who carried an injured dog in his sled? The dog had broken its leg in a hole stomped into the trail by a moose. Rhodes was invited to inspect the dog's leg while the official and the musher looked on. Rhodes was pleased by this sign of acceptance, even when the musher said, 'Women got good hands.' The animal seemed comfortable, closing its eyes and falling asleep the moment she finished her inspection. 'It's had a broken leg before,' the musher said, not quite able to disguise the apprehension in his voice. 'I'm a lot more upset than he is, I can tell you. Thing is, he's my leader. My other leader was hurt in that big dog fight back in Anchorage.'

'You'll find another leader in your pack,' Rhodes consoled him. 'What about your swing dogs?'

'I'll try them but neither of them takes to responsibility, you know what I mean?'

Rhodes knew. A lead dog must want to be a leader, must glory in the responsibility, otherwise the other dogs

71

would never accept it and would certainly not follow it simply because it ran out front.

When the musher had sympathized with Rhodes's problem and resumed his race, Rhodes said, 'I'd better declare my twenty-four-hour layover as from now.' She looked at her watch.

'What I can do, I can book it from the time we first discussed it. That'll save you an hour, okay?'

'Hey, I don't want to get you into trouble.'

The checker winked. 'The Iditarod is a family affair. This early in the race we like to give the mushers the benefit of the doubt. Here comes that guy with the fancy sled, whatsisname.'

'James Whitbury,' she replied automatically, feeling blood rising in her face from anticipatory embarrassment at the humiliation he would certainly inflict on her as soon as he heard she had made the most elementary error in the book, losing her post packet. *What would have happened to the children of Nome if Leonhard Seppala had lost the serum-parcel?* But she would not ask the checker not to mention her loss . . .

'What's he think he's in, a twenty-mile sprint?'

'He must have taken a break. He was right behind me when I took the trail this morning.'

'That's strange. I mean, here's the natural place to take a break if one is due. He could get acuppajoe here and be warm. That reminds me of my manners. You want acuppajoe? It's on the stove in the shed there – pour me a mug too. I'll just check him through and then we'll radio Anchorage and ask them to fly you out a new post packet, okay?'

But, instead of accepting the offered escape, Rhodes waited. Better to get it over than let James think she hid from his scorn. She watched him draw up. He too carried all his mandatory gear on top, including his post packet.

72

He stood beside his sled, smiling pleasantly at Rhodes but saying nothing, while his gear and food was checked. He was ready to go, reaching for the drivebow, when the checker asked him the same question he had asked the other mushers who had come through: 'You didn't maybe find this little lady's post packet beside the trail, did you?'

The smile grew broad – Like molasses running sickly sweet out of a barrel, Rhodes thought, *Here it comes*. Without comment, he pulled a packet from his parka pocket and threw it to Rhodes, who instinctively fielded it. Turning aside quickly to hide tears of relief and fury at being succoured by her chief rival, she secured the post packet under the net.

'Hey! You shoulda reported that first off.' Surprise and outrage grated in the checker's voice.

'Slipped my mind in the excitement,' James said mildly. He turned to Rhodes. 'The smart thing, instead of just waiting aimlessly, would've been to declare your twenty-four-hour layover and call Anchorage for a new post packet.'

'She did,' the official said flatly.

'I certainly hope you cross Rainy Pass before the weather closes it down,' James said to Rhodes, 'otherwise you'll win the red lantern.' The red lantern is the symbolic 'prize' given to the tail-end musher in a sled race. He pushed his sled, shook the drivebow and called softly, 'Come on.' His dogs carried him into the night.

Rhodes stared after him. He was a hundred yards away, disappearing into the darkness, when she found her voice. 'Bastard!' she said through clenched teeth.

'What's going on here?' the checker demanded.

'A private race between us,' Rhodes replied shortly.

'He found your post packet, so why are you calling him names?'

Her mind gnawed at the twenty-four frustrating hours

she would now have to spend here. 'What is the weather forecast for Rainy Pass, do you know?'

'Bad. You can call Anchorage for an update. But you could waste a lot of time trying to get through to them. If I was you, I'd just push on.'

Rhodes was puzzled. 'You mean, go now?'

'Sure. I don't normally chase off pretty girls but you're obviously serious about racing that guy Whitbury. He'll get a permanent start if he's across Rainy Pass when the weather locks you up this side.'

'But what about the twenty-four-hour layover I've already declared here? Doesn't – '

'Doesn't matter a damn, see? You can declare your twenty-four any place you want, as often as you want, every checkpoint you want. The rules only say you must *take* it once. They don't say nothing about not *declaring* it more than once. Rick Swenson now, he's a big one for declaring his mandatory layover every once in a while just to keep the other front-runners guessing.'

'Ye-esss,' Rhodes breathed. 'I wonder if Master Whitbury knows that little bit of strategy.'

'One thing before you go?'

'Sure.'

The checker hesitated so long Rhodes thought he would never speak. Suddenly, knowing what he would ask, she wished he would not. At last he blurted, 'You think he snatched your post packet?'

Rhodes could only look at him. She would not lie: James Whitbury had opportunity, while she repaired her sled; and he had inexplicably arrived here hours after her, long enough for her to despair and declare a layover which, with the forecast weather, could knock her out of the race. But she would not condemn him on such flimsy evidence. And he had brought the post packet to her. If

74

he was guilty as charged, the smart thing would have been to bury it, and he was not stupid.

'You can protest, you know,' the checker persisted.

Rhodes shook her head. 'My Dad always says, "Winners are made running behind their dogs on icy trails, not whining protests in overheated committee rooms." Thanks for your help!' She shook the drivebow. 'Hike!'

'Good luck!' the checker shouted after her.

She first knew she was lost when Toots, Gee'n'Tee and Seven'n'Seven became tangled in brush. The long train of dogs, sled and musher stopped, not abruptly, but with unmistakable finality. She untangled the dogs and studied the ground ahead. They had lost the trail, that was certain even in the weak light of her headlamp. She turned the team around, tangling them in the brush again, and extricated them patiently. 'We can afford the time to do the job right, Toots.' She did not want to run so fast that she caught up with James and let him know she had not taken her twenty-four-hour layover. With determined calmness she led the dogs by the gangline back along her trail glittering in the moonlight like a zipper cut in the snow by the sled, her own footprints centred in the crossing teeth. Finding the main trail again was not difficult: which direction to head from there was another matter. It was plain what had happened: the musher without a lead dog had lost the trail here and trampled all over the landscape before making his choice. Pawprints, bootprints and sled-drag trails struck out to all points of the compass. The pink tape used to mark the trail predictably had blown away. Rhodes stood beside her sled, steadying her compass, as another team emerged from the brush. The dogs sniffed each other. It was one of the mushers who had passed her at the checkpoint while she searched for her post packet: he should have been at least an hour ahead of her. That James Whitbury, who had left between them, was not here proved that *he* had not lost the trail.

'Not that way.' He pointed in the direction from which he had arrived.

'That way, nothing but scrub and brushwood,' Rhodes answered, pointing to her own trail.

He ran his headlamp around the other trails they could see. 'That leaves a lot of choice, Miss. What's your compass say?'

'One of those three trails over there.' Rhodes pointed again and offered him the compass to check for himself. 'But I'm not heading that way. We were veering right when we lost the trail. I'll veer left until I find the open spaces of the river. The checker at Susitna told me the trail follows the river. Too many trees here for that.'

'Woman's intuition?'

'If you're an Eskimo or Indian, I'll follow you.' She was carefully keeping her light out of his eyes, as he was keeping his out of hers; not looking at each other gave the conversation a slightly offbeat quality.

'Hell, no. I used to be a Beverley Hills hairdresser 'til I got fed up and came up here three years ago. Lead on, Sister.'

Ten minutes later Toots veered right again but this time there was a wide expanse between parallel lines of trees. No pink ribbon remained here either but Toots had her nose to the ice, sniffing the trail of the teams ahead; Rhodes knew they were back on the trail, though the going was not as flat as she had expected, probably when it crossed islands, and often led up the banks, piled in places to a hundred feet with snowdrifts. It was on the steep downside of one of these that the hairdresser lost control and overturned his sled. There was no way Rhodes could stop until she reached bottom. She made a wide turn to reduce speed before returning to look up to where his dogs and his sled were dark splotches almost fifty feet above her.

'Are you all right?'

One of the splotches moved around the others; the creeping rorschacht was the musher examining his dogs for injury. 'Yeah! Can you wait until I check the dogs and turn my sled right side up?'

'Of course.' Toots and her other dogs were lying down already, as sled dogs will at every opportunity. Without thinking about it she started up the wall of snow.

'No! Stay there. If you help me, I'll be disqualified.'

'Sorry!'

'It's okay. It's easy to forget.'

Yes, she thought. Easy. One's natural inclination is to help.

When at last he brought his sled and his dogs level with her, he said, 'Thanks for waiting. You go on ahead. You set too furious a pace for me. This is my first Iditarod.'

'Mine too,' Rhodes called over her shoulder as she drove her team into the night.

'Then you're mad,' he shouted after her.

For another ten minutes she enjoyed the wind whipping against her body where it rose above the sled, the sensuous pleasure of speed on the even ice of the river, the rollicking fifty- and sixty-foot descents down sliding loose-snow banks, the crunch of crystal-ice underfoot. Then she started talking softly, reassuringly to her dogs, especially to Toots, so that they would not think they were in disfavor with her, would not feel guilty for losing the trail and becoming tangled in the brush. Soon they settled into a steady pace. *Right*. The same pace James Whitbury would keep. Perhaps even a little slower. Good! Let him think she had taken her twenty-four-hour break: she would do nothing to let him find out she had not. All she would have to do then would be to judge the moment to 'catch up' – and he would think she was *twenty-four hours ahead* of him. The right moment would be just when he called his own twenty-four-hour layover; she could then make a big effort to gain a march on him, call her own layover and exert herself only enough to stay ahead while he burned up his dogs trying to catch up . . . Of course she would have to make sacrifices too, the first coming up shortly at Skwentna checkpoint. She had planned to take her scheduled nine-hour break there at the log-cabin of the famed Joe Delia, sleeping upstairs in the loft he reserved for the women on the trail. She had been looking forward intensely to meeting Joe Delia, who was said to have rerouted the Iditarod, when he broke trail for its modern incarnation, to protect his beaver, lynx and marten trap-line. In more recent years, after Delia had moved his trap-line away, the trail had been restored to its rightful position. Rhodes thought that a great story, symptomatic of the *living* nature of the race and the trail along which it was run. She cared not a *poof!* for historical exactitude if it endangered a man's livelihood. But James Whitbury undoubtedly would take a break at Skwentna so she would have to camp before then and forego Joe Delia's hospitality. Still, there was no problem about camping short of Skwentna: she was now on the last of the flat – well, mostly flat, early part of the race and there was no shortage of camping spots.

She calculated she was about two hours behind James, made up of an hour when she lost the trail and another hour waiting for the ex-Hollywood hairdresser to sort out his shunt. It was a large enough margin, she decided, and kept to her steady nine miles per hour. Routine. In the dark, with nothing to look at, her unoccupied mind recalled the kindly red-faced checker. Why is it, Rhodes wondered as she ran behind her dogs into the night, that all the good men and true I meet are getting on in years? Or, if they are younger, have that sedately smug look of men happy in the bosoms of their loving families? 'I'm twenty-three,' she said aloud, 'and the only unmarried men I know are hyper-competitive rattlesnakes. Feeling sorry for me, Toots? Well don't, because we'll beat him hollow.' When, soon after, she found mortal danger on the trail, she did not consider an instant bright shaft of cheerfulness paradoxical at all; rather, a reminder that self-pity was an indulgent insult to her intelligence. She had recalled Margery's view of Rhodes and Rhodes's men: You set your standards too high, Margery had told her once. You can be good and dull and see only the best in everyone, like Lorette; or you can be a sharp-tongued bitch like me and enjoy yourself. But you can't have it both ways, unless you enjoy being miserable . . . *The hell with self-pity!* And then, *You're pretty free and easy with the swearwords now you're on the trail. As well your daddy cannot hear you, girl.*

When she first saw the moose she felt a shaft of good cheer – it was a *natural* danger, not some prank contrived to interfere in her race or caused by stupidity or unforeseeable accident. Then, as she caught the malevolent eyes of the animal, she could not restrain a startled 'Damn!' It was the biggest moose she had ever seen. In that uncertain half-light of an Arctic winter dawn, it rose from the lacy ground-mist like evil from another age, reclaiming its heritage from the interloper and her dogs. It was also the nearest she had ever been to a moose: they are not uncommon in these parts but Alaska is vast and previously she had seen them only from an aeroplane, following the gray-green track of a moose munching its way across the frozen landscape until the trail was lost or, rarely, they sighted the sulking dark-gray bulk that could be nothing else. But from that safe distance she had never imagined

79

a moose could be as huge as the beast now straddling the trail a hundred yards ahead, glaring at her. Perhaps, she hoped, it is the half-light magnifying it. She travelled another thirty yards before a shouted 'Whoa!' and her weight hard on the brake brought the sled to a lurching halt. A moment of uneasy silence. The moose lowered its head to glare more directly. Ears flattened, nose flaring defiantly, lips drawn back from big square teeth, repeatedly it slashed its tongue out over its nose. Its anger was tangible, even without the other signals: sharp cloven hooves lashed out a warning; for emphasis, it reared on its hind legs and pawed the air, a prelude to stomping her into the earth.

It *was* even larger than she had feared. In the sled Rhodes had a heavy Russian pistol her father had brought back from Korea; all the mushers had been advised to pack a weapon but hers was at the bottom of her gear after the search for her post packet at Susitna. Even if it had been on top, and if she could have unclipped the net in time, it would not have been much good against three-quarters of a ton of enraged moose charging to contest the trail with her. One moment the moose was a quivering mountain of rage pawing the earth, the next an irresistible force ten yards nearer to her and accelerating, head down, horns leading, hooves pounding, intent on crushing her and the dogs.

Toots whimpered and her fur rose. But she stood her ground, sensing the unrest of the dogs behind her but waiting for Rhodes's command. Rhodes held the brake down against the tension of the towline, held position, reminded God 'I haven't been a bad Christian,' waited, waited longer for the moose to come too near and be running too fast to swerve and kill them when they made their break. Now she could see its eyes more clearly in the growing light as it was almost upon them. Soft brown, mournful almost, belying the wild flaring nostrils, snorting breath, intimidating bulk, terrifying charge.

Three more seconds!

'Hike!' While her voice still rang in her ears the bitter taste of defeat was on her lips; and her stomach knotted in the knowledge that her ill-judgement and failure of nerve would result in her dogs being stomped. Desperately she tried to rectify her error by stamping on the brake and in that moment hope flared.

'Gee, gee! Come gee, come gee!' She could *smell* the moose now. It towered over her. She jerked her foot off the brake.

The straining Toots and the two swing dogs felt the moose's snorting breath on them and they frantically jerked the sled forward, turning right at the same time. Even in her numbing fear Rhodes nodded approval as the swing dogs followed in Toots's footsteps rather than take a short-cut that would distance them from the danger. The other dogs whinnied and pulled for life, each hard on the heels of the one in front. But she had trained them well: they all pulled in the same direction. Terrified, she still felt a flash of pride in her dogs.

The last-second pressure on the brake delayed them that vital extra moment to bring the moose so near that it could not reduce momentum and turn to attack them when dogs and sled literally side-stepped.

A blast of hot musty air from the moose's breath and shaggy hide sickened Rhodes. Her elbow struck the massive hindquarters as the sled bumped sideways across the ruts of the trail. The pain was vicious and the animal's foetid odor almost made her vomit. 'Olé!' she shouted, defiant still despite fear, panic and rage. She had never been to a bullfight and had once dropped a boy who invited her to one south of the border. Hemingway's

81

descriptions of these blood-feasts had been enough for her.

No time for reminiscing now.

'Haw, Toots, haw!' She wanted the dogs to swing back onto the trail. They were too spooked to come to another dead halt while she again tried that bullfighter-trick. She could only try to outrun the overgrown elk and she had to be headed in the right direction or would become hopelessly lost.

Toots looked uncertainly over her shoulder at Rhodes. She had been told to come around and she was an obedient dog: regardless of the moose turning ponderously a hundred yards away, wallowing like a tanker in heavy seas, Toots was leading the team around towards it. Rhodes pointed the way she wanted to go and made a throwing motion. The hurt look disappeared from Toots's eyes and she brought the team around in the direction of Skwentna.

Already the moose, charging again, was only twenty yards behind Rhodes. She could almost feel its breath upon her neck – *hearing* its angry snorting over the barking, whimpering dogs and the thunder of its hooves was *not* imagination. She shook the drivebow frantically for more speed, then jumped from the runners and pushed behind the sled. The dogs' breath heehawed in their throats in an all-out sprint; they no longer had breath left for barking or whimpering. They, too, were terrified.

Rhodes risked a hurried backward glance. The moose gained on them even as she turned. It was only ten paces behind her and she could clearly see the crazy paving pattern on its nose even in that uncertain light. Running easily, its snorting a sign of fury rather than exertion, the moose's skin barely rippled but flowed casually with the smooth coordination of its motion, like good poetry.

It will catch and trample us. Oh, my poor dogs!

2
Siberia

Even at the height of the wolfhunt by the salvagemen and the logging Indians, wolves and men saw each other infrequently, the men because wolves are difficult to see even under ideal conditions, the wolves because they soon learned it was fatal not to run at the first whiff of men or, more often, the baying of dogs carried three miles or more on the chill still forest air. The wolves were nervous, strung out by sudden pressure of change in their environment.

Over the years they had come to accept Man as another hunter with whom they shared a territory. Collectively – the individual wolf being less intelligent than the sum of the group-consciousness – they knew that in time they would test and eventually eat him, if he did not eat them first. The flesh of the human-fed aircrash survivor had been good and taken with less danger than even a weak moose cow. In general though, Man did not approach them and they avoided him, except for an infrequent stealthy look. To the wolves, this was the balance of perceived power, a Mexican standoff, entirely unremarkable in that it was their natural manner of cohabitation with all other animals of the forest: they would test those naturally stronger or bigger than themselves but only when these superior rivals seemed old or weak, ready for killing and eating, and then always in order of the oldest and weakest and least dangerous first. The men they saw in their forest fastness were not old, ill or weak. But the wolves were patient: Man's turn for destruction would come. Except that now the men had reversed the natural process and inexplicably – to these wolves – hunted them unremittingly. That the persecution rang an echo in their blood-memory did not console the wolves: it frightened them all the more by the implication that persecution could be the natural state, rather than the Eden they had been inhabiting. The negative mental state of the wolves was reinforced by their physical deterioration.

Winter is never the best time for wolves – though these had started very fit indeed – and now all their time and energy was spent in running and hiding from the hunters. There was nothing left for their own time-consuming scouting and testing of each animal in their territory, killing only one out of every eight they tested. So, on a day when the men did not appear, a Sunday, the wolves, restless with their growling-empty stomachs, were ready to hunt again, the natural time to howl. Rubbing playfully against each other, they formed a circle, noses together, tails wagging outwards, and raised their heads to the sky and howled their call of community spirit, their dedication to those who had died on previous hunts and others who might die on this one. That was how the men, having left behind their noisy dogs, found them by approaching downwind. On that single day they scored their biggest tally, fully half of the wolves they would kill in several weeks of hunting.

The wolves were weak with hunger. They had to eat before they could run again. They skulked, as for many days now, on the outermost edge of their accustomed hunting territory. The men stood between them and the forest which, until now, had been their own. Beyond lay more forest, to human eyes the same forest, but to the wolves forbidding and dangerous because it was not theirs. Serendipitously they had howled, and so been found and attacked, on the northwestern border of their memory map. They stood on the promontory of their territory nearest Siberia.

Fear snapped another link in their genetic memory: the founding father, Big Jim, and the whole troupe of wolves, all linked by shared blood and consciousness, had survived by escaping northwestwards. Reinforcing the threat of Man's guns firing relentlessly at them and the tug of recent salvation was the vaguer, older, but still powerful ancestral pull of their origin: their genetic memory discards nothing, and long, long ago wolves had arrived here from Siberia, by way of the frozen Bering Strait. Northwestwards was safe. The wolves, individually, did not want to die at the hands of these men; like all living things, they strive to maintain their individual lives. The struggle between the group taboo on crossing the line of their own territory and the individual fear of the shouting, shooting men barely two trees behind was resolved for some at the border of their erstwhile lives with the unknown: several of the wolves the hunters killed were shot while pausing involuntarily at the precise margin of their territory, sniffing their own urine-warning to would-be trespassers. Those escaped whose fear was greatest.

Having outrun the men, they found a bull moose. This moose was in its prime but the wolves were ragged with hunger and some would starve to death before they found a weaker animal. With no alternative, they attacked the strong moose, two of their company dying on its horns before they brought it down. They were so uncomfortable outside their own territory that they ripped into the moose while its antlers still swept dangerously, not waiting for blood-loss to weaken it, ripping away hide and flesh, slashing veins and arteries to eat the heart while it still beat. There were none of the usual fights for choice morsels. Gorged but uneasy even though they had lost the men for that day, instead of sleeping while part of the feast digested they ran with uncomfortably joggling bellies back to the security of their own territory.

3
Tatina

'Lamb chops.' James handed over the parcel. 'You seem to have enough food for the dogs – ' he glanced at the lines of dogs earlier mushers had dropped ' – so put these in your own food store.' He had not dropped any dogs himself.

'Thanks. You feed your dogs Grade A lamb chops?' The quality was printed on the box.

'It works for Swenson, so I thought I'd try it.'

'And?'

'I don't know if it makes any difference. I had planned to feed a fish combination but a friend in Fairbanks thought there wasn't enough fat in it for the dogs to last the distance.'

'I heard you trained for the Olympics on a potato diet.'

'Yes. Lamb chops with the fat left on, protein *and* carbohydrates. It's the same thing. Then you burn it off again. It works for people – for dogs too, I hope.'

'You'll be all right. Twenty-eight pounds of good chops will go quite a ways here.'

'Thanks for your hospitality.' James shook the drive-bow. 'Hike!' The dogs came to their feet slowly, still enjoying the long leisurely break at Skwentna. 'Hike!' He jerked the sled to help the wheel dogs break it loose from the ice, then let the dogs set their own pace. Joe Delia had told him that after another ten miles on the Skwentna River the trail would turn northwest and then rise gently over the forty miles to Finger Lake. After that the real climb to Rainy Pass Lodge would begin, then another ascent to the divide, and after that the descent on the far side of Rainy Pass – that part he wanted to cover in daylight if possible. On the other hand, Armed Forces Radio had reported a coming storm, driven by the winds that had plagued the early part of the race; he wanted to be on the other side of Rainy Pass before it hit, sometime in the next forty-eight hours.

He wondered how far behind was Rhodes, whether she would make it over the mountains before the storm locked her out. It would be a shame if she had to scratch so soon because of an accident that could befall anyone on the trail. He had seen the tears in her eyes and the turn of her head to hide anger and frustration. He would have felt the same; they shared a keen competitiveness. She probably thought he had kept her post packet until the last moment simply to make her burn. But not so: after finding the post packet beside the trail and picking it up without knowing whose it was he had lost the trail; running hell-for-leather to catch her, he had been so relieved to find her at the checkpoint, obviously having trouble with her sled, that he had forgotten about the post packet. There was no reason, having seen the net securing her gear, to suspect the post packet was hers. But there had never been any point in explaining to a furious woman until she calmed down.

She had done him a favor by challenging him to this race: though long interested in the Iditarod he had always shied away, fearful of making a fool of himself. She had provided a reason. And now, away and running, he was doing much better than he had expected. He did not want her to drop out: he wanted a real race.

Now that she had taken her twenty-four-hour layover, he could not afford to wait until she caught up with him so he could keep an eye on her. He had to gain as much time as possible so that, when he took his own twenty-four, they would start level or with him not too far behind her; then the advantage of fresher dogs could work for him.

The trail rose here, all the way to Finger Lake, at the gentle rate of about fourteen feet in every mile, something the dogs might not notice. He settled them and then kept them running briskly over the frozen marshes and along the riverbank, rising gradually through the spruce forest towards the Alaska Range which massively divides the white man's Alaska from the Interior. Running at a steady whack, just short of a sprint, he reached the Finger Lake checkpoint in just under seven hours, snacked his dogs and asked the vet flown in by the organizers to check his dogs.

When the vet rose from the last dog, he said, 'Fine dogs, son. What was I supposed to be looking for?'

'Just that they'll pull me over the Pass. I don't want to be stuck if the storm strikes early.'

'Rookie?'

'Yes.'

'They'll get you over. I wish everyone would be so careful.'

'D'you have advice on how I should stage it over the mountain?'

The vet looked down at his hands. 'Well, I'll tell you what I did when I ran. I came in here just like you did, my dogs still fresh. Then I went halfway up, camped, went again, took my long break at Rainy Pass and left there so that I finished the final ascent at dawn and could see the way down. I did that twice. The third time I ran, I decided I didn't want to see. I went down at night. A lot less frightening. You take your choice and you take your chances.'

'I was planning to hit the final descent in daylight, right after dawn.'

89

'Yes, that's probably wise. Though a lot of people say the ascent to the top is as frightening as the descent.'

'Thanks anyway.'

'Sorry I can't be more definite.' The vet laughed shyly. 'I mean, I actually like giving advice. But this mountain is something you can't tell anyone about, you have to experience it for yourself. Anyway, you're doing all right. You're the leading rookie, did you know?'

James was delighted. 'Is that so! I must be lucky. I talked to the other rookies in Anchorage and they struck me as competent and confident.'

'Still a long way to Nome. They could be pacing themselves different.'

James grinned. 'I'll keep that in mind.'

While James readied his team to leave Finger Lake, the vet offered a last piece of advice: 'In the Happy Valley, you'll be running down as often as up. A nasty shock that, when you're expecting a steady climb. Wrap your sled runners in chains to slow you down.'

'I haven't any.' Chains would damage the light alloy of his toboggan; the metal was sensitive to nicks and laboratory tests had shown that with most induced breakages the fracture had started at a nick.

'Then drag a log.'

But James had the city-dweller's reverence for trees and hated chopping them down; amongst the profusion of trees here he rationalized his sustained reluctance as due to lack of time. He saw no suitable log lying around, so instead carried his snowhook in hand, ready to throw in an emergency.

He rejoined the river for about ten miles, then turned up the Happy River Valley and into Rainy Pass. For the next twenty miles the trail would rise a hundred feet in every mile, a truly steep ascent.

At first he thought the mountain leaning forbiddingly

into the sky over him, caps glinting in the quarter moon, must be Mount McKinley but soon he came much nearer to the peaks and realized that the highest of them, even at the rate he was rising, was far short of the twenty-odd thousand feet of McKinley. He sorted through the maps imprinted on his mind, found the one he wanted, decided which direction was north-east and turned his head. The dark bulk blackening the horizon must be McKinley. It was unimportant that he could not see it clearly now; tomorrow he could look his fill. By dog sled it would take a long time to pass out of the glowering sight of the highest mountain in North America. The Athabascan Indians, who live in its shadow on the far side of Rainy Pass, call it Denali, in their language The Great One. Sensing its dominance even in the night, James thought, Denali is a far better name than that of some President who wanted to stay on the gold standard; it says something about the mountain that 'McKinley' cannot.

His toboggan teetered on the edge of the precipice at the switchback where the narrow trail turned to cross the Happy River Valley gorge for the first time. He swore and flung the snowhook he carried in his hand into the darkness. The snowhook gripped just as the sled slid over the side of the three-foot-wide track. His headlamp swept the bottomless pit below him as his feet scrabbled for purchase. The threatening drop was all the more frightening for being ill-defined. He could fall ten feet – or five hundred. He had no breath for cursing but was grateful for tying the line short on the snowhook. 'Stand!' he shouted at his dogs. 'Stand still! Stand!' He hung from the sled, feet swinging free. He looked down: there was a rock, a vague shadow protruding from the ice but it seemed firm. There was nothing else. His feet found it, pressed. It took his weight, held when he pushed against his toboggan. He stood still, breathing deeply, recovering strength. *Amid the heartrending beauty lurks heartlurching jeopardy.*

If another musher came along the trail now there would be an accident. Then he gathered his strength, gave thanks for his lightweight toboggan – and heaved. 'Hike!' he shouted at his dogs.

The toboggan slid over the precipice-edge onto the track. He knew it would ride over the snowhook, jerking the dogs to another standstill; after that the sled and dogs would slide back, over him, dragging him with them into the pit below. Unless he was quick. But he had to time his move precisely. He held to the sled and was dragged over the broken edge with it, feet swinging and knees bumping painfully on the ice-teeth. Back on the trail, he immediately rolled towards the snowhook, hoping not to roll onto its spikes in the dark. His hand slapped against it: he jerked it free and scrambled erect just before the line snapped taut. He jumped for the runners, the sno-whook a disembowelling instrument if he misjudged.

His feet thudded onto the milled serrations of the runners. He teetered as his terrified dogs took his weight and accelerated. Throwing the lethal snowhook forward into the sled, he grabbed the drivebow just before his feet slipped off onto the hard, smooth ice. He flung his other arm forward and slapped his hand onto the drivebow just in time.

For minutes he hung there, face down, loose snow whipping from the ice into his face, the toes of his boots dragging a furrow in the trail. Then, by stages, he hauled himself up until he could regain the runners.

He was surprised to find that the dogs had slowed to little more than fast walking pace.

'Delilah,' he told his leader, 'you have more sense than me.'

She did not look around to his voice but kept her nose close to the trail.

Three times more the trail crossed the Gorge and James let the dogs set their own pace. If he tried to hurry them these treacherous mountains would kill him and them. He was coming to understand why the organizers insist that a prospective Iditarod entrant must be recommended by two recognized mushers before they will consider his application: they did not want anyone's life on their own conscience. It made sense.

It was eerie, riding on a trail at places only three feet wide and not knowing whether the downside was a dip a man could put his foot in and reach bottom or a crevasse into which man, dogs and sled could disappear without trace.

Don't let your imagination run away with you. Nevertheless he grasped the snowhook firmly in one hand and remained alert: no more admiring glances at majestic Mount McKinley, lit by a quarter moon; the temptation was now reduced since from this part of the Gorge only its own rim is visible. *What a tourist attraction, if only it were easier to reach.* In the season, he knew, guides conducted people on horseback hunting trips from Rainy Pass Lodge, but the hunters flew to the Lodge, on the plateau around Puntilla Lake, halfway up the Pass; the dire grandeur of the Pass itself was experienced only by Iditarod racers.

Even at walking pace he spent most of his time off the runners, pushing the toboggan. On this uncertain footing the dogs simply could not manage his weight as well as the steep grades. Where powdered snow had fallen or blown onto the trail the going was better. But it was too dangerous to try running in the snow beside the trail: once, off the trail in a dip, he immediately sank to his chin in the snow and recovered without major delay or even disaster only by instantly spreadeagling himself behind the sled and letting the dogs, still on the trail, pull him and the sled out.

On that ascent James met only one other musher, kneeling in the snow beside the trail and vomiting from his exertions. It was fortunate that James was moving slowly, carefully negotiating a boulder, or his team would have piled onto the other standing on the trail.

James waited for the other musher to finish. The man hauled himself erect, put a mouthful of snow in his mouth, chewed, gargled, spat it out.

'Anything I can do? I have glucose to – '

'No, thanks, I have some. Sorry to hold you up.'

'Trying too hard?'

'Yeah. I want to be on the other side of this mountain when the storm hits.'

There was no room for James's team to pass. To save the other man embarrassment he said, 'I had a narrow escape so I'm in no hurry.'

'It's okay. I'm camping first chance I get.'

James followed until the other musher pushed off the trail and started erecting his pup tent. 'All right now? I can wait a while if – '

'Thanks but all I need is rest.'

James decided to carry on for another two hours, telling himself he was not so much tired as frightened. Yet every muscle ached separately. He passed a camped musher, then another. He was the leading rookie: now he must be overtaking veterans. It was the wrong time and place to be precocious. But forward motion carried the same exhilaration as downhill racing or the giant slalom. Except, he thought wryly, only fools ski in the dark.

He found himself on his knees on an incline, his dogs lying down in their traces. He did not know how long he had been there like that. He dug the snowhook, still in his hand, into the ice, wrapped the line around his wrist, curled up and instantly fell asleep.

His father, an internationally rated polo player, prodded him in the ribs with the round toe of a Church riding boot. Sealskin of course. Not now, James complained, I'm resting on a stage of the Iditarod, the toughest race in the world. Rise and run, his father said in that mild voice which cloaked the volcanic impatience of his nature. You haven't reached the target you set yourself. Not yet, not by several miles.

In common with most Americans, James Alderston Whitbury III had never been to Alaska. Unlike most people, he had the Trust: it was part charitable foundation, part conglomerate, part family bank. It had been created by his grandfather to protect the family's wealth from Washington's depredations and the stupidity of family wastrels. James's father had been a prime wastrel and many expected James to go the same way. James knew that this view was based on the similar sporting careers he and his father had chosen but he did not care enough for ill-informed opinion to point out the much more important dissimilarities. His father had never earned a penny from his polo (indeed, the suggestion would have horrified him), his only interest in the Trust being that it should allow him to keep strings of polo ponies on three continents. James knew the accountants and lawyers must have some glimmering of the scope of the Trust but so far he had not been able to spare the two or three years necessary to familiarize himself with its ramifications; his chief interest lay in designing and building things, not shuffling corporations. He was comfortably off even without the income the Trust paid him; doting uncles and aunts had seen to that. His tastes were simple – when in New York, he still lived in his mother's apartment. He acknowledged that other people worked for a living but considered he worked equally hard at being an outstanding athlete. Thus far an agreed correspondence. But James would have thought it ill-mannered to explain to outsiders that, unlike his father, he had actually added to the family wealth: his innovations in ski gear had earned the Trust useful sums and himself substantial royalties. Dog sled racing appeared to him another field of competitive endeavor where the gear was, if not outmoded, at least in need of updating.

He spent three hundred thousand dollars of his own money on specifying and building a lightweight sled of revolutionary design and, like the man who designed a better mousetrap, found a queue outside his door. At its head was Frontier Construction, which had pipeline building and maintenance contracts in Alaska. Frontier's President, Bill Swift, was personally committed to conservation; he persuaded his board that, considering future contracts on which they were tendering and the mounting conservationist protest, it was good business to use dogs and sleds instead of snow machines. Frontier ordered a thousand prototypes of James's sled and promised to take many more if the first batch worked. They would also sponsor James in the Iditarod. Swift knew and recommended Dave Cohen, a professional dog-breeder, whom James immediately hired until after the Iditarod. That was a wise move because for the next six months James was busy putting the initial thousand sleds into production, which proved easier to promise than deliver. A small specialist smelter had been used to cast the single demonstration sled but the operators at the bigger smelters lacked the skill of the prototype foundrymen in working with the unfamiliar new materials. After 'productionizing' the process, James worked with Tip Durrell, Frontier's Chief Engineer, on a program to test the sleds in the laboratory and under field conditions. After that he modified the other gear he would be carrying, most of which lent itself to lightening and much of it to innovation. Next, problems with the sleds emerged in extensive field tests, demanding more development work, more tests on beta prototypes and finally putting the finished version into production. More orders had come in but it would be well into another year before they could deliver even Frontier's full quota, so James made no promises. Despite teething troubles, the sled venture was a runaway success and had become a substantial business, employing nearly thirty people. Managers were hired but James still had to see the sled into full production before they could take over from him. And there were the thousand and one things an Iditarod runner had to take care of, even one who was wealthy or had extensive sponsorship; even if, like James, he had Dave Cohen to choose, buy and tend his dogs, or could call on the other facilities of a corporation like Frontier. Most of his fellow mushers preferred to entrust their lives to traditional, proven gear rather than to newfangled items for which no spare parts would be available in the middle of nowhere; they copied everything from the successful applications of their predecessors but, even so, there was still so much to learn that this acquisition of knowledge could become a fulltime occupation, especially in that most arcane of subjects, feeding and caring for racing huskies. Much had been learned on earlier Iditarods but everyone James spoke to conceded that much remained to be discovered; paradoxically, a great deal was known about the strains and stresses on humans in long-distance ultra-endurance events and everyone had an opinion on how James should train. He listened politely but had decided already to train on a slight modification of the schedule and diet he had followed as an Olympic skier. He abhorred the prospect of all those potatoes but he was convinced the high-carbohydrate diet worked for him; there would be no time for experimentation and he knew from experience that a diet and schedule which suits one athlete could easily defeat the ambition of another.

Bill Swift hired an animal nutritionist first to advise James and then to apply the knowledge gained to the growing dog population now supported by Frontier. Her report ran to eight hundred pages and James read it carefully, spending several days with her to be certain he understood it. Then he told Swift that feeding long-distance huskies was still a matter of guesswork and luck. There were too many variables: temperature, the diet the dogs had been fed before, their psychological condition, how hard they were being worked – these and other considerations could all affect what the dogs should be fed and what they would and would not eat.

'I guessed as much.' Swift was unruffled. 'Swenson ships a ton and a half of food. He can't use it all, so he must be preparing for all eventualities. We'll ship every kind of food to every checkpoint for you. That way you can't go wrong.'

James was not so confident. 'I could, if I chose wrong. I'm sure this nutritionist of yours is the best available but all she can tell me is that I should include more fish in the diet when it is hot and not to feed the dogs the beaver meat too soon because they won't want to go back to anything else.'

Swift laughed. 'Hell, most mushers had to learn that the hard way. You're handed the wisdom of generations on a plate. It isn't much – '

'But it isn't scientific!'

'Neither is human nutrition, the way I understand it. It's an art. Dogs are creative creatures, just like people. You want scientific feeding, go into battery hens.'

James shook his head. 'I mentioned that. She says that there are as many mixes on the market as there are manufacturers. I don't want to knock her trade but it seems to me nutritionists guess even worse than doctors.'

Swift clapped him on the shoulder. 'The delusion that all problems have solutions is peculiar to us engineers, my boy.'

James was not satisfied but he had run out of time. In the Fall he and Dave Cohen and their dogs retired to bush Alaska to train, going north as far as Shugnak on the 67th parallel, 400 miles from Anchorage, searching for the permanent cold in the shadow of the Brooks Range, beyond which lies the Beaufort Sea and the Arctic Ocean. Nearest to them were the Baird Mountains and James often ran the dogs that far in search of physical fatigue to drive from his mind the vivid images of Rhodes riding her sled around the foot of Skull Mountain; Rhodes standing beside her table at the club, first laughing, then with rage illuminating her face. He had meant to call her after the Olympics but the reporters had blown an innocent joke out of proportion. Then Rhodes had retaliated with her joke about the armed guard at the ranch being hired through his Mafia connections: this had upset his mother because her uncle had been jailed during Prohibition for smuggling Scotch whisky on his yacht and she was extremely sensitive about it. James was in no way a mother's boy but he had a strong family loyalty and that would have been an awkward time to introduce Rhodes to his mother; Rhodes had struck him as the kind of girl one had better not call unless prepared to take her home and introduce her to one's family. So he had not called. James Whitbury knew he was often awkward with people for fear of undue deference to or resentment of his wealth, but with himself he was ruthlessly honest.

When his dogs were acclimatized James and Dave took

99

them further north still, to the Frontier base camp at Prudhoe Bay. It was here, partly out of frustration at being whited-in for days on end with the reporters Frontier had flown in, that he had gotten them off his back by telling them that Rhodes was at Emmonak.

Afterwards he wanted to kick himself. He admired her sense of private dignity, her belief, held by so few of the women he knew, that one's reality does not depend on appearances in newspapers and on television, and here he was helping the hounds of the fourth estate to find her. After that it was too late to call.

James rolled away from the prodding of his father's riding boot. He wakened – not a boot, but a rounded mound of ice, cut up by the friction of a passing sled, then frozen again. A reminder that, while he might be the leading rookie, more experienced contenders were out in front, away and running. He rose groggily. He should not block the trail; it was not only against the rules but he was inviting disaster if someone should come along at speed. He moved among his dogs, coaxing them, calling their names, giving each a piece of the squaw candy – strips of dried fish – Dave Cohen had taught him to carry in his pockets, and chewing a piece himself. Then, without command from him they took the trail again, off and running as strongly as if they had rested for hours. He looked at his watch but, since he did not know when he had fallen asleep, he could not tell how much time had passed. Certainly not hours, or some angry front-runner would have crashed into him or kicked him awake to move his team off the trail.

Again he let the dogs make their own pace. His lead dog, Delilah, a purebred Siberian husky, knew what she was about and was used to rough terrain. At one point, where the trail should have turned left, he was flabbergasted to see her turning right and then straight back at him. Before he could do anything to correct her, she came up on his right. He looked left to where the trail should be; the turn was too sharp for any dog team, èven pulling the shortest of sleds, so the trailblazer had made a figure of eight to the right on an outcrop of rock. His light swung over the side as the sled turned. He saw the ice glinting between his boots, then the deep dark drop, the light not reaching bottom. The rock outcrop lay at an angle outwards – 'reverse camber' his engineer's mind described it, gently sloped but enough for him to have to strain to keep his toboggan from sliding over the edge on its plastic undersheet. *An old-fashioned wooden sled with its extra friction would not be in such danger*. Then he remembered: even the Eskimo and Indian sleds now had plastic strips on the runners. Unprotected wood would never last over 1200 miles of ice and exposed rock to Nome. The oldtimers had rebuilt worn-out sleds along the trail, using whatever grew nearby for replacement runners, but in a race there was no time for this.

The dogs crossed behind the toboggan and he let the incline of the outcrop add to the sled's momentum as leverage for him to swing it around. He heaved, felt his feet sliding on the ice, and caught the drivebow just before his dogs pulled it out of reach, knowing instinctively just where he would find it even before his head swung around and his lamp lit the hand already on it. Sled, dogs, trail, the night, all had become extensions of himself. Now there was the race and nothing else. Even so he wanted to vomit, like the man down the trail: fear and exhaustion pulling in tandem. His feet found the runners and he was grateful to stand resting on them on a long downhill section, recovering his breath and equilibrium.

He hit the ice bridge at no more than nine or ten miles an hour, already slowing but still too fast. His headlamp picked out the broken ice. He knew what had happened: a full creek had frozen and then, later, the water underneath had receded, leaving a thin layer of ice over a void. Earlier mushers had cracked the ice and now it reared up in jagged blocks frozen lethally to each other.

'Haw, haw!' he tried to steer the team around but the rear corner of the toboggan caught a large block of ice squarely. He could feel the impact in every bone as he flew through the air, hunching his shoulders to crash into the whiteness his whirling light revealed, hoping it was snow and not ice. It was snow. He rolled only once before its mushy texture absorbed his momentum. He rolled onto his knees, flailing his arms for purchase in that winter quicksand, and saw the sled, travelling backwards and sideways, aimed straight at him, closing fast. He ducked, falling flat in the white powder, face buried, hoping he would not suffocate. When he managed to raise his head again, gasping for air, one of the dogs being dragged back by the weight of the sled planted a paw firmly in his face and pushed him over backwards.

For a moment he lay spreadeagled – *This would be comical if it weren't so serious* – too stunned to move; then he half-crawled, half-swam through loose snow towards where his dogs and sled had come to rest not more than twenty feet away.

The lines were tangled but the dogs, except for a couple snapping at each other, were lying down. The incline was steep and all that had stopped them sliding over the edge was a small buildup of the wave of loose snow they had driven before them and the toboggan. His light could show nothing below. He found the line of the snowhook and at first thought he had lost the hook itself because the line was slack but when he tugged hard it caught, held, and he had some insurance. He found the gangline and patiently sorted out the dogs, hard work in that soft snow. By the time he had finished though, they were in a hole tramped three feet deep into the snow and the footing was almost good. Leading the dogs out was less easy, especially since he had to stay behind the sled and push. He put his best command leader, General, out front. Halfway to the trail, the snowhook's line length ran out and he had to crawl back to loosen the snowhook and carry it further forward while his sled and dogs stood poised to slide away from him into the darkness. With the snowhook once more affording an anchor and a little peace of mind, the last part of the recovery was almost easy. Back on the trail he realized he was drenched in sweat. He changed clothes, bearing the discomfort to avoid frostbite later, grateful that there was no wind to aggravate the cold. He had heard that in these parts the wind chill factor – the combination of wind and cold – could fall off the bottom of the US Weather Service Chart, which ends at 130° below zero. *Is this the still before the storm?* He felt the dogs but they were not wet. No legs had been broken, no tendons pulled in the tangle, nor any other injury sustained. But his dogs were as pooped as he.

'So far and no further,' he said aloud. 'Dead heroes win no prizes.'

He rewarded the dogs with a one-pound block of Philadelphia cream cheese each. Then he proceeded slowly and camped on the first level patch he found, setting his wrist alarm to continue at dawn.

After all that his last mishap on the way to Rainy Pass Lodge was almost anticlimactic, an enjoyable excitement, though potentially dangerous enough.

When they sighted the Lodge's free-roaming horses, he and his dogs were threading their way across the plateau among the sharp white peaks, covering the winding trail to the Lodge, east of Lake Puntilla, in no great hurry because James had decided to leave the Lodge so that he could complete the whole descent in blessed daylight. The dogs, rested and in high spirits, took off after the horses. James wiggled his feet into the serrations on the runners of his toboggan and held on tight. It was a ride to remember as the horses led them into the dingleweeds. The dogs barked their pleasure, the horses neighed, blowing steam in the cold crisp air, the sled bounced here and there where it touched, which was not often. It was the same exhilaration of spirit and body he had experienced on the mountain the night before, only a great deal safer. After a while he made no attempt to slow the dogs. The horses would tire of the game and outdistance the dogs, or it would be time for them to return to the Lodge to be fed. All he had to do was to stay on until then, or until the dogs became bored with chasing horses which stayed tantalizingly out of reach. Since the dogs would have a long rest before he continued up the mountain, he was not concerned that they would wear themselves out. So inured had he become to the near-disasters of the trail that his thoughts were, more than anything else, on how much of this kind of bashing his alloy toboggan could take.

Near the lake they crossed the trail and without change of pace the dogs abandoned the horse-chase and set out on the trail again.

'You're coming in steamin',' said a musher who was preparing to pull out. 'Hey, you're the guy with the ali sled. How's it holding up?'

'A couple of times I wished it were a bit heavier or I'd loaded it a bit more.'

'Yeah, I know what you mean. A heavy sled won't budge in the wrong direction so easily. But once it starts moving, it takes a lot more to stop it too, just remember that. Go!'

James stood for a moment looking after the other musher. 'Is he running out front?' he asked a hovering journalist whose plane could be seen tethered on the lake.

'Honea and Peters are an hour ahead of him but at this stage of the race it doesn't mean much. You figuring to stick with him?'

'No. He's running down Rainy Pass at night. I frightened myself badly just coming up this far. I'll wait for daylight.'

The journalist laughed slyly. 'Hey, you gave Swenson something to think about: maybe there's a rookie he's got to contend with. He doesn't know you're laying over here nearly half a day.'

'Listen, don't you write I'm setting myself up against the front runners. He'll run a long way in the twelve hours I'll wait here.'

'You're still the leading rookie, you know. You're about twelve hours ahead of the next one, that girl who looks more like a *Playboy* centerfold than a dog sled racer, the one you say – '

'Enough,' James said quietly.

The reporter looked into his face and shut up.

James, embarrassed at his overreaction, said, 'She's just twelve hours behind me?'

The journalist waggled his hand. 'Give or take a couple of hours. It's tough coming up the mountain.'

James thought that a bit rich coming from a man who had flown in but he let it ride. Rhodes had caught up twelve hours already! She would not give up. Good for her. But that was pushing too damned hard, even with dogs like hers. Or perhaps she knew something he did not . . . 'What news of the storm?'

The journalist waggled his hand again, the gesture of a

non-combatant who cared little except that trouble brought excitement. 'Thirty-six hours away, says the Weather Bureau. Couple of Indian mushers in there – ' he gestured at the Lodge ' – say it's forty-eight hours away. Take your pick. If you see the Eskimo and Indians leaving in a hurry, you want to be hot on their tail 'cos a storm's the only thing that fazes them.' The hand waggled again.

James was fed up with the journalist's disdain and badly camouflaged racism. But he nodded politely before wandering away. He would avoid the man in future; it was bad enough allowing the reporter to see his anger at that lipsmacking description of Rhodes. James had once scoffed at the manners he had been taught as the 'Code of the Whitburys' but with each misadventure he came to appreciate a little more that there was much to be said for showing the outside world at all times a bland face. (His father had actually called it 'the stiff upper lip'.) Ill-mannered slobs like this reporter gained much by angering others into displays of emotion.

James prepared food and fed his dogs. A plane landed. The vet, black bag in hand, climbed down and walked towards James.

'It was worse,' James told him, taking up their last conversation as if neither time nor distance had intervened, which on the Iditarod did not feel strange at all.

The vet smiled. 'No, I told you, it is impossible to describe. Frightened shitless?'

'I couldn't put it better myself. Would you give my dogs Vitamin B shots please.'

'Refusing food? Diarrhoea?'

'No. As a preventive measure.'

While the vet worked he told James across a dog James held for him, 'You want to worry less about the dogs and more about yourself.'

106

'I'm in better condition than I look. I just ran into some private nightmares on the mountain. About the dogs, there aren't any muscles strained from last night's accidents, anything like that?' The vet had given each dog a quick once-over, almost as a reflex, while injecting it.

'Don't worry, your dogs are all right. Come, the pilot told me there's a baron of beef laid out in there.' As they walked towards the Lodge, the vet added, 'A dog running in the Iditarod stands more chance of being alive at the end than one of the general dog population. Put another way, out of every two hundred dogs in this race, maybe one will die in the next two weeks. Out of every two hundred dogs just running around the streets and back-yards, two or maybe three will die over the same period. At first we used to worry a lot about the dogs but less now. Mushers know more about the limits of dogs, their feeding and care. And we've found out you can't work a dog to death. He'll just quit on you, lie down and refuse to go. Dogs are smarter than people.'

'Yes,' said James, remembering his night in the Gorge. 'But you still do an autopsy on every dead dog.'

'We call it a necropsy. It's a public relations exercise. If we ever find a musher maltreating his dogs we'll kick him out well before he actually kills one. I don't expect it ever to happen. A dog on the Iditarod gets treated very well indeed.'

'I can't see anybody illtreating his dogs and finishing.'

'Exactly. But, to reassure people who're suspicious of mushers and think sled racing "exploits" dogs, we do necropsies. You know what a working sled-dog pulls?'

'I've heard the rule of thumb that a dog pulls its own weight. But the old-timers often had dogs pulling two or three times their own weight over the long haul and more over short distances.'

107

'Right. Do you see any dogs in the Iditarod pulling even half their own weight?'

'No.'

'What do yours pull?'

'I worked it out. 16.8% of body weight.'

The vet whistled. 'And I thought that sled of yours was just a gimmick.'

'It genuinely weighs just twenty pounds. But all my gear was selected or specially made to weigh as little as possible. I even thought of slimming myself but decided that wouldn't be clever. I'd lose twenty pounds running the race and couldn't afford to lose more than that.'

'Smart decision.'

They paused in front of the building to enjoy the sun.

'What do the other racers pull, relative to dog weight?'

'With the exception of Joe Redington and Herbie Nayokpuk, who always carry gear to cope with every possible emergency, I reckon the average would be between quarter and half a dog's weight. That counts the sled, the gear *and* the musher.' The vet, a short dark man with a pot belly, peered up at James to make the point.

'Yes, I counted myself into the total.'

'Amazing.' He took James's arm and they walked into the Lodge. The bundles on the couches and the floor were sleeping mushers, seven or eight of them, the leaders of the race. Later arrivals and 'campers' would not rate the same hushed voices. The vet introduced their hosts. 'This is Jules and Leslie Mead. They own Teeland's Moonshine Shop in Wasilla. They're old-time members of the Iditarod family.'

'You're welcome. You want to eat or sleep first?'

'I'm already fed up with my own cooking.'

The Meads either had a very big plane or had made multiple trips. The spread they laid on would have done a Fifth Avenue hotel proud, never mind this remote outpost

108

of civilization: true to the spirit of hospitality James had already noticed in Alaska they welcomed all comers and not only mushers and race officials. There must have been fifty other people, James guessed, including two television teams with a third said to have gone already by helicopter to Farewell, a delirium tremens of reporters, and a number of people who were following the race. He looked around for Rhodes's father and friends but they were not there.

Later, replete with soup, ham off the bone with fried eggs, thickly-carved juicy beef, two beers and coffee, he took over the couch Victor Kantongan had just vacated. At once he fell into a dreamless sleep.

Late in the afternoon, he listened to a tale told by Joe Redington, the man who inspired the modern race and, at over sixty, was still running it just behind his brilliant protégée Susan Butcher. Redington told how C. C. Chittick and John Jacobsin had died in a snowstorm on a trip of which a listening musher said, wonderingly, 'But that's only four, maybe five hours of easy going!' Chittick and Jacobsin had nearly completed their journey before freezing to death in their parkas less than a mile from their destination, the Pass Creek Roadhouse. They were only a hundred feet off the trail. . . That had been in 1913 and nothing had changed since then. C. C. Chittick's body, which was never found, could still be frozen underneath the huge snowdrift that marks the location.

James spent nearly ninety minutes putting booties on his dogs. His weight saving did not extend to his dogs' footwear. He used a modified version of the design first made popular by Joe May, from whom many mushers copied running schedules, food mixes, gear innovations and – some of the younger ones – even his style: May *looked* like a publicist's dream of a musher. The traditional bootie was a pouch made from sealskin or other leather and tied with a drawstring: since these booties could not be tied tightly for fear of cutting the dog's blood circulation, inevitably they were lost and caused delays while they were found and retied. The May booties were made with a tuck just above the foot and a wide band of velcro attaching to a small square beyond the tuck, so creating a more retentive shape without endangering circulation. James had his booties made of 'breathing nylon', complete with the May tuck and velcro strip, but added a snap at the top of the tuck to take the strain off the velcro and provide a failsafe fastener; he added pieces of the plastic compound used in stick-on soles, moulded to the shape of a dog's paw and bonded to the nylon pouches. These booties took a little longer to put on because he had to match the size to the dog's paw and they could be put on only one way, like a human shoe. In training he had run eighty miles with twelve dogs and never lost a bootie.

Other mushers, preparing to leave or just arriving after making the last part of the ascent in the late afternoon, ribbed him goodnaturedly. 'Hell, you can see he's got superior dogs. Of course they wear shoes. He wouldn't ask them to walk to Nome on anything but the best.' But they carefully inspected his booties. The competitive spirit of the Iditarod runner is legend. One said, 'You got a patent on these booties, Whitbury?'

James nodded. 'But nobody will worry if you make some for yourself, as long as you don't sell them.'

'That's right generous of you. Where's the catch?'

'If they prove good all the way to Nome, I'll have tens of thousands made for sale. With those economies of scale, you'll spend more making them than they sell for.'

'Who's going to buy tens of thousands?'

'Frontier. All those dogs of theirs will need mushers and – '

'Jobs for us!'

James nodded. 'But there aren't enough experienced men. Inexperienced mushers won't know how to tie on the old-style booties. It'll be cheaper for Frontier to buy booties that don't fall off.'

They digested this. One said, 'For an inventor, you're a real regular guy.'

James looked down at his work to hide his pleasure in such acceptance.

As he pulled out he looked over his shoulder, half expecting Rhodes to be rounding the end of the lake, hot on his heels. He had decided to cover the last part of the climb, another twelve hundred feet to the divide, so that he could start the descent at dawn. This reverted to his original plan but with time and rest the fear instilled in him the previous night had faded – and other mushers had reported worse incidents, one hobbling in on a stick he had tied to a broken leg and having to be flown out to Anchorage for surgery. Besides, he could not afford to linger another fourteen hours if Rhodes had already gained half a day on him.

'She must be one of the wonders of the world,' he said to the night. 'It's just not bloody possible.' But it was. Sports reporters, the least unreliable of their breed, do not normally make mistakes about facts as elementary as who runs where in a race. 'Tungsten Woman Strikes Again!' he shouted, then listened for the reverberation and echo to bounce off the mountains rising five thousand feet into the darkness above him. 'Not quite sixty hours into the race and she's picked up twelve on me. And I thought I was running like the clappers. I'll tell you what, General,' he said to his command leader, out front because on this dangerous mountain he wanted control

111

over his team that his fast leader Delilah could not offer him, 'she doesn't even have to push any more, just keep up that pace, and she'll win unless we get lucky.' There was a fortnight yet to Nome but, if she had gained a twenty per cent advantage on him so quickly, she could gain still more. If she kept up the same punishing pace – could she? – he would never catch her.

But could she? The veterans of the race, and Dave Cohen, had agreed her dogs were good and tough and well trained. His own dogs were marginally better, if only because he had more money, but he lacked her experience as a dog sled racer. Did that matter? The Iditarod is unique. In Colorado Rhodes was a 25-mile sprint champion. No, even her unchallenged supremacy in 200-mile races in civilized Colorado would not count for much in Alaska. He had to conclude that she was simply pushing so much harder than he. 'I can't believe it,' he said aloud. 'It just isn't possible to push *that much* harder.' He went round and round the argument but there was only one answer, and it too was a question: If she pushed so much harder on this hazardous stretch up the Pass, how much harder would she press on the less dangerous flatlands of the tundra?

Would her dogs survive such a pace? He studied his own dogs. Fresh as daisies.

One of the old-timers at the pre-race banquet had recalled when general opinion held that a woman could not win a race this long because she would never push her dogs hard enough. That opinion had been quietly buried, the old-timer said, since the rise of Susan Butcher. Anyway, Rhodes would know the stamina of her dogs to the last ounce and also exactly how to preserve their strength. She would never make so elementary a pacing mistake. Unless. . .

Unless she was trying to trick him into a mistake that would put him out of the race, after which she could slow

112

down. Dave Cohen was a fine teacher but time with his pupil had been limited, while Rhodes had virtually been born a dog sled racer.

Perhaps she was just in a hurry to clear the Pass before the storm closed it.

Perhaps the storm was a myth, a rumor spread by a tactician like Swenson to make everyone else worry. James saw a clear night, the aurora borealis competing with his feeble headlamp; as the dogs settled down to a steady pace he switched off the headlamp without cutting visibility markedly. The black spots on the trail were lichens and rocks showing through a thin layer of snow. The rest of the snow had been blown from the trail, except in the ravines, where the mouth had a little extra bump over which he had to hold on tight or lose his sled and dogs: he soon learned, having to run after the sled only twice. Most of the time he was not riding but pushing. It was hard work and he kept a pace just short of perspiration, riding the sled to slow the dogs every time he became too hot. He had no more fresh underclothes until he could do his laundry at Farewell where the weather station personnel enjoyed the luxury of a tumble drier. *Contracting frostbite from my own sweat is just about the most stupid thing I could do.*

The turquoise and yellow northern lights were bright and sharp – better than Times Square, it seemed to him – but cast eerie shadows as he ran up the mountain, always upwards, nearly twenty miles up and up and up.

'Soon I'll start hallucinating,' he said aloud. The experience was addictive.

More to rest his mind than his dogs, he took a break when he found open water at Pass Creek. He ladled some of the shockingly cold, clear water for himself and then let the dogs dip. He was about to commit the fatal mistake of chucking the water undrunk in the mug into his face –

113

in sub-freezing temperature – when he saw the white shapes jumping off what appeared a sheer cliff face. He knew they were wild Dall sheep but the fancy lingered that he stood in a graveyard and the spirits of C. C. Chittick and John Jacobsin had arrived to inveigle him into their world. When he shook his head to free his imagination of the ghosts, he saw the dipper poised to throw the water into his face, to seep into his clothes, to freeze and maim or kill him. He cursed aloud.

By then his dogs were already thirty paces away. The water from the dipper scythed out as he ran after the dogs, shouting like a madman to make himself heard over their barking. 'Goddamn mountain sheep are tough, you stupid mutts. Tough! Stop! I give you Grade A lamb chops and you want Dall sheep. . .'

He had to save his breath for running. His dogs were driven by demons, straining after those sheep. The northern lights showed him shadow under the sled most of the time as it flew along, touching only here and there. Several times his hands reached, only to have the sled jerked away by some unevenness in the trail. Once he fell over a crumpled ice bridge and had to make a special effort to catch up. Finally it was another ice bridge that helped him; the sled stuck, momentarily, behind one of the big blocks of ice left standing where a previous musher had struggled through. The dogs jerked, the sled broke loose and the drivebow flew neatly into his outstretched hands; he even had enough momentum to plant his feet firmly on the runners before the dogs were off again. He stood for a long time, panting, simply holding on, without breath to shout at the dogs.

He had joked to the vet at Puntilla Lake about nightmares but this was the true black velvet from which they were cut. Involuntarily he glanced over his shoulder for Chittick and Jacobsin but, of course, where were the white shapes but in front of him. He found himself laughing wildly as the sled, with his two hundred pounds not restraining it much, crashed over a big ridge in the trail and then down. . .

He had planned to camp at the top of the mountain and commence the descent at dawn, well rested, alert, able to see the dangers of the trail. Too late. He was into the ice chute in the dark, his dogs out of control. Pitch black. Straight. Left. From above, green and yellow lights reached out for him but to no avail. He had gone to the dogs, was lost to men, to reason, even to fear, not a man but a speeding demon hurrying on an unknown errand behind the hounds of hell.

The descent from Rainy Pass is legendary, even among the hard men of the Iditarod, a maze of narrow ledges, dangerous defiles, switchbacks, hairpins, sudden slides on wind-driven banks of loose snow, ravines with sides a hundred feet high only inches from dogs, sled and racer.

James had known all this in advance, of course: a naïf would never be allowed to start the race. Dave had told James much about the descent, other mushers had shared details of their experience, much of the conversation at the compulsory pre-race banquet had centred on this descent. But he had never imagined it could possibly be this bad. Not that he discounted what he heard, for he lacked the true cynic's instant distrust (though he had the New Yorker's modicum required for survival); in addition he had some experience of the solitary type of person who never tells an untruth because everything in his world is strange. James had believed what he was told. But this was worse. No-one had even attempted to describe the psychological side-effects. . .

His lightweight toboggan shot over a rise and rose twenty feet into air. He looked down at the length of his shadow created by the northern lights and calculated how high – before he could finish his calculation the sled crashed back to the trail – no, they were way off the trail, he could see it over there, a forlorn scrap of pink ribbons fluttering in their passage –

'Get on the trail, you stupid canines!' he roared. 'At least run in the right direction.'

How cool and calculating I am, he thought, knowing that he was no such thing, that he was riding to certain death. He should jump now and walk to the trail, where he could sit and wait until they could send a helicopter from the next checkpoint, Rohn River, to pick him up. All this he knew with startling clarity yet his fingers, resting lightly on the drivebow and ready to tighten instantly if the sled should hit something and rise into the air, would not let go even that minimal purchase –

– he felt he could let go and ride without any further purchase than the serrations milled into the runners – the cost of milling the serrations into the prototype had shocked him, nearly ten dollars per serration –

'Look, Ma, no hands!'

He raised his hands, clapped them above his head, put them back on the drivebow and did not fall off and was a god of the ice age and of any number of ravishing maidens, all of whom looked like Rhodes –

Greedy!

– and his dogs, at the bottom of Rainy Pass, lost interest in the sheep.

'Is there any animal more stupid than a dog?' he enquired gently as, still panting, they settled into a steady run of nine miles per hour. 'Or sheep,' he shouted after the wraiths of the Dall sheep now turning back to their high eyrie.

'Horses,' he answered himself. 'Especially polo ponies.'

He knew where he was: the Interior. More specifically, in Pass Fork. Or perhaps already in Dalzell Creek, of

116

which Pass Fork is a tributary. Wherever, he was in a canyon of spectacular beauty. Even in that light from the far north, which he now distrusted intensely as a hallucinogen, he had to appreciate the wonder of it.

After a while he whoa-ed the dogs and went forward, his stiff limbs crackling, to inspect the sled. The right-hand runner had been nicked in two places and, as he expected, fractures were developing from the notches. He rigged a spinnaker-weight tarpaulin as a windbreak and changed into the thermal underclothes he had worn the previous day; they were still damp but drier than the wringing-wet set he now discarded.

'Now get me to Rohn River before I freeze,' he commanded his dogs. 'Move!' If the cracks grew into breaks before he reached Rohn he would be in serious trouble.

It was pitch dark, three hours before dawn. He should still have been camped, resting at the top of the mountain behind him. He thought of what would have happened if he had met another musher on the trail, and shivered convulsively.

On the Tatina River he found overflow. Late in winter the water begins to flow again but many rivers and creeks are frozen all the way to the bedrock. The water has nowhere to run except on top of the ice. It is difficult to spot and, worse, when it freezes again, causes glare-ice which offers man and dog no purchase. Any light glints differently on snow, open water and glare-ice, and James now learned it glints differently on overflow as well. He cursed as he received a faceful of spray, then another. There was no point in stopping.

The dogs headed for the bank, trying to find purchase and avoid getting wet. Before they reached it, General fell into a hole in the ice concealed by the overflow. The two swing dogs followed their leader into the hole but the rest of the team overran the spot. James shouted and hauled frantically at the back of the sled, first to steer it around the hole, then to clear space to work in.

He hauled the dogs out by the gangline and such parts of their anatomy and harness as came to hand, cursing the other dogs nuzzling his back: there was no time to unharness them before the dogs under the ice drowned. The swing dogs came out first and were inclined to linger near him, shaking themselves, drenching him from the back as well.

'Back!' Frantically he forearmed them away. 'Give me room to work!'

He hauled hand over hand on the line in his mittens and saw wet fur. He grabbed General by the scruff of his neck and hauled. The dog popped through the hole in the ice and James fell to slide on his back on overflow and ice, the coughing dog on his chest, the rest of the team perforce trotting after them. General recovered first. He jumped off James and brought the team behind him to a halt. Then he stood shaking himself, coughing up water.

James felt cold water flow down his back as he jumped up. He was exhausted, wanting only to lie there and enjoy the northern lights. But what he *had* to do was reach Rohn River checkpoint and dry out within fifteen minutes; otherwise he would have all eternity to contemplate lights.

There was no need to worry about the three wet dogs. The soaking would negate the insulating qualities of their thick undercoats but the dogs could dry out on the run, which he could not. He needed to be indoors, before a fire.

'Thank God for checkpoints,' he said aloud. If this misfortune had befallen any of the old-time mushers they would have frozen to death. He still could: fifteen minutes was all he had. He stood on the runners and shook the drivebow. 'Run like you've never run before,' he told General. 'Run!'

It was impossible to make great speed on that overflow and glare-ice, even if they no longer cared how wet they became. There was simply no purchase for human or canine feet. The dogs kept trying to head up onto the bank but James knew that breaking trail in the blown snow there would be even slower than slithering and scratching along the overflow and glare-ice on the river. In places the trailblazer had found the overflow too much and cut the trail up the bank. These detours slowed him but James gritted his teeth and followed the trail as marked – if he lost it now he could certainly die.

His eye caught a flash of blue as the northern lights lit something moving on the bank of the river. There was a snow machine and a man in a bright blue parka standing amid the trees with his back to James. He would stop and ask how far to the Rohn River checkpoint. If it was further than five minutes by dog sled, he would ask the man to take him in the snow machine. That would mean throwing the race but scratching was preferable to spending the rest of his life without toes, fingers, ears, even hands and feet. He was not so insanely competitive that he would rather die than lose.

Eyes now accustomed to the night light, James saw the man in the blue parka reach into the snowmobile and bring out a black box. A camera freak enduring great hardship for his hobby? If so, he was in for a surprise when James and his team came upon him out of the night. . . James opened his mouth to shout a greeting over the intervening half-mile, a wilderness courtesy, but. . .

The river mushroomed white ice and black water. The flash of explosion overtinted the northern lights' kaleidoscopic yellows, greens and blues with shades ranging either side to diamantine white and mourning purple. The blast of sound overtook the head-on wind he instinctively leaned into and the concussion drove him through the air. He saw the ice reaching up for him, saw the northern lights glint differently on overflow and the bald spot where wind and blast conspired to bare the glare-ice before it too reared up in great sheets. *Now Rhodes will win by default.* He turned in the air, gravity accelerating him into the darkness. But another darkness overtook him before his body struck the ice.

4

Conservation

Big Jim and his offspring gradually established a 400-square-mile pocket of Alaska as their exclusive territory, not out of greed or need but simply because Nature's normal restraints on expansion of pack and territory were absent. The usual territory to sustain a troupe of eight wolves is 200 square miles; neither hunting ground nor troupe is normally bigger because neighboring troupes of wolves will ferociously defend their adjoining territories.

But Man had interfered disastrously in the ecology of Alaska, as so often happens even when he acts from high motives. Conservationists and ethnic specialists had blinded themselves with the obvious fact that the Eskimo's livelihood depends solely on free-roaming herds of caribou, whose only natural predator was the wolf: eliminate the wolf and the survival quotient of the Eskimo must perforce increase. Altruistically these conservationists and ethnologists exposed themselves to great hardship and danger to hunt down every wolf in Alaska; such was their persistence that they killed 99% of Alaskan wolves.

Like most such grand schemes conceived in ignorance, this one backfired catastrophically and predictably. Without the wolves culling the old, sick, and weak caribou, and the new calves least likely to contribute to the genetic pool, the caribou population doubled, trebled and quadrupled in a few years. The Eskimo looked on glumly: they knew what would happen next but no one had consulted them for they did not proclaim themselves experts. The sparse vegetation of the tundra could not support the population-explosion of caribou and soon it was over-cropped and crumbling underfoot. The caribou were virtually exterminated in a famine and many Eskimo – for whose benefit the wolves had been killed – came to the brink of starvation. Now, several decades later, the caribou herds have recovered almost to their natural-balance numbers; however, many previously self-sustaining Eskimo still live on government handouts, and the tundra will take another half-century to recover its prior splendor . . . if Man does not interfere again.

There is no possibility whatsoever of the timber wolf ever regaining sufficient numbers in Alaska to replace men with rifles for the essential annual chore of culling caribou.

Big Jim's pack did not know all this but they did not need to. They established their original territory by instinct alone: since they found no contesting wolves on it, it was theirs. They claimed only enough to feed the troupe but, when the pack grew larger in the good years and to feed all its members tentatively explored beyond its instinct-drawn borders, it found no packs hunting on adjacent territories to contest expansion. Conversely, if there had been packs hunting on contiguous territories, the big pack could never have grown because its expansion would have been blocked; Big Jim's troupe would have refrained from breeding beyond the food-capability of its own territory. By destroying Nature's constraints the conservationists created a mutant wolf-pack six to eight times bigger than the natural maximum.

Yet at each stage of expansion instinct drew the wolves a new border, to be crossed only in great need and with dread. Thus, the first few times that hunger and the men from the logging village and salvage camp drove them to search elsewhere for food, they returned to their own territory as speedily as they safely could. But soon they learned that no danger lurked beyond the boundaries of instinct and did not return along their own tracks, falling asleep where they fed.

Finding no resistance to enlargement of their hunting range, the wolves continued to expand it as opportunity offered: they followed the available food, though in a north-westerly direction whenever that was possible, as in the Spring the caribou trekked north from their forest wintering grounds. It was as though some instinct to travel away from the sun and Man had replaced the territorial instinct. True, this expansion conflicted with the prior instinct and caused several wolves to behave neurotically. But wolves normally are highly strung and, while their body language is a marvellously complex and effective form of communication, it is also intricately specialized towards satisfying another instinct: hunger; it lacks the range of human communication. The few wolves whose territorial instincts were stronger than their fear and hunger could not deflect the ravenous will of the majority and either were disciplined by the pack – one was killed and eaten while a stronger wolf was driven out to die a lingering and lonely death – or submitted to their even stronger instinct for pack-conformity.

Wolf society is not so different from human society.

Thus the largest wolf-pack ever recorded was created by men, set on its travels by men, even guided by men in a direction which was bound to intersect with the Iditarod racers and their sled dogs on the way to Nome.

5
Farewell

The moose behind her ran easily, athletically. Her dogs would tire before the moose: they were flat out, using every last ounce of reserve, while the moose could at any moment call up an extra spurt of speed and trample them.

It flashed into her mind that she was running from an attempt at rape. 'What?' she asked herself aloud, then shouted to the moose, 'You stupid elk, I'm not your kind. Go find a doe.'

Perhaps her shout enraged the animal, perhaps it was tired of the game; whichever, the moose huffed and puffed and closed the gap at frightening speed. Rhodes breathed deeply, then jumped into the snow beside the track, grateful for the small mercy of not falling on cut-up and refrozen ridges of trail-ice. She rolled upright and ran, hoping to lead the moose away from her dogs: the dogs were tied to the sled whilst she was loose and free to act. The snow dragged at her calf muscles. But soft snow, unlike hard ice, would protect her, act as a cushion when the moose trampled her. Behind her she heard branches break and the thump of snow sliding off disturbed trees. Through her feet she felt the thundering hooves though, strangely, she could not hear them. The thumping reverberated in her body and head; after a while they fell into step with her and she realized she no longer heard the moose but her own frantic heart. She dared to look over her shoulder and a branch hit her across the side of her face. She fell to the snow to lie panting, without energy to rise, waiting to be trampled to death. It was a mercy to black out.

Later, when she recovered consciousness and opened her eyes, she saw the moose foraging twenty paces away. It had lost interest in her. She was tempted to curse it aloud but, instead, rose inch by inch, as quietly as she could, checking for broken bones, then raised one foot, looked at the moose to see if it would come after her again, turned to see where she was putting her hovering foot, took one step, glanced at the moose, praying there was no dry twig to snap under the blown snow, took another step –

Thirty excruciatingly slow steps later the moose turned to stare incuriously at her, then wandered away.

'And the same to you!' she whispered to the retreating back of the largest deer in North America.

Retracing her footsteps towards the trail, she laughed in nervous release. Whatever humor had been in the whole episode was pretty sick comedy: moose contesting the trail often trampled six or eight or ten dogs before they were shot, and there were reports of people badly trampled and even killed by the animals. A man – or a woman – could not expect to be a match for a 1500-pound moose. Nonetheless it was insulting that the moose should chase her for miles only to lose interest when she was beaten, literally down and out.

'Watch it, Rhodes,' she admonished herself. 'That was a moose, not a human.'

Still, a moose looks like an animal designed by a committee, having the face of a camel on the neck of a horse with mulelike ears under a huge spread of antlers, all on the body of a water-ox carried high off the ground on the legs of a giraffe.

Blue. In her raggedly tired mind rose the sad specter of her own failed genetic experiment. An Eskimo had given her the little Arctic or Blue Fox and Rhodes had hand-reared him as a pet. About fifteen million years ago the wolf, the fox *and the dog* had sprung from a common ancestor, Tomarctus (who, a vet told Rhodes, had probably been short and squat with stumpy legs, not unlike a Corgi). Rhodes therefore had high hopes for Blue. . . The Arctic Fox, in common with the polar bear, has hair on the pad of its paw. Dogs do not. If she could cross-breed an Arctic Fox with her dogs and the pups inherited the hairy footprint, they would have better-protected feet and – much more important because booties could as easily *protect* their feet – the hair would give them better grip on snow and far superior purchase on ice. And that no bootie could do, even when made of moosehide with the hair outside and guardhairs still in place: the moose-hair wore off too easily. The musher who bred dogs with hairy undersides to their paws would steal a march on all other competitors, worth as much as two or three miles per hour – a devastating edge in a race as long as the Iditarod.

Blue, the Arctic Fox, had done its duty by Rhodes's malemute bitch and then run off into the night in search of greater adventure; the Eskimo had warned that this would happen even with the most affectionate fox but Rhodes could not bring herself to chain Blue. The bitch pupped and – hallelujah! – the pups had hairy footpads. The pups grew apace. But there was something wrong with them. At first Rhodes thought only that they were uncommonly incurious and unadventurous, especially considering their parentage, staying *too* close to their mother all the time. Then the truth struck her and she brought a torch into the gloomy shed and shone it into their eyes. Not one of them blinked: they were all blind.

Her landlord, sent by his wife to call her to supper, found her standing at the shed door, peering at the unchanging sky. She hugged her body with both arms under the transparent plastic cape she wore, rain running off it distorting her body, lending her an air of fragile sadness. He was not a particularly sensitive man but, still ten paces from her, he asked, 'What is it?'

'My puppies are blind.'

'All? You sure? Let's see.'

But they were all blind.

'You'll have to put them down,' he said, returning the last pup to its mother's teat and resting the six-cell torch face-down on the shelf above the box.

'I hate it! I know it's necessary but I hate it.'

'It's crueller not to do it.'

'Tomorrow. Tomorrow I'll do it.'

'The longer you put it off the worse it will be. I'll do it for you.'

Relief flooded her. She would not have to look into the pups' blind eyes and then kill them. She knew it was weak of her to let him do it: she had tried to subvert evolution and was now evading the punishment for failure. But she could not. . .

'Hold the bitch here.' He took the five pups in his two hands and walked out of the shed.

With shock she realized he would kill them immediately. She opened her mouth to call out that tonight, after dark . . . but he was gone. She talked to the bitch, gentling her, scratching her ears, trying not to look into those trusting eyes. She knew the Eskimo was right: those pups would have grown up to sit staring at nothing all day. But their lives had been so short; they had harmed no one. After a while she carried a spade outside, closing the shed door on the bitch so that she would not see what had been done to her pups.

The Eskimo stood beside a paraffin drum on which the pups lay spread in a fan, heads outwards. He had crushed their skulls with his heel. She gagged, turned away, blinded by tears, and started digging a hole. She could not go in to eat. When he returned from his meal he took the spade from her hands and pulled her by her elbow out of the four-foot-deep hole she had hacked in violent distress through permafrost that engineers routinely dynamite.

They buried the tiny still-warm bodies to the sad accompaniment of the bitch whining softly for her pups.

Rhodes would never again be tempted to meddle with nature.

Rhodes wiped the tears from her cheeks before they could freeze on her skin. She was wrung out. She wanted to lie down in the snow to sleep, to recover her selfness, not to be blown hither and thither by the winds of chance. But she had chosen to run a race and she had always prided herself on being a finisher, not a fader. And she had a responsibility to her dogs. Before she could rest she had to find her team. She sat with head between her knees and counted slowly to one hundred. From seventy-nine, at each new number she saw Countess Mayo, Toots's mother, jump over a stile. In a small corner of her mind she knew it was ludicrous to have hallucinations in broad daylight. First Blue and now Countess Mayo. She rose and marched determinedly along the trail she and the moose had cut. It was faster returning than coming – well, almost – because the moose had broken so many branches and trampled the snow. She found the main trail with its cheap lipstick-pink surveyor's tape and started trudging along it. The dogs could have come back and passed the place where she had rejoined the trail. She hoped not. She headed for the mountains. That was the right way, forward. While she was moving, there was hope. She started jogging, a pace she could maintain for hours.

'I told them they shouldn't let any bloody women on the trail. Of course they didn't bloody listen. Now look at that bloody Susan Butcher, making us all look like bloody fools. You can guess who my wife is rooting for and it isn't bloody me.'

He was short and slight, had jet black hair and wore yellow shooter's glasses. For a moment she fancied he might be Emmitt Peters because he looked exactly like the legendary musher. But no, he was another trim, fit, Indian. He sat on a log beside the trail, holding his team and hers, waiting. Head down, she had not seen him until he started talking.

She stood on the trail, stared, then walked over to take her team's gangline. 'Thank you, Mr Bloody,' she said, stroking Toots. 'Oh, sorry.'

'It's all right. A lot of people call me Bloody Bobby Franks. What happened?'

'A moose thought we were on its trail. My dogs weren't going to make it so I jumped. After a while the moose lost interest. I hope I didn't hold you up too long.'

He shook his head, then rose to look searchingly at her; he still had to look up at her. 'The moose didn't get you.' Not a question; a statement. His fingers traced the bruise on the side of her face.

'A branch. How bad does it look?'

'Skin's not broken. If you don't keep bloody touching it, it'll go away. You feel all right?'

'Yes, thank you. You can carry on if you like.'

'I can camp near you.'

She was tempted but James Whitbury had gained several hours more while she played catch-me-if-you-can with the moose. 'Thanks, but I have a schedule to keep.' She looked at her watch. 'I'm four hours behind and my dogs look all right.'

'They're bloody okay. They bin bloody resting for about three mebbe four hours looks to me. You go first, I'll follow to see you're all right.'

After encountering the moose, running up Rainy Pass in broad daylight with the experienced 'Bloody' Bobby Franks behind her seemed more like a Girl Guides proving trip than a notoriously dangerous section of the Iditarod. Several times as she flashed past rocks that could shatter sleds or bones, she thought, I'm like those kids at college I sneered at, high on something. Only not drugs. Danger. She made Rainy Pass Lodge an hour before Franks, had cared for her dogs and when he arrived was fast asleep, having wolfed a meal from the Meads' bounty.

'That bloody woman is crazy in the bloody head.' Bobby Franks circled his finger at his temple. 'She came up that mountain like she was running into town late for the bloody hairdresser. She frightened the bloody hell out of me. Wake me a bloody hour after she's bloody gone.'

Rhodes left in good time to make the divide at dawn. She was back on her schedule and only seven hours behind James. The beauty of the final ascent exalted her and she felt sorry for the kids she had met at college who needed a fix but would never be able to experience this genuine high. Dawn broke as she entered the ice chute.

She felt an intense need to thank God for beauty, for what He had made. Normally she was not religious. When she was thirteen her father had told her that he had not been religious until he had met her mother. Her father still went to church and Rhodes with him, less from overwhelming belief than from established duty. What had been good enough for his wife was good enough for her father and what was good enough for him was good enough for Rhodes; no further reason was necessary. But the grandeur of the ice chute, reaching on each side for a sere sky, was enough to turn agnostics into believers. Or into mystics, she told herself. But as a civilized and educated woman she could not permit the pathetic fallacy to interfere with her schedule, with her race, with beating James Whitbury to Nome.

Still, she ran down that mountain, driven by the exhilaration beyond reason of beauty, of fear, awe, terror and the self-destructive urge that lingers in the cobwebby corners of every mind, on a roller-coaster of glee, joyously speeding around huge rocks that her inviolate sanity remonstrated were best negotiated with extreme care. Though conscious of the danger she could not stop herself. 'Fool!' she told herself aloud and thought of how spiders and crabs breed young to live on their backs, eating them alive, dying excruciatingly for a natural impulse; she had read that the male black widow spider *knows* the female will eat him after mating, tries to escape and sometimes succeeds, to mate with another female and *then* be eaten. This is precisely how Man pits himself against danger. . . As she steered it aside to avoid a huge chunk of ice rising out of the trail at one of the bridges that had broken up under the weight of passing racers, the sled clipped a rock. It took her four hundred yards to halt the team, sparks flying from the rock as the brake cut through a thin layer of snow and ice into the mountain itself.

She was shocked cold sober, as if someone had emptied a bucket of icy water over her. A stanchion was cracked. It was not serious; she decided not to replace it unless it broke through before the Rohn River checkpoint. She set off at reduced pace, grimly restraining the impulse to watch the dropside of the trail at the difficult sections: something about this mountain induced suicidal tendencies. Even at this lesser pace she passed another musher who had started out from the Lodge before her. But she refused to take that as a sign she was still travelling too fast: she had chosen what her bones told her was a good-sense speed and she would stick to it. It cramped her stomach to reduce speed and keep it down but the dogs trotted easily and Nome was a long way ahead. . . That burning desire to *go*, to get ahead, lead, would only betray her. A cool head, strategy, that was what she needed, not to go loco and kill herself and her dogs on this mountain, no matter how beautiful a memorial it would make. And what seemed like plodding obviously was faster than the pace the other musher she had passed thought safe.

She came to Pass Fork, then Dalzell Creek, and allowed the dogs gradually to pick up speed on the smoother trail-surface. She also permitted herself to look up from the trail to the spectacular beauty of the canyon formed by huge mountains rising over 5000 feet on each side.

They sped over a bank and onto the Tatina. Overflow soaked her boots before they could stop and almost immediately she felt the water starting to freeze her toes. Sitting on the sled, taking her boots off, she studied the water. It was several inches deep. It was unlikely that anything more had melted than could be expected at this season – the temperature was steady at around thirty below zero. She concluded that the trailblazer had decided not to make it easy for the mushers. She would have preferred shoe-pacs with rubber soles and leather tops but they too would soon be wet through. She flung her soaked mukluks into the sled and put on vapor-barrier bunny boots.

In that brief pause to change her footwear the sled froze to the ice. Before trying to loosen it she inspected the booties on her dogs; she did not want her dogs' feet to freeze either. The sled was frozen fast and she and the dogs could not pull it loose. Rhodes was terrified that her dogs would freeze to the ice where they stood. She took her axe to the ice, leaving splinters of her sled runners stuck in the ice under the overflow. She had to work quickly: the water flowed into any crack she made on one side and froze again while she worked on the other side. This happened twice. She straightened her aching back briefly while she considered. Then she bent again, chopping beneath one runner, a small, deep, square hole rather than the elongated channels she had been cutting until then. She stuck the head of the axe into the hole and called to the dogs: 'Hike! Go!' Then she jumped on the axe handle, thankful that she had chosen a workmanlike axe with full-size handle (handcarved out of hardwood by her father) rather than a hand axe like those of many other racers – some made of light alloy after James Whitbury's example. The leverage broke the hold of the ice, tilting the sled dangerously; it teetered as she dived for its side to haul it down. The sled slammed back to the ice and surged forward violently. Rhodes jumped for the runners. Then she remembered her axe; without it she would be disqualified. She scooped it up and ran after the sled, slithering wildly on the glare-ice, shouting at her dogs to wait, hearing the hoarseness in her voice, the note of fear.

Fortunately the dogs were averse to scrabbling on the glare-ice and hated the overflow worse than cats; quickly they lost the exuberance of being able to move again and turned towards dry going in the snow on the riverbank.

Rhodes ran straight on in the splashing water: here she could run faster than the dogs could in the loose snow. Gaining on the dogs, she too turned into the snow, treading in the trail of an earlier musher who also had found his dogs reluctant to stay on the river with its overflow and glare-ice. (This had been James's team, but Rhodes could not know that.) She slowed to let her dogs pass, then grabbed the drivebow and stepped onto the runners as the sled swept by.

It's at times like this, she thought, that I wish dogs are

driven by reins and a whip instead of just your voice and the respect they have for you.

When she recovered her breath, she called 'Gee! Gee!', jumped off the runners and pushed the sled sideways to steer the dogs back onto the fast, if uncomfortable, river. The soft snow on the bank was too slow, a couple of feet deep in most places, deeper still in unpredictable patches, all of it slushy going.

On the river, travelling much faster, Rhodes became apprehensive that Toots, her other dogs, even her sled and she, could fall through a hole in the ice hidden by the overflow. She ran past the sled and took the gangline to lead her team from the front. From here it should be easier to spot the holes in the ice underneath the overflow. 'We don't want to wake up to a fanfare of winged musicians,' she told Toots. Rhodes no longer glanced up at the scenic wonders: she stared grimly ten feet in front of her loping boots. 'Anyone who comes down here at night is plain crazy and deserves everything that happens.'

She led the dogs and sled past a gaping mini-lake and then over an ice bridge between two patches of deep-blue water, adding, 'Anyone who comes through here at *any* time is plumb loco.'

And, she thought, if Toots ever answers me, I shall stop mushing.

'You know,' she told Toots, tempting fate, 'the old-timers had the right idea. Before your time, before my time, the musher didn't run behind his sled or ride the runners. He rode on skis in front of the sled, behind the wheel dogs. He was tied into the gangline and steered the sled with a pole tied to the righthand side of the sled. Called a gee pole. Obviously. But the lighter racing sleds could be steered from the back and went a whack faster without the gee pole, so they did away with it. Except they didn't foresee situations like this, did they?'

She reached a huge dark patch of open water surrounded by jagged upright slabs of ice. At first she thought she had lost the trail: she could not believe there could be so much open water where many teams would be passing at night. But pieces of pink ribbon survived here and there. *Whoever cut trail here isn't just making things difficult for the mushers. This is so dangerous as to be malicious.* She looked over her shoulder to see if Toots had the scent of other teams veering right or left: Toots had her nose to the ice, pointing straight ahead. *This is impossible!* Perhaps it was not open water, merely black glare-ice recently covered by overflow. She would not take the chance. She led her team towards the bank, choosing the northern bank because the race was heading northwest and when in doubt she always turned in the direction of the race. From the bank she looked down at the large dark patch. Was she paranoid, losing time over some imaginary obstacle? Losing her nerve?

She grasped the pattern.

Slabs of ice, jagged points, cracklines, everything radiated from a kernel of violence, spreading a circular message up and down the river, towards each of the banks, to all points in between. She could not accept what she saw, though she knew it was true. She stared at the fallen trees on the far side of the river, leaning away from her, split and shattered trunks pointing accusingly towards her. On her own side of the river, around her, were more shattered trees. She picked up a jagged piece of branch and flung it as far as she could into the dark patch. It sank quickly, spreading ripples to within six feet of her feet.

Someone had blown up the river. And recently: the tracks of a snow machine were visible right under her nose.

She led her team around the destruction, searching for anyone hurt in the explosion and needing help. If there

135

had been anyone, he was now under the ice, with dogs and sled. She set off on the trail at a rollicking pace that soon had the dogs' tongues hanging out. She had planned to rest her dogs and feed them short of Rohn, so that she would not run into James before he left there. But this was more important than tactics.

She was already turning off the river, following signposts to the checkpoint, when she remembered that she had left the gaping hole in the river unprotected. But no, she had nothing to mark it with and those jagged teeth of ice surrounding it would warn any musher not asleep on his sled.

She made Rohn in just over seven hours from Rainy Pass Lodge, a very brisk time compared to the ten hours she had allowed.

'Someone blew up the river five to six miles back,' she told the checker.

He finished checking her gear.

'I said, somebody blew up the river back there.'

'Spectacular, was it?'

'I don't know. I came afterwards. There's a hole right across the river under the overflow. A musher could have drowned there during the night.'

He studied her carefully.

'I'm not hallucinating. I was leading my dogs. There are sheets of ice standing up, pointing outwards. Exploded trees, pointing away from the epicenter. The man who did it left snow-machine tracks. Look, you don't have to believe me. Just check that everyone who left Rainy Pass Lodge before me arrived here.'

He stepped back before her vehemence. 'Strange things happen on the trail.'

'Yes, I know. I was starting to feel religious.' She *had* given herself over to that mountain. She shook her head

136

to clear the memory. 'But I was over all that when I saw the Tatina all blown. Just check, please!'

'Sure. We check all the time. But that won't tell us much. Four years ago, when I ran, I was lost for five days before I found the trail again. Still, at least half a dozen mushers took longer than me to make Nome. Go look after your dogs. Paul Fleming's here if you want him to look at the bust stanchion this side. There's a packet of spare stanchions waiting for you in the shed. Your father sent them with the food-plane. Also a message of love and good luck; they'll see you in McGrath.'

'Thanks. Can you send someone to put up a warning marker?'

'Hey, the Iditarod isn't the highway patrol! Guys who can't look out for themselves aren't allowed to run.'

'Whoever you send with the marker can see for himself I'm not just talking.'

He had the grace to look embarrassed.

'And you'd better radio the police about people with explosives blowing up the river.'

'Police? You from the city, Miss? It'll take the cops weeks to get here. Anyway, what do we tell them? That somebody blew up a piece of frozen river? Let's not panic, eh?'

She shrugged and went about the routine of feeding her dogs, inspecting their paws for snow or water freezing between the pads and for cuts needing attention.

As always, Paul Fleming was there to enjoy the race. But he knew from experience that Rainy Pass would not be kind to lightweight racing sleds and had brought the tools of his trade. He inspected the stanchions Rhodes had tied in and pronounced it a competent job: he saw no need to retie them. He fitted a new stanchion in place of the last one broken and inspected the rest of her sled professionally. Her father had made it well, he said.

137

Rhodes lay in her sleeping bag in the old cabin that might have been part of the original roadhouse there; she tried to sleep but the explosive rose of violence on the Tatina bothered her. When it was time to leave for Farewell she was tired and tense. But she had to stick to her schedule, start running at night again now that she was over Rainy Pass. Fondling her dogs and checking their booties before setting out, she wondered if anyone had fallen into that gaping hole on the Tatina.

'Who didn't turn up from the Lodge?' she asked the checker.

'Only one. But Darryl Edge – you passed him on the mountain – saw the hole and he also thinks it was explosives. So I popped out there on the snow tractor and you're right, somebody blew up the river. There's no sign that any musher was there at the time, though.'

'There wouldn't be. His tracks will be covered by the overflow.'

'Sure. But there would be *some* sign. A musher and his sled and twelve dogs don't just disappear like that, leaving no trace.'

'How long has he been missing?'

'He hasn't actually been posted missing. But he left Rainy Pass Lodge eight, nine hours before you and he hasn't arrived here yet. But you'd expect a rookie to take a long time down that mountain. Not everybody is in a crazy hurry like you. Though this one was the leading rookie when he left the Lodge. Now you're the leading rookie, which isn't bad for a girl, huh?'

'Yes, thanks,' she said dejectedly.

'We're not making a big thing about it yet. Maybe tomorrow, if he doesn't turn up roundabout midday, we'll start looking. He won't be the first musher to get lost on the mountain or in the canyon. I'm waiting to see his sled.

138

They say he built it of the same metals that fly on the space shuttle.'

She had not even considered the possibility. 'It's James Whitbury missing?'

The checker responded to the tone of alarm in her voice. 'You'n'he got something going?'

'Not like you think. A race within the race.'

'He'll turn up. He's just lost. That hole in the river, that's some trapper too lazy to set a trapline. He blows up the river once, goes downriver, blows another hole in it, scoops up the dead animals, goes downriver to blow another hole. There *are* people like that, you know. Only other people are so embarrassed by them, they don't say much about it. Your James Whitbury – '

'He's not my James Whitbury!'

He raised an eyebrow. 'He'll turn up, a bit shamefaced about getting lost and letting you take the lead. Use it while you can.'

Well, she thought, these people are vastly experienced in the ways of the Iditarod; there's nothing more I can do.

She hoped to cover the thirty-eight miles to Farewell in ten hours or less. It was mostly flat and good going, except for the – by now expected – overflow on the shallower rivers and creeks. She flipped memorized notes in her mind until she came to one reading 'Bison country'.

From Rohn Roadhouse she ran almost due north on the South Fork of the Kuskokwim. The glare-ice here made fast going but at places there was overflow that terrified her, and terror exhausted her beyond the demands of the trail. She did not want to slow the dogs by running in front. By now she had convinced herself that James was only lost, that he would soon find the trail again and clear Rohn, pressing hard on her trail because he would believe she was now twenty-four hours ahead of him. She was too tired to work out the implications of this but it was clear that, by becoming lost, he had upset her strategy; he could hurry right on past her, they would both take their twenty-four-hour layover, he would be ahead with rested dogs and she would then have to push much harder and use up her dogs' reserve long before they reached Nome. Unless . . . unless she pushed so much harder now that he could not possibly catch up, unless she raced ahead now and then rested her dogs, unless, unless. . . Thinking was too much bother.

The trailblazer had decided to give the mushers a break after the horrors of the Tatina and she thanked him fervently when the trail left the river to enter the thick spruce forest. Once, on a narrow cut through the dense trees, she passed a dark hulk just off the trail and realized with shock that it was a bison. The animal was not native to the area: bison were introduced before World War II and had flourished. Her light swivelled with her head and she saw, high on the trunk of a tree, four or five times her own height, a blaze that appeared as old as time itself. Though she was alone, chasing the shadowy legend that was Leonhard Seppala, there had been people here before her, before Seppala even – twenty and thirty feet of spruce growth meant perhaps a hundred years ago. These veterans, who had expected others to follow, cut and marked the trail for the followers, of whom she was proud to be one.

She was already on the Post River, silently cursing the overflow while she tried to keep her dogs from heading up the bank to the surer footing and dry going, when the moon rose over Tunis Mountain. Now she knew how the ancient Druids felt. The huge open expanse of ice before her was Lake Veleska and they zipped over it without incident. She had time to study the sky and the distant horizon of trees. 'Severe, clear,' she said aloud in weather forecaster's tones. It would not last. There would be a

140

storm – Nature also subscribes to Murphy's Law because Murphy *is* Nature, random event piled onto random event. Unlike in a Colorado sprint, where bad weather would give her heavier dogs an advantage over competitors who mostly preferred lightweight sprinters, here she would prefer clear weather and easier going. Here a storm could catch her out in the middle of nowhere and she could die: she did not want to challenge Alaska that way.

Open water again. She led the team. Terrifying. She found herself thinking of the courage of little Daniel Brook, who was crippled by polio but refused to admit the limitations of leg irons, running, jumping and playing football just like other boys. He had been at school with her and Margery and, instead of going to college, had asked his father for a rundown Toyota agency that now, only a few years later, was making him rich. He had once told her his personal mantra was nothing oriental, just the words 'I can, I can, I can,' repeated endlessly. 'Thing is,' he added, 'you mustn't grit your teeth and carry on grimly. The light touch, right? Then you start thinking it's fun. I can, I can, I can. Like can-can, with bright music and the Rockettes twirling under the lights.'

She wanted to sit down and wait for the dawn so that at least she could see better than by the twee light of her headlamp.

'I can, I can, I can,' she started chanting and soon *she knew she could* and shook the drivebow so that the dogs sped up from the crawl her fear had reduced them to.

'I can, I can, I can!' she sang full-bodiedly, ringing the far mountains.

She felt a glow starting from her and looked around to reassure Toots should it startle her. Light flowed from her until dogs and sled too glowed with her determination and belief that she would survive.

She thought it was about minus twenty. The northern

141

lights found her and she switched off her light until she returned to the trees. Trees flashed past. Trees, trees, trees and more trees. Spruce had taken over the world. Guttenberg's Revenge, she thought tiredly. Why do I always have my best ideas just when I'm falling asleep and know they'll be lost when I wake? Her aura had faded and disappeared when she entered the forest. Primitive man feared the forest and burned it for more reasons than just to drive animals before the fire. Until recently Indians burned the forest to create clearings to grow corn, encourage new growth to attract game, destroy hiding places for enemies. They believed a man could spend only five days in the forest before the dread Wendigo claimed him or he went mad. Better to burn it.

She woke in the snow. She rose and plodded wearily until she remembered she was in a race, then broke into a reluctant trot. Her team had stopped no more than half a mile from where she had fallen asleep and off the sled. She wondered if that was what had happened to James in the mountain. . .

Perhaps the line of red repeatedly glimpsed on the horizon was James's blood blown into the ether and the pulsing red light in the center of it his heart still pumping vainly, uselessly, angrily.

Dawn broke and stole the red lights. Her eyes adjusted and she saw the red light still blinked on its tower in front of the dawn. She was travelling eastward, back towards Anchorage. . .

'You're lost, Sister,' a cheery female voice greeted her from shapeless Carheart overalls. 'Nome's thataway. But since you haven't checked in here, just as well you came back. If you miss a checkpoint, you're disqualified.'

This must be Farewell, a village of five souls and more buildings, all dedicated to giving pilots weather forecasts and reorienting those who inevitably lost their bearings in the vastness of Alaska. 'This *is* Farewell?' Dawn was too soon to reach Farewell, Rhodes thought. I should be on the trail for another hour yet.

'Sure! You're three hundred miles from Anchorage, a quarter of the way to Nome. We have buildings with beds to sleep in. We have hot running water. Wonders to behold, we have a clothes dryer. We'll give you a hot meal. Lot of mushers take their twenty-four here. You look like it wouldn't be a bad idea for you to declare here too.'

'I'm meeting people in McGrath.'

'You don't look like a barfly to me.'

'What?'

'There's only three bars between Anchorage and Nome and two of them are in McGrath. Declare your twenty-four anyway. If you want to continue after your rest, that's okay.'

'All right. Thanks.'

'You're the second woman and first rookie through here. You're lying ninth. Can you believe it?'

'Never dreamt. . .'

'Yeah, right!'

'Right now I just feel like lying – down.' This woman was a tonic. 'Is all my gear present?'

' – and correct. Dog food's arranged in that building at the end of the street. Big circle, alphabetical. Just walk around until you come to the Ds. And remember, I'm proud of you. Alaska is proud of you.'

Rhodes, already leading her dogs towards the food hall, felt her back straightening involuntarily.

Alaska is proud of you.

She turned around. 'Is Susan leading?'

'No. Swenson and Peters were an hour ahead of her out of here. You racing her?'

'No, I'm racing myself,' Rhodes said sadly, convinced

143

that James was out of the race, even if still alive. 'I just want to finish.'

'You're only five hours behind her and that's pretty good over three hundred miles for a first-timer.'

'Mmm. Any news from Rohn?' She had an irrational impulse that mentioning James's name would somehow lessen his chances of survival.

'Nope. Business as usual.'

Rhodes hesitated. But the checker at Rohn had told her they would not declare James missing until noon today, perhaps not even then. She turned away.

There were only two other mushers at Farewell, one taking his twenty-four-hour mandatory break to allow dogs drained in the dog fight in Anchorage to recover their strength; he was fast asleep in a spare house of the three facing Farewell's lone 'street'. The other musher was preparing to leave, chasing the leaders. He was a big Eskimo of about fifty and nodded distantly to her as she passed, but the words he called after her were friendly: 'You're doing okay.'

She was startled: in Colorado the front-runners had not welcomed the girl who rose so fast in a man's sport. 'Thanks.'

'See you in Nome. Hike!' And he disappeared into the crisp morning like something from a magic tale. She was too tired to remember his name but he was a past winner and consistent high finisher.

The laundry room, where she found her flown-in food, almost overwhelmed her with fumes of Blazo and Coleman fuel, the lingering traces of heavy red meat the other mushers had cooked with as much as half by volume of fat. The smell was nauseating. She swallowed, stopped breathing for a moment and then was all right.

While the dogs' meal – ground lamb and chunks of horsemeat with an equal volume of fat to counter the cold

144

– cooked on the double Coleman her father had modified to burn separately off each cylinder, she fed each dog a quart of sour cream: this she substituted for the expensive cream cheese James Whitbury and other mushers with big sponsorship used for a quick boost. Rhodes, too, could have used cream cheese but refused all sponsorship because she would not paste sponsors' stickers over the sled her father had handcarved for her. The sour cream had been cheap, the dogs loved it, and it worked just as well.

After feeding her dogs she showered and changed into her last fresh clothes – *oh, luxury! Emma Bovary in your louse-brown, what would have happened to you if your creator had instead a vivid scarlet in mind?* She threw her laundry into the washer and then spun it in the dryer. She found an empty room with a made bed and crawled into it. But could not sleep – she had crossed the border of exhaustion into washed-out wakefulness. The question nagged: how had she become lost and started travelling eastwards, arriving at Farewell fortuitously though from the wrong direction? It would forever be an unsolved mystery; she consciously put it out of her mind.

She thought of the smell in the laundry room: it reminded her of what she loved about Colorado in winter, why she felt so instantly at home in Alaska – *Alaska is proud of you!* – and suddenly she was rejuvenated. *Alaska has no smell.* Alaska always smells clean, as does Colorado in winter. She loved Spring, Summer and Fall in Colorado too; but Winter, the mushing season, had always been her favorite.

Her schedule called for a layover of nine hours here at Farewell, her main rest of the day. Two hours were now gone but still she could not sleep.

Race officials, pressmen and television crews had flown in to watch the front-runners pass and quite a few lingered to enjoy Farewell's comforts while the racers slogged their way to the next checkpoint with an airstrip. She sat in the kitchen of a house and listened to the pilots talk of south winds blowing into McGrath, heralding a storm perhaps two days away.

The other storm had struck Rainy Pass. A race official told her it would be 'eight-ten-maybe-twelve-fourteen' days before the last backmarker passed through Farewell. Two mushers had scratched at Rainy Pass Lodge and another at Rohn.

While she had been in the shower another musher had come in and declared he was scratching here. It was the man she had met back . . . back where? An eternity ago, just out of Anchorage. He had lost his lead dog and, with no other leader, had brought his team this far only by willpower. He sat at the corner of the table, haggard face almost in his bowl of soup, spooning a mouthful every minute or two, forcing himself to eat politely the food his hosts had offered him. When someone commiserated with him, he looked up with deadened eyes, nodded, returned to the soup he was scarcely eating.

'It's a magnificent feat for him to reach here,' a man with a spread moustache told Rhodes. 'Most of us, the officials, ran at one time or another. I heard they were thinking of telling him a couple of checkpoints back he should scratch. I told them not to be stupid. Sure, I'd agree if he was a danger to himself or other mushers. But he's tough and experienced. You don't tell a man like that he doesn't know when to give up. Some other day you could be in trouble on the trail and be rescued by a man who doesn't know how to give up. Three hundred miles – over Rainy Pass – without a leader! Can you believe it?'

Rhodes shook her head. The official she was talking to

was a past winner and now president of the race organization; she was too tired to remember his name and too embarrassed to ask. He thought she was doing well but cautioned her against breaking trail for others all the time. 'Sometimes, give your dogs a break and follow another musher even if he's slower than you. Let him break trail for you.'

The woman in the Carhearts was large and plain but her smiling face radiated kindness. She told Rhodes, 'That building wind you met coming in will turn into a right smart storm. Not now, maybe when you reach the far side of McGrath. But already it has chapped your skin. Wait, I'll get you some creme.'

When she returned with the lotion Rhodes was fast asleep, upright in a kitchen chair.

She did not want to wake, especially not to Harry Coignton of the Washington *Post* telling her she was dead. It was a nightmare, dream within a dream. She told herself, Soon I will wake once and be back in the dream, then I'll wake again and be back in the Iditarod.

Coignton shook her shoulder.

'Mr Coignton,' she said coldly,'I came here running behind a dog sled, not sitting in an airplane. Go away, let me rest.'

Coignton studied her face closely. 'Listen, James Whitbury is missing, presumed drowned.'

The alarm on her wrist bleeped plaintively, a mouse in a catless land. Time to go.

She noticed the journalist staring at her, trying to discern her reaction. She looked away, staring blankly at the corner of the ceiling.

'Hey, what are you crying for? You keep telling us there's nothing between you.'

Every sparrow that falls.

147

She rose and jerked her bright orange parka from the back of the chair and pulled it on as she stumbled out.

She had a race to run, to Nome the fastest and best she could. For herself, for James, for all those vanquished by Alaska.

The reporters followed her, asking more questions. She ignored them while she harnessed her dogs and checked their booties, then drove them into the dusk gathering as slowly as a cinema queue. The journalists protests against exclusion from her thoughts rang hollow in the cold air, brushed aside by the crisp wind to startle a flock of ptarmigans into the sunset. Soon, puffing from the unaccustomed exercise of shambling runs beside her, the reporters fell away unnoticed by Rhodes.

Nikolai was forty-five miles away, McGrath another forty-five. Her father, with Margery and Harvey, would be waiting at McGrath, steadfast beacons of her life.

Ahead of her ran Number One, Leonhard Seppala; at her heels snapped the grinning skull of James Whitbury, picked clean by the fingerling spring salmon of the Tatina. After a while she stopped looking over her shoulder: he would forever be behind her, just as Leonhard Seppala would always lead the way.

6
Black Death

Within a week the troupe of wolves, no longer persecuted by men, in following the available food left the last trees behind, casting many fearful glances backwards; they dawdled for two days on bare ice, still within sight of the last few straggly trees, before hunger drove them north-westwards in pursuit of the migrating caribou. Two of their number remained among the trees, too timid to leave the beloved environment for the embrace of the naked white space.

Not far across the tundra the pack paused six weeks. Before the logging Indians and salvagemen started hunting them the pack had enjoyed many good years, including the last, and all pairs had mated freely. Now the females cast large litters of four and five cubs, each with a birth-coat of gray hair curled like a husky's, not yet proof against moisture or drifting snow. If the cubs had been born one week earlier or later the adults would have killed them for they could not then have offered them either food or security. But now the troupe stood safely and squarely across the path of La Foule, the migrating caribou. They could spare the six weeks the cubs needed to stay in their holes; these refuges were dug into the snow on the sides of ninety-foot-high eskers that snake like railroad embankments of ice, white sand and gravel across parts of the tundra, serving the caribou as roads.

When the cubs had developed their weatherproof coats – already with more white and cream about them than their forest-gray parents – they were strong enough to travel. Now the wolves joined the tail end of the migration that served them as a movable feast: the weakest and most easily eaten caribou sustained the troupe all the way to the Summer grazing grounds; there they arrived in late May to feast once more on the caribou-calvings of May and June. The wolves had never fed so well before: they grew sleek and confident again – and providentially so for, here on the tundra, even more sparsely populated than the cold northern forests, they saw men much more frequently. But these men were Eskimo, who have never shared the instinctive revulsion of other races towards the wolf. The Eskimo consider wolves to be no more dangerous than other predators to caribou, which the Eskimo feel belong to them, even though not coralled or branded; they regard wolves much as overgrown foxes and do not fear them as they fear bears. An Eskimo, even with a high-velocity rifle in his hand, will show a musk ox a great deal more respect than a wolf. Many Eskimo consider the wolf as a partner in caribou-management. The wolf-pack, in contact with Eskimo for the first time, may have sensed this; certainly they soon learned that it was necessary only to stay out of rifle range of any Eskimo they met. In wolves, as in all other species, familiarity breeds contempt; on the open tundra they soon became so used to Man that they lost some of their age-old wariness towards him.

The further north they travelled, and the more their symbiotic relationship with the Eskimo clarified itself in small contacts and sightings, the greater became the impact of another blood-memory refreshed by present geography and circumstance: across that ice bridge to Siberia, whence came their ancestors, wolves had been used deliberately by survivors of the Black Death to dispose of corpses they lacked the energy to bury.

For the same service the vultures that devour the dead in Nepalese 'sky burial' are still revered and protected.

150

Yet the instinctive revulsion with which almost all men now regard wolves dates from the Black Death – to which the Eskimo were not exposed.

Every time the wolves saw a human, the taste of the man at the crashed airplane welled up in their throats. And it was good. While the caribou provided a feast, they would not hunt Eskimo, for they were dangerous, nor would they steal huskies from the line of a camped and sleeping Eskimo. But once they did come upon a lone musher through a flurry of unseasonal snow and against the wind; confronted without warning by wolves close enough to touch, he allowed his fear to show. The wolf with the crippled leg, now one of the betas, crashed through the Eskimo's warding arms and tore out his throat. The man was ripped apart and eaten before the tail-end of the wolf pack arrived. His dogs were eaten in their traces. The mental stimulant of human flesh was reinforced, even for the half-grown cubs, who licked the blood-soaked snow where their elders had eaten the musher.

Eating the musher invigorated the wolves' confidence in their command of the tundra, their new hunting ground; they had taken the most dangerous animal without loss of a single wolf. But they were not misled into turning their attention from caribou to Eskimo: circumstances at every turn increased the pack intelligence of these wolves, amply demonstrated by their accommodation to the unexpected and unsettling events that only months before had unbalanced several of their fellows into fatal neurosis. Only two of the new cubs were lost on the 700-mile trek to the caribou's northern grazing grounds and now the pack was almost sixty strong. In the forest it would have split through internal tension, but here they were continually moving after the bountiful caribou; abnormal friction had no time or space to develop so they stayed together.

7
Frostbite

The northern lights shone bile green, threatening fungus yellow, at least where he could see them past the diamond-white flash still imprinted on his retina. He realized the dirty green and yellow was not reflected from the northern lights: he lay in his own vomit, staring at pure black glare-ice. The overflow washed the vomit away slowly. The throbbing in his head was not pain but the chug-chug of the snow machine disappearing into the night. For a moment there was no doubt in his mind that the snow machine driver had intended him to disappear into that hole, dogs, sled and all. Missing without a trace. *Dogs, sled and all?* No, this was not an Alaskan version of a Central Park mugging. The man on the snow machine had not seen him, still did not know he was there. He called out but his voice was weak and he knew it would not carry. He did not call again. He would need all his strength.

Delilah lay with her face only inches from his, nose to nose, staring gravely at him. General stuck his head between them and licked James across the face. The snow machine chuffed softly, ever more softly, out of earshot. 'I'm sorry,' he told his dogs. But they would soon find their way to the next checkpoint or be found by another musher along the trail. He would be the one to die.

No, damn it, I will not. Anger spurted adrenalin. He flexed his leg muscles to keep blood circulating. He had at most a minute before he started freezing. He found himself dancing on the ice, splashing huge sheets of overflow in every direction, shaking his head and fists in

152

frustration. He reached a shattered tree and beat his fists against its trunk, listening to the ice crackling as it splintered inside his mittens. Being blown to bits or drowning would have been preferable to freezing to death. He hit his head against the tree and felt the skin split like a sheet of paper torn between the fingers: without pain, faintly, far away, of little concern.

The dogs jumped up and barked at him, unsettled by the smell of his blood. Their yapping brought him to his senses. He had not yet escaped certain death: being briefly warm and gaining psychological relief was not constructive.

The flow of blood across his eyes brought the automatic response of trying to wipe it away with his sleeve. His arm was heavy and the cloth crackled as if full of electricity. His dogs were soaked and freezing.

'Get going, you stupid mutts!' he shouted at them. 'Run yourselves dry.' He stood, turning his head to look out of the corners of his eyes because he could only bring objects into focus in his peripheral vision – concussion, he thought – but the plentiful splintered wood was too green to burn and the gas in his stove would not dry even him, let alone the dogs. 'Hike!'

Delilah stared up at him with her soft brown eyes and shook herself to rid her fur of water. But the oily underpelt was soaked and shaking would not help: she needed to run until the icicles standing like spikes in her fur melted in her body heat and ran off as water, and then run and run until the fur dried out completely. Humans cannot run themselves dry. They need fire. James felt frost start in his toes. 'Just proves dogs are superior to people,' he said. The words slurred in his ears. Could his tongue be freezing first? Or had he bitten it when he was blown away from the big hole in the river?

The digression nearly killed him. He found himself

bending to unharness the dogs from the sled to give them a better chance of survival: his fingers would not work the towline clip. He rose from the sled in what seemed to be slow-motion and hit himself on the forehead with his frozen mitten. The blow made a dull thunking sound and hurt excruciatingly but it woke him enough to concentrate. What killed people within sight of cars passing on a nearby road, he had read, was the lassitude that accompanies the freezing process. The victim suddenly does not care any more, even if he can still move. He shivered in his clothes, already stiffening with icicles. He would probably die – but he would die on his feet, straining for the warmth of the Rohn River checkpoint, running his dogs dry. He owed them that much.

He fell on the drivebow. 'Hike!' Perhaps Delilah heard him or perhaps the vibration of the sled set her off. The dogs dragged James along behind his toboggan, his hands clawed around the drivebow, the toes of his stiff-frozen boots dragging a dual furrow in the snow.

Perhaps, James thought, we're heading the wrong way. But he had no energy, no will to command the dogs to turn. He could not even find the strength to pull his feet up on the runners. He hung there, a dead weight frozen to the handlebars, an added hazard to help kill his dogs. *I should have let them go while I still could*.

He saw the warning yellow of the drums and at first thought it an hallucination. But it stayed in his peripheral vision as the dogs dragged him past it. He tried to call out to the dogs but could only croak: or was the sound only in his head? The brain still works even if all the rest is ice.

I can't even remember any Famous Last Words. Was it worth a smile? Did his lips still move? And, when they found him, would he enter legend as The Smiling Musher?

No, you don't remember Famous Last Words, you make them up, every man for himself at the appropriate time.

154

His vision cleared for the briefest moment. Long enough. The drums were carefully stacked in a pyramid, plain yellow fuel drums without even a name on them. But that they were there at all was a sign.

Impetus.

In these parts there were no filling stations; gas was brought in Summer by river-barge and whoever had any in midwinter was unlikely to sell it to passing tourists except in a grave emergency – inwardly he smiled at the macabre joke. The snow machine had brought its own fuel. And perhaps left half a drum.

Slender hope.

Perhaps already too late.

The dogs would not stop. With an effort he turned his head to watch the yellow drums flash past.

Emergency.

He shouted, 'For Rhodes!' this time making a sound he heard clearly in his ears as well as his mind.

A desperate gamble. If the drums were all dry. . .

Almost too late.

With the last of his strength he dug his toes in and tried to fling himself away from the drivebow. But nothing now seemed to happen as he planned; like a Victrola with a weak spring his world was grinding to a halt. He lacked strength for flinging. But his hands were closed on the drivebow only by the vestigial friction of his will; once relaxed, the drivebow slipped out of the frozen tubes formed by his fingers and palms.

Painfully slowly – he could clearly see the tube of fingers and palm on his right hand flying through the air above him – he tried to dig in one toe and raise the other. He wanted to roll. If he fell flat and stopped, he would never rise again.

Freezing to death is really rather painless. Pity that euthanasia is morally repugnant. And suicide for cowards.

The hell with sophomoric chat. There's work to do. Get on with it!

He rolled, with seeming slowness (his perception had slowed: he was rolling very quickly indeed); he tried to keep his hands, feet, arms and legs close to his body so that they would not slow or stop him. Or stick in the snow and snap like an icicle flicked by a fingernail.

He crashed into the drums, setting them tumbling. One cracked him on the head and he passed out, thinking, It wasn't for lack of trying.

Only a full drum could knock me out.

He was too tired to move his head; and he worried that the spike of ice in his jugular would snap and pierce his neck, causing him to bleed to death. His line of sight was onto his hand and right there in his hand lay the cap of one of the fuel drums, with the drum foreshortened behind it. His fingers clawed for the cap but it happened only in his mind: the fingers remained a frozen tube and the knuckle side of his mittens brushed the cap ineffectually.

He was amazed to feel no disappointment.

'Now what?' He was surprised he could still speak aloud. Or perhaps not, perhaps speech was like those fingers he could feel obeying him but see remaining as a tube. *Like people with amputated legs still suffering from ingrown toenails.* He decided that, under the circumstances, the joke was gruesome and in questionable taste.

General licked his face. Delilah whimpered at his distress. Or perhaps from fear. The other dogs whined miserably.

I should have shot that idiot in the snow machine. Then we could have dried out by the flames of his infernal combustion engine.

He carried a revolver in his sled, because all the

156

mushers had been advised to carry a firearm. Many carried revolvers at the waist, but James felt selfconscious with even a knife on his person and had left the Jim Bowie act to those who knew how to use the things.

If I can't shoot up the snow machine, I can shoot up its fuel drums.

He tried to measure the distance between him and the sled but his eyes would not focus. He breathed once, twice, thrice, then rolled. He intended rolling over and over and over but managed only to roll once, halfway, onto his stomach. He lay with his face in the snow and cursed just once. Then something hard hit him in the side. He saw the dull glint of his polished toboggan even in the darkness under the trees and knew what had happened: his sudden movement had startled Delilah and General, who jumped, followed by the rest of the dogs, and the sled had swung around until it hit him and was stopped. He felt no pain.

He hooked his clawed hand into the netting. He would never manage untying it. He did not even try; instead, he scythed his whole body around in one last desperate motion, flaunting Fate by his will, ripping the net out of its moorings by main force.

His axe slid off the other mandatory gear on top of the sled and onto his arm. He felt nothing but did not think the light alloy axe, its only steel a thin sharpening sliver at the cutting head, would break his arm. Not that a broken arm would make much difference.

The revolver was packed on the other side of the sled. He reached for the toboggan to pull himself around it but Delilah and General chose that moment to return to their master's side; as they turned, the other dogs dragged the sled away from James.

He grabbed at it and missed. He watched it go, his last chance. He shook with frustration.

157

His eyes refocussed on his malformed hands. 'But how would I have pulled the trigger anyway?' For the first time it occurred to him that he would have died in the explosion caused by firing into the fuel drums, and his dogs with him.

His arms twinged. He saw again the axe falling on his arm.

The axe had a tubular handle of the same ergonomically correct diameter as the drivebow around which his fingers had been molded into tubes.

He groped with his whole arm in the snow but could feel nothing. He could see his arm moving at a different speed from that his mind instructed and reported. It could be right on the axe and he would feel nothing. Slowly he wiggled himself around in the snow, hope giving dead muscles impetus, until his eyes found the handle of the axe in the snow. With infinite care he arranged his clenched hands next to the top of the leather-wrapped axe-handle. It was slow work but he would not let his concentration lapse. He was probably dead already. He had an infinity to perform one last simple task, to build a funeral pyre for himself. A small fire by which his dogs could dry out.

Dogs tried to nuzzle him. 'Shoo! Scat!' His low croak drove them back a step.

He tensed for the critical part of the operation. He imagined that he could feel ice being crushed within his flesh as muscles stretched towards the last oxygen coursing his blood. Slowly he slid his hands along the snow towards the axe-handle. Since he was unable to close his fingers for extra friction, the axe would slip out of one hand: he had to place both clawed hands because, in two finger-and-palm tubes, he could angle his hands to lock the axe in. Like the stiction caused by misaligned bearings, he thought.

'Old MIT graduates never die,' he said aloud. He smiled. When it was time to enter college he had lacked clear direction to his life except the negative one that under no circumstances would he fulfil his mother's romantic notion of her son as a medical researcher; he had chosen engineering by sticking a pin into a college prospectus. His mother and the President of the Trust had insisted on MIT. Now his training would save his life. Perhaps.

He was losing such perspective as he still commanded. First he put his hands too far, then too near, each time sliding them past the axe-handle. 'Listen, do you want to die?' he asked himself. He stopped concentrating, took a quick impression, closed his eyes, moved his hands as steadily as he could towards the tube-mecca. He opened his eyes for another quick impression. Almost there. He closed them again and moved his hands another three inches.

When he opened his eyes again, his hands were around the axe-handle. He breathed deeply and slid both hands down the tube until they rested, one beside the other, next to the head. He dragged the axe towards his face, arms crackling as they bent. Good. I can still bend my arms. *But do you want to live without toes and fingers and a nose, without feet and hands and a face?* He pushed the axe-head into the snow and slowly rose onto his knees. He no longer listened to the obscene crackling. He felt nauseated and all became black before him.

When he came to he was teetering on his knees. If I black out again all is lost, he told himself. How melodramatic. Nothing seemed to matter any more. But he had always finished what he started and this would be his final task; habit dies hard. He gathered the dregs of his strength and swung the axe as fast as he could past his own ribs and over, holding his hands at acute angle to each other

159

for as long as he could manage. He was glad of the searing pain in his left hand – the pain proved that the hand was not yet lost to the cold. He gave the light axe as much momentum as possible: the force with which it hit the fuel drum would be its weight multiplied by the velocity he managed to impart to it. There would be no second chance.

Too late, he thought of the axe striking a spark against the drum and turning it into a bomb. Too bad if that happens. He fell flat on his face as the axe-handle slipped out of his hands but heard it strike the drum.

He lay there, not trying to raise his head, resigned to his fate. Then he sniffed. *I am a finisher*. Nothing. He was mortally tired. He wanted to weep but that would use too much energy. Instead he thought of Rhodes. Pity we got off on the wrong foot. Life would never be complete without some regrets, a few unfulfilled ambitions. Pass the saccharine, this snow smells vile. Very unlike Alaska. Perhaps the highway is just over there and I'm too lazy to live, a textbook case of death by hypothermia.

'Gas!' Good God, he had split the drum and there was fuel in it, flowing out onto the snow.

Now to roll out of the fuel and set it alight.

Suddenly he had energy for rolling and so much of it that his momentum carried him onto his knees beside the toboggan. His luck held: the click-spark for his Colemans lay close to hand and required no intricate work even for his clumsy robot-hands: only to be held between his two wrists, the lever arms slid inside his mittens – never mind the cold metal stripping skin from his wrists, and to be pressed and –

A glorious yellow fire sprang into life immediately. He reared back from its heat.

He kneeled devotedly before that flame until it started licking at his knees, then rose painfully and rolled the

160

other drums away. He found his fingers unfrozen enough to remove the cap from another drum and pour the evil-smelling liquid into the hole in the snow where the first drum's contents were about to give up the last of their warmth. His dogs crowded around, yipping excitedly, thinking he was preparing food, crowding the fire to dry themselves. He kicked the drums with his still thumping, unfeeling feet – like a very severe case of circulation loss, say after sitting an hour on the lavatory – and found them all full.

'Thank you,' he said aloud. 'Thank you very much, whoever you are.'

It struck him that trees too were repositories of gasoline. After all, he thought, a log is made up of cellulose, oxygen, hydrogen and carbon, a store of years of sunlight. When it burns it offers a sudden, controlled explosion of light and heat. The hydrogen and carbon, released, combine to form octane, butane, propane, methane, ethane, heptane – 'And a few more -anes,' he said aloud – which together are gasoline. He considered the conundrum that a burning log reacts chemically with the atmosphere to create twice the weight of the log in water; he wondered if the first fires of creation had drowned themselves. 'They must have, until the fires became hot enough to evaporate the water and keep burning.' It was a comforting thought.

He poured the contents of two more drums into the hole, then stood in the snow beside the fire and stripped to the skin. Much skin tore away with his clothes, especially from his back and behind his knees, but he was not overly concerned about that, feeling no immediate pain. What did cause him excruciating pain was the return of circulation to his hands and feet as the fire warmed him. Blood flowed where a frozen sock tore a big-toe nail and James smiled conspiratorially at it. 'We'll live,' he said to his big toe, feeling not at all ridiculous to stand naked in winter in the middle of Alaska, watching blood drip from his big toe to freeze on contact with the snow. He thought it likely, if blood still flowed from his blue and wrinkled feet, that he was not frostbitten and would not lose toes or his foot. For a crazy moment he contemplated cutting his equally blue hands to see if blood flowed but in sub-zero temperature any cut takes ages to heal. . . The pins and needles were enough evidence of returning circulation.

He had a pair of dry shoe-pacs in his toboggan and wore these while he arranged his clothes on branches over the fire. He emptied another pair of drums into the fire and wrapped his padded sleeping bag around his shoulders. He cooked for his dogs and made broth for himself; he could not face solid food.

When all of the fuel had burned away his clothes were bone-dry and his dogs were dry and rested. He dressed, harnessed the dogs, bent back the alloy hooks he had wrenched apart to pull the net off, packed his sled and set off for Rohn. He was not in good shape but he could not wait in the middle of nowhere until he felt better; soon he would need professional attention.

If he did not rest soon he would fall asleep and from the runners into the eiderwhite snow. He knew he was concussed because things were hazy in his peripheral vision as well as straight ahead. It was not merely fatigue; there was a different quality to the haziness, like after that bobsled crash at Aspen. But Rohn River checkpoint could be no more than six or seven miles from where he had met with his explosive accident on the Tatina. He had long since run six or seven miles. Several times over. He looked at his perpetual Rolex and for the first time it struck him that it was silly to bring a solid gold watch on a dog-sled race across Alaska. Especially when things became rough. He chuckled at the joke. When he held it to his ear, the Rolex ticked fine. 'Well, what would you expect from a twelve-thousand-dollar watch,' he muttered. 'Of course it works.' But he could not focus his eyes on the hands. He tried to focus on just one hand at a time, bringing his wrist closer to his eyes and then taking it far, far away. Finally he gave up. The hell with time, he was out in the wilderness, he would use the sun, moon and stars to tell time. Just a moment while I study the sky, he told himself, then, aloud, 'It's now double-oh, zero-zero Whitbury time. This is where the world starts counting. Boinggg!'

He decided to run for another hour and then turn back on his own tracks. He knew he was well past Rohn but he was in no mental or physical condition to estimate how long he had ridden the runners at such and such a pace that should have carried him so far and no further. 'When in doubt, forge ahead towards Nome,' 'Colonel' Norman Vaughan, at over seventy the oldest man ever to run the Iditarod, had advised mushers. And, 'If you're really lost and don't want to die, turn south. If you'd rather die than give up, remember which way Nome is: north.' The Colonel had also coined the aphorism: 'Next to the pipeline, the Iditarod is the biggest cause of divorce in Alaska.'

But he was not lost, not really. Delilah had her nose down, following the trail by smell, running confidently, without hunting about. Here and there he caught a flash of surveyor's pink and knew they were on the trail. But the question was: where on the trail?

When next he noticed his surroundings it was full daylight and his dogs were lying down. He fed them but could not stomach food himself. All over his body there was the bone-bruised ache he had experienced only once before, when he had crewed on a shorthanded yacht across the Atlantic into a constant near-gale that had almost killed the whole crew. His head ached abominably. He could see no further than three feet. He crawled into his sleeping bag and stretched out in it on the ice. If overflow came, too bad. He probably would not wake. One symptom of concussion is that the victim is reluctant to wake.

He woke at four in the afternoon because General was licking his face; he could see as far as his sled and, nearby, in perfect perspective, Delilah looking on with approval. He pushed General away and looked quickly at his watch, reading the time aloud so as not to forget it; but when he tried to study his surroundings his vision clouded over again and he could see only white glare as if he were on the middle of a large frozen-over lake. His head throbbed worse than ever. He tried to visualize the maps of this part of the race. Lake Veleska, a small lake on the way to Farewell? But no, in his state he could never have come that far. He was suffering from eye strain or hallucination.

He climbed painfully from his sleeping bag and packed his sled mainly by feeling for it, then let the dogs continue in the direction in which they were pointing. Soon there was some overflow and they turned west into a forest. Elder, he thought, not too tall, but he could not be certain. Trees anyway.

He wished people he could not see would not insist on speaking to him. 'We have not been properly introduced,' he reprimanded them.

'Are you all right, buddy?'

A concerned female voice.

'Where's this?'

'Wow, you're certainly lost! This is Farewell. Hey, now I got you! James Whitbury. They posted you missing at Rohn a couple of hours ago.'

'Oh. Sorry. Man blew me up on the river and now I don't see too well. Are you as pretty as you sound?'

'My friends say handsome. We'll see to your dogs. Come, this way.'

He took the hand on his elbow and put it gently aside. 'First I'll care for my dogs.'

'We'll do it, don't worry.'

'Against the rules.'

'You missed a checkpoint, James,' she said reasonably. 'You're in a bad way. If you go back to Rohn, you'll be running with the campers. You don't look to me like a backmarker.'

'She's right, you know,' a male voice said. James received an impression of a mustache trying to take off independently of its creator. 'Go with her. I'll send the vet to look you over. There's a doctor running with the campers; he'll be here in thirty-six hours.'

'The quiet voice of authority,' James said. 'I'll still care for my own dogs.'

The man with the wings on his lips laughed easily. 'Right. President. For my sins. I'll look after your dogs myself, okay? Emergency. I'll also talk to the other members of the race committee about overlooking the fact that you missed the Rohn checkpoint. Exceptional circumstances, okay? Now for chrissake go lie down before you fall over and we have to carry you.'

James numbly allowed the girl to lead him away. She laughed warmly at something he said but a moment later he did not recall saying anything at all. Inside a building that he did not remember entering, she started removing his clothes.

'You strode in here like a giant,' she said, 'but after the parka, the fur vest, the insulated overalls, the thermal underwear and the woollen longjohns are off, you could do with some fattening up.'

Once more he must have said something amusing. She laughed again. 'These clothes must've cost the same as a Charles Atlas course but they do make you look like you got muscles in your sleeves.'

The vet started prodding him. 'The problem with muscles,' James said, still to the girl he could make out only as an overalled shape, 'is they're like a loan, you have to keep servicing the interest.'

'Do you know what you hit your head against?' the vet asked.

'Ice. A tree. Will I keep my toes and fingers?'

'Probably.'

'Eeowww! What the hell do you think you're sticking that needle into, a horse?'

'Hey, there's a lady present!'

'Then let her do the injections. She has gentle hands.'

'I'm no lady,' she drawled in a Texas twang, 'I'm an officer of the US Weather Service.'

'Bless the US Weather Service.' James fell asleep, chuckling, before she finished zipping him into his bag.

When he woke twenty hours later the hand on his shoulder was Bill Swift's. On the other side of his bed stood Frontier's staff doctor, a youngish man who specialized in cold weather medicine. No-one spoke while the doctor examined James. When he finished he said, 'About six weeks' rest and recreation in Honolulu should put you straight. Lie in the sun for six hours every day and take your pills after every meal and you'll live.'

'I'm in a race, not a vaudeville act, dammit!'

'Well, you can't carry on.'

'Can't or shouldn't?' James had never been keen on doctors and this one had a very superior manner.

'All right, shouldn't.'

'What's wrong with me, exactly?' James asked more politely, having won a small concession.

'Exactly, nothing more than exhaustion, abrasions and the aftereffects of a very close call to frostbite. But the skin will part from your body. With skinless fingers and toes, racing will be extremely painful.'

'Is there any *medical* reason I can't run?'

Bill Swift reacted to the atmosphere between the two men. 'Hold on there, James. Holly is the doctor here.'

But Holly answered the question. 'There's a medical reason all right. If you contract a secondary infection through the bare flesh of toes or fingers, you could lose them, perhaps even bigger parts of you.'

'I knew I could lose fingers and toes through frostbite before I started this race,' James said mildly. 'Nothing's changed. Thanks Holly, it's decent of you to come all the way out here for me.'

'It's my specialty, chum. If you had a broken leg I wouldn't make house calls.'

Though the doctor had not intended a joke, everyone else laughed, including the man with the flying mustache, who had come in unnoticed by James.

'What do you say now? I can see and my doctor pronounces me fit to run.'

Holly snorted.

'It's a free country,' the race official said. 'I can't stop you going to Nome if you insist. But – '

James groaned. 'So I have to return to Rohn to check in and then come all the way back here. You guys are all heart.'

'Actually we *are*. We've decided we're so damned grateful you're not dead that we won't disqualify you for not checking in at Rohn. But you can't collect any prize money, even if you finish in the top twenty, okay?'

James waved the prize money away. 'Thanks. That's good news.'

'We also won't disqualify you because I cared for your

167

dogs. We won't disqualify you for accepting assistance from a motorized vehicle – that's the fuel you burned. That was clearly an emergency and you had to dry out.'

James had a sinking feeling. 'Then for what did you disqualify me?'

'We didn't. I declared your twenty-four for you last night and in three-and-a-half hours you can leave.'

'Thank you!'

'But,' the race President said, 'my advice to you is to pack it in. For what you did already, your name will go down in the Iditarod record. Why expose yourself to further danger?'

'Your toboggan is proven,' Bill Swift said quietly. 'Tip's examined it. You came over Rainy Pass and then were gelignited with no more damage to the sled than a few haircracks. Going all the way to Nome is simply not necessary.'

James shook his head. Yesterday, when he thought he would die, he had resolved to finish the job. Not to do so, now that he was alive, would finish him. Once, at a sports celebrity fundraiser, he had been seated next to Nicki Lauda, the motor racer who drove in a Grand Prix only forty-three days after crashing so badly that he received final rites; the Austrian told him he had raced again so soon because every day of reflection on the sweetness of life made it harder to return to the cockpit. Delayed too long, return would be impossible and self-respect lost forever.

'You can *tell* him to stop,' the doctor said. He ignored the angry glance James cast him.

The race official looked the doctor up and down before answering. 'With all due respect for your reputation, Doctor, this is the Iditarod. If we thought Mr Whitbury incapable of reaching Nome under any and all circumstances, we would never have let him start. After that,

168

there are only two possible reasons for disqualifying him: if he misses a checkpoint or if he maltreats his dogs.'

The doctor was unimpressed. 'You had your missed checkpoint and you let it slip.' To James he added, 'Nothing personal. Professional responsibility.' Without waiting for a reply he turned to stare at Bill Swift.

'James isn't an employee, Holly. I can't *order* him to do anything. He knows my opinion.'

'Right, then we're all agreed,' James said heartily.

'What about his concussion?' a female voice asked behind him.

James hurriedly rearranged his sleeping bag over most of his nakedness. Then he recognized her voice. She had put him to bed. He turned his head and said, 'Hello again.'

'Hi. About the concussion. . .'

Holly shook his head. 'It's gone now. But it could come back. James, if your eyes start playing tricks on you, don't go to sleep. Hurry to the nearest checkpoint and seek medical advice.' With that he left.

They stood, uncomfortably looking at one another while James tried to swallow a chuckle. Bill Swift said, 'Funny how a man can live for years in Alaska and still not fix the spread of it in his mind.'

The woman, who said her name was Jo, stayed when they all trooped out. She showed James to the bathroom and waited to put salve on his back after his shower. He was stiff and sore and glad to let her help him dress. His body was just one large bruise. She advised, 'The best way to live with a big bruise is not to stop running until it goes away.'

'Yes. Only the first million steps will hurt.'

He had to laugh at the large eyes she made. 'Go on, don't let anyone hear you talk like that. You're now a hero of the Iditarod. It would embarrass us if people

169

found out you're really a city slicker who can't stand a little pain.'

'You mean I'd better live up to my legend?'

'Right. I've often wondered why Iditarod winners are such loners. Maybe it's because they can't handle the emotional investment people make in them as heroes.'

'Perhaps there *is* a Clark Kent syndrome. But I bet most of them started out as loners.'

'I thought you'd know, with your Olympic Gold.'

He did, but would never let on. 'Where I come from, everyone has an Olympic Gold.'

She turned away, ostensibly while he shrugged into his woollen longjohns, but he sensed her disappointment. He had again failed to connect with another human being. But trying to undo the damage would only aggravate the breach. He knew. He had been there before.

'Come on, I'll make you a meal,' she said when she had laced up his boots. 'Better not try to change your socks until you're thoroughly warmed up or you'll pull a tendon.'

At the door he pulled her around by her shoulders, held her face between his hands and kissed her full on the lips.

'Mr Whitbury!' she said when he let her go but there was a twinkle in her eye. She was a plain girl, with a bone structure that would make her beautiful all the way from forty-five to seventy-five: for another ten years, until she reached forty-five, she would have only her engaging nature and enquiring mind to sustain her.

'Please call me James. After all, we've been intimate.' He winked as she blushed. 'Next time you take a vacation come stay with me in New York.' The blush deepened and she squirmed in his hands. *Quickly before you disconnect again!* 'Not like that. I stay with my mother. I'll introduce you to some guys who really are gold.' Al

170

Wagstaff, President of the Trust, was a widower who would treasure such a woman.

'I'd like that.' She squeezed his hand and they went out into the passage.

James wolfed his food. He could not remember being so hungry since he gave up a high-protein diet at college.

A flock of plump white ptarmigan rose almost vertically into the sunset ahead as he crossed Sheep Creek. He looked back to where Bill Swift, Tip Durrell and the company doctor stood at the end of Farewell's 'street' to see him off. Jo had joined them. She pushed both thumbs into the air. He waved. The ptarmigan decided he and his dogs were not a threat and settled like down falling from a tearing pillow-fight. The trail was not as frightening as coming down Rainy Pass but he was apprehensive. Twenty-nine mushers had passed before him, the friction of their sleds melting the ice and cutting it up to refreeze unevenly, constantly jarring his toboggan as it rode the corrugations; he could turn an ankle or one of his dogs could break a leg. But he could not leave the trail to make his own way: he would certainly lose his bearings in the spruce lining both sides of the trail. The South Fork of the Kuskokwim, on which the trail ran when it had nowhere else to go, made even worse going because of the ankle-deep overflow; he decided it must be a very shallow river. But, when he reached The Burn, he was sorry to leave even these unpleasant conditions.

The Burn is over 360,000 acres that caught fire in 1977, leaving only charred sticks. For now, James thought. The destruction of the forest was a disaster for him and his generation but in a thousand years it would have been only a minor mishap. Spruce and fir seldom survive fire but the roots of aspen and birch remain alive in the soil to grow again, even when the tree has been burned level

171

with the ground; jackpine seeds not only survive fire but positively *require* it – will, in fact, not germinate without the heat of fire – so that after a burn jackpine are spread far and wide among the new birch and alder suckers, shooting up to fresh dominance. He thought of the colors the flames would have made from the trace elements in the wood: sodium burns yellow, potassium burns blue and violet, copper burns green, and the black smoke is unburned carbon. The remaining ash, perhaps one hundredth the weight of the tree, contains potassium, sulphur, copper, magnesium, boron, sodium, all the minerals needed to nourish thrusting young trees. *The everlasting cycle of the forest.*

Trees, he thought, probably our most precious natural resource. Perhaps three or four per cent of all new natural green growth would, if Man could only learn to tap it, provide enough alcohol to power all the world's cities, industries, automobiles, planes and trains.

James sniffed the wind, then hurriedly closed all his zips and snaps. The wind as yet blew only thirty to forty miles an hour, difficult but not impossible, about the same strength as the winds just out of Anchorage. But this was a different sort of wind – cold, bitter and mean. He was a full day's travel from McGrath – if he did not lose the trail or have an accident – and he hoped fervently the storm would not catch him until he could take his next long break in the comfort of the town.

His immediate problem was that the wind, with no trees high enough to break its direction and scatter its force, had swept the snow from the trail, leaving it composed of gravel, burnt sticks and often exposed treetrunks. He worried about the weakened, cracked runners and spars of his toboggan. He was in a race first, a sled-testing program second. Tip Durrell was up there in a comfortable plane on his way to McGrath, not down here jouncing around and trying to stay on the runners; his opinion on the strength of the runners was theoretical. Every bone in James's body jarred, every bruise cried out for mercy, but he kept his pace. If the toboggan broke, the time lost in jury-rigging it with birch saplings would have to be made up either before it broke or afterwards.

Hey! he thought – and *Ouch!* as the toboggan landed after becoming airborne over a burnt stump – this storm comes *from* McGrath, so it could be worse there. Rhodes might be sitting out the storm. So, if I don't let the weather stop me, I could make up all or most of the time I've lost. And, beyond McGrath, there are another eight hundred miles to Nome even if she does decide to run in the teeth of the storm. A cheering thought, but first he had to reach McGrath.

'Get a move on, Delilah! I want to be within striking distance of McGrath when the storm bites.'

She perked up her ears and gathered a little speed but slowed again almost immediately to the speed she had been maintaining before. Any faster would be dangerous, she seemed to be saying, but see how I humor you.

'Smart dog. Take note, General. You're good at taking commands but sometimes a lead dog must think for himself.' Dave Cohen had told him the professional musher never talks to his dogs except to command them or offer encouragement in difficult conditions; only city-slicker converts to mushing feel the need to talk in the barren middle of desolate nowhere and, having no one else, talk to their dogs. 'Rubbish!' James said aloud to The Burn. He had read in a newspaper that Rhodes talked to her dogs all the time and she was not city people, she was from a Colorado ranch. But he understood the sense of Dave's remarks: one had to be born in Alaska not to be awed by its vast emptiness – even native

173

Alaskans had a healthy caution of the wide white world out there.

The hulking dark shapes out in The Burn were bison, he realized with a shock. God, they are big, he was tempted to say but could not get the words out for fear they would hear him and decide to contest the trail with this intruder. He shook the drivebow silently but Delilah sensibly ignored his plea. The cindered, threatening Burn – almost metropolitan in its blight – rolled on forever and there were more bison, and still more of them now that he looked closely, so big and near he could almost touch them, hovering in the folds of their suppressed anger, more jeopardy per ton of flesh than the killer whale he had once seen over the side of a fiberglass launch. He had never been so alone in his life.

When he came once more to the familiar aspect of the taiga, The Burn and the bison behind him, he stopped the toboggan to inspect the runners. He felt an urge to throw himself down and kiss the earth, like a Polish Pope, in gratitude for being alive. Yet another part of his mind reasoned that it was the dreary depression of The Burn that had frightened him, that the bison were grazing peacefully and that he should not have felt threatened by them. What marvellous recuperative powers the human psyche has, he thought; I wish my body would recover as fast.

He crossed two creeks with open water, the fords clearly marked by the passage of twenty-nine mushers before him, and another pair that were frozen, then arrived at a bigger river. The Kuskokwim. A musher coming towards him shouted, 'Nicolai's the other way. Marker got blown away.'

'Thanks,' James shouted fervently. For the first time in his life he understood the abiding satisfaction of having others nearby, simply nearby. He turned his team and followed the other musher.

Three crosses floated on the horizon, then a vaguely oriental church appeared. The rest of the village was log. James checked in at the community center. When he turned, a boy of about sixteen was carrying a bag of food labelled 'Whitbury' towards him. It was too late to refuse help: another villager already had his double Coleman burning and an old Indian was inspecting his dogs' feet with brisk professionalism.

James looked resignedly at the checker, waiting to be disqualified. Oh well, he thought, next year is another race. 'We don't worry about it too much here,' the checker told him. 'Everybody gets the same treatment, so everybody's equal. And how're you going to stop them helping?'

A woman offered James a bowl of food. He hesitated; these Indians looked very poor. The checker, understanding, nodded almost imperceptibly. James took the bowl and smiled at the woman, who bobbed and scurried away. He was glad he had not insulted her pride by rejecting hospitality. Whatever was in the bowl was delicious.

'Reindeer stew,' the checker said. 'You're not taking food out of their mouths, you know. How much did you ship that your dogs won't eat?'

James brightened and started to enjoy the stew. 'I'll be leaving about two hundred pounds of lamb chops, chopped steak and some beaver. A couple of boxes of butter and the same of cottage cheese. But none of the fat.' He would increase the fat content of the dogs' food in preparation for the storm. Frontier, true to Bill Swift's promise, had shipped piles of food all over Alaska: even in the unlikely event of a heatwave he would be able to feed the proper dog-diet wherever he arrived.

The boy studied James's toboggan. 'I got a lightweight sled too.'

175

James smiled at him. 'Alloy?'

The boy's intense features broke into a slight grin. 'Wood. You want to see?'

'Yes, I do.' He was rewarded by the quick smile that flashed across the boy's face as they turned around one of the log cabins to the shed behind. The sled was on a bench, still under construction.

James whistled. The sled was built of wood planed so thin it was almost shavings, barely thicker than veneer, then laminated into the most sensuous curves he had ever seen on a piece of equipment. 'Now that's a thing of beauty.'

The boy nodded shyly and stroked his sled, his bravado burst of communication apparently exhausted by daring to invite James to view his sled.

'Are you building it yourself?'

'Yes. My dad cures the wood, though.'

'Will you race it?'

'Maybe when I'm eighteen. I already made one and sold it. Maybe I'll sell this one too. We got six dogs but I can borrow more for the Iditarod.'

James guessed the boy and his family would not need – and could not afford to keep – the number of dogs required to select an Iditarod team. Even top mushers ran with borrowed dogs. 'You want to sell me this sled when it is finished?'

The boy shook his head. 'Maybe this one I'll keep. I. . . My dad said he heard on the radio you sell sleds for money to enter the Iditarod, so I wouldn't want to take your money.'

James, properly chastened, nodded gravely at his fellow sled-builder. 'Thanks for letting me see it. Would you help me check my dogs?'

'Yes, please!'

* * *

176

Before the race James had estimated eight hours for the forty-five miles from Nicolai to McGrath. For him that would be fast. Emmitt Peters had taken just under six hours, as he had last year and the year before; James particularly asked after Peters' time because he estimated that on any section of the race his own probable fastest speed was Peters' time plus one third. The checker obligingly radioed McGrath for Peters' time this year. As his possible slowest speed, James doubled the time taken by Emmitt Peters; on sections where there were known to be special difficulties, such as over Rainy Pass, he added a safety margin of another ten per cent. Peering into the soft, swirling snow, James realized he had chosen a clumsy way of setting objectives: over Rainy Pass the racer's 'special difficulty' could be seriously injuring or killing himself, which would put him out of the race rather than needing a larger margin for speed variations. Here on the flat the possibility of becoming lost, perhaps taking days to find the trail again, required a much larger margin than the dangers of Rainy Pass. Before leaving Nicolai he revised to ten hours minimum his estimate of the time needed to reach McGrath, taking account of the snow.

At first he wished it would snow harder: the dogs wore their booties and the snow could not ball up between the pads of their feet. But the snow lay so thinly that he worried about the cut-up and refrozen trail hammering away at his dogs and toboggan. The powdery snow appeared smooth and solid but there was not enough of it to carry any weight before giving way to the spikes and crevasses below.

Soon he stopped worrying about the condition of the trail. Now his concern was to find it at all. Everything was hidden under a cushion of snow, including, where the wind had not consumed it, the pink tape that was supposed to mark the trail. Loss of the tape would not have bothered him except for the coincident snowfall. But he had been counting on his positioning, running right behind the leaders, to give his dogs something to follow by touch and smell. Now, with the snow obliterating all trace of preceding teams, the surviving shreds of surveyor's tape became desperately important to him.

'It's not a storm,' he told himself, 'just a gentle snowfall.' True, it was gentle. But also persistent and close. Visibility was down to Delilah's ears. 'It's not even as uncomfortable as that wind yesterday.' It was warmer than before, without being too warm for his Alaskan dogs. Nonetheless, it was an unsettling experience. But James decided not to stop unless he lost the trail and became disoriented in the whiteout.

He took one of his scheduled breaks with another musher who had pulled off the trail and was camping until visibility improved.

'Sure,' the musher said over coffee, sitting knee to knee with James in his small tent, 'you could reach Nome before me and steal my place in the prize money. But you could also lose yourself for good. Then you can keep my place warm in Heaven.' He thought this a great joke and slapped James's knee. 'Seriously, boy, unless you got very good reason to be out there in zero visibility, it's obstinate to risk your life. It's your turn to get the coffee.' James poured and replaced the pot on the small stove standing in the snow just outside the flap, then zipped them in again. The other musher added, 'Of course Swenson and Peters and May and the others aren't stopping for lost visibility. They want to win real bad. Maybe they need the money. But I'm running mainly to get away from my wife. And my two kids. I scrape and save all my life to send them to college and they come back smartassed and foulmouthed. On the Iditarod is the only time I can hear myself think. Back in Seattle you'd think I was the patented American Mr Nothing instead of listening so attentively to me.'

James grinned. 'I bet another thing is you can never get a word in edgeways. I talk to my dogs.'

'Right! They never answer you back. You know, it's a pleasure to talk to you. That's one of the joys of the Iditarod, being alone in the silence, then speaking to people again. Words assume a responsibility out of proportion to their meaning and value. You want to sleep?'

'No thanks. How many times have you run?'

'Five. Last year I came eleventh.'

Later, with James about to continue into the deepening snowfall, the other musher offered him advice. 'When you get near McGrath don't bother with the trail. It's cut by too many irrelevant snow-machine tracks. In bad visibility that's the guaranteed way to lose yourself in the forest. Stick to the river. It's longer but surer. And, until you get to the river, don't rush it. Better an hour longer on the trail than a day spent trying to find it again.'

'The voice of experience and caution.'

The other musher laughed. 'You could say that. You know what I do for a living?'

'No. Tell me.'

'I'm a movie stuntman.'

James laughed. 'I'll do exactly as you say.'

Despite heeding the good advice he lost the trail twice, adding just over three hours to his journey. When he stumbled onto the Kuskokwim, after being lost the second time, he decided to stick to it until he reached McGrath, no matter that he might follow its serpentine wandering for thirty miles while the trail, if only he could keep to it, would carry him to McGrath across the empty sides of the bulging S-curves in no more than ten miles.

Snow fell more heavily. He was dead-tired, wanted to sleep. He thought about tying himself to the drivebow.

179

'Hibernation is a wonderful capability,' he told General, who was running with the team dogs. Delilah and the swing dogs were out of sight beyond the curtain of snow that receded every time he rushed up and tried to tear it aside.

He found himself on an airfield.

He looked at his watch. He had been on the trail sixteen hours and now he was back at Farewell. Oh damn, damn, damn!

'Delilah! Come haw! Down that road there and let's hope it isn't another runway.'

He saw a plane parked in front of a bar. He blinked and stared through the snow. The plane was joined by another, stationary, but appearing slowly out of the white blanket of the night.

It *was* another runway. It was also the main street of McGrath.

8
Hunger

In the Fall the caribou returned to the forests in the south but the wolf-pack did not accompany them; the wolves yearned too strongly for Siberia to follow their food back to the forest. This break with the tradition of wolf-generations was unwise. Winter is a bad time for wolves, even in the forest with the wintering caribou. The caribou has a foot with two toes and a hollow underneath which is much better adapted for running over slippery ice or through deep snow than that of the wolf. Among other forest-animals the weaker ones die early in Winter; some retreat into impregnable castles of snow and ice and logs, so well stocked that they need not emerge until well into Spring, when the rivers start flowing. The remaining foraging animals, including the caribou, are the stronger survivors who fiercely protect the placental young they carry or their pregnant females. Winter is the time when the weaker and older wolves themselves perish as the forest settles up with its commission agents. Each wolf needs thirteen pounds of red meat a day, two and a quarter tons a year – equal to three full-grown bull moose or one hundred and thirty beaver. The first really harsh bite of Winter kills the weaker prey and provides the wolves with a last gargantuan feast; from then until well into the Spring when the new calves are born – the yearling calves being too fleet for the wolves and the adults the toughest of their species – the wolves have a lean time. If they want to eat, many of them must die on the horns of rampant deer; since they must run further and faster for each meal and fight harder when they corner it, old and weak wolves often fall beside the trail before the prey is brought down. In a really bad winter, if the pack is large after several easy winters and abundant summers, as much as a fifth of the diet of the pack-members who survive into the Spring consists of wolves that fall by the wayside or die of wounds sustained in desperate forays against fit and angry deer.

In the forest the pack had grown greatly past Nature's normal instinctive balance: seven to ten wolves is a viable pack, twenty a very large pack. Fifty wolves together are an Alaskan freak of consecutive bountiful seasons in which the moose too can grow larger and fiercer, to be brought down only by many more wolves than would succeed in normal times. When the pendulum swings the other way then inexorably Nature will reduce such a wolf-pack. But the troupe was no longer in the sheltering forest. And in this winter, out on the desolate tundra, they met the worst weather for a longer period than any pack-member had known. Even in the forest not all wolves would have survived that winter and been fit to hunt through the first hard part of the Spring until the newborn caribou calves made easy prey.

On these barrenlands life for the wolves would be even more precarious. True, there are animals on and under the tundra all year round: lemmings, moles, hares, Arctic Foxes, bears, a very few birds; at the seashore seals and other basking sea-mammals; domesticated caribou (sometimes called 'reindeer' to distinguish them from wild caribou) and their Eskimo-masters. Sometimes wolves will dig for burrowing prey but the tundra's permafrost defeats much better adapted digger-raptors than wolves. Hares are too fast for wolves to catch, as are birds and Arctic Foxes. Bears are too big and vicious but wolves often scavenge the carrion left by bears. Most basking sea-mammals are too wary or too fast or simply too big

182

and violent for wolves (but not for bears, from whom wolves inherit the uneaten excess); even hooking seal-pups from their aglos requires special skills not easily learned by forest-bred wolves.

As for the domesticated caribou, penned and apparently easy prey, their Eskimo owners are marvellously adapted and equipped to protect their livelihood. Eleven wolves fell victim to Eskimo rifles while attacking the tame caribou. Another was trampled by the penned reindeer. It was an expensive lesson.

The pack was too large for the age-proven expedient of attaching themselves to a bear and living on his leavings, though they soon learned to follow any Arctic Fox trotting purposefully in a given direction without casting around for scent; such an Arctic Fox usually was bound for a bear's kill. While they could not injure a bear without suffering fatalities, some of the younger bears could be pestered into leaving their kill by several wolves snapping at their flanks but it was a dangerous business and the wolves had to be desperately hungry to attempt it.

For a time they fed well on the half-frozen waste of a fish factory (not the one where Rhodes had worked) left over from the Summer. When that was finished several died of hunger and hypothermia while they scavenged for carrion on the beaches and tundra. They found an almost whole walrus left by a bear and lived another day; but when they attacked a pod of several walrus they were beaten off with heavy casualties and the walrus contemptuously did not even re-enter the water.

The wolves preserved their remaining strength by reluctantly retreating southwards from the 50° isotherm line. By now it was too late to follow the caribou south: they would all die before they reached the forest. The wolves looked hungrily at the Eskimo, remembering in the backs of their throats the good taste of men. But the Eskimo

would defend their own lives with even greater skill and
energy than they did their chattels; the wolves were not
yet suicidally hungry.

That left the musk oxen, with which they were unfamiliar. They had to attack the hulking sweep-horned animals or starve.

9
Grizzly

McGuire's Tavern was jumping. At a table near the back an Indian woman solemnly strummed a guitar, now and again picking sad Alaskan-Western schmaltz when the mood took her; she never smiled. Across the table from her sat a smiling Indian. On the table lay a beaver carcass. Occasionally a musher would break away from the serious business of drinking at the bar to inspect the carcass. How much? Thirty dollars. Too much. Twenty-five? Okay. Money would change hands. 'My sled's parked under Crazy Horse's plane,' the Indian would conclude the arrangement. 'Help yourself.' He never went outside to check that only the paid-for number were taken. Crazy Horse's plane was the one almost in the doorway of McGuire's and the sled stood under its wing. For every beaver carcass he sold, the Indian ordered a Seven-and-Seven but he seemed quite sober. The woman drank Schweppes sparkling orange. At the bar they were taking bets on whether the trapper would be able to keep to his feet once he rose; in eight hours he had not stood up once even to relieve himself.

Rhodes looked at her watch; her mandatory twenty-four-hour rest stop was over: she could go whenever she chose. Outside she could hear the wind whistle even over the excited buzz of the tavern crowded by the Iditarod to three or four times its comfortable capacity. They had been anxiously following the reports coming in every ten minutes from the blue steel and glass FAA tower: the weather was worsening. She had slept, the dogs were fed and rested. She had received an emotional charge from seeing her father and her friends; the pain of the Iditarod is, she now knew, only secondarily in tired muscles and aching bones – the main effect, given that the racer is physically in shape, is the unexpected *aloneness*. She was accustomed to loneliness but the singularity of the Iditarod runner was a different order of pain. The wild white spaces hurt her, wore her down, with their suggestion that she was the only person left in the world and that she did not matter. Seeing people – especially those who cared for her and hugged her as her father and Harvey did or cried in happiness at seeing her as Margery did – told her that the wild white spaces deceived: she was not alone, she mattered. Refreshed, she was ready to start the remaining eight hundred miles to Nome as soon as the weather would let her.

She listened to Dave and Margery discussing Thoreau's idealized wilderness versus the observable reality. She had found Dave sitting in the booth with her father and the Mannesmans when she came in. Dave had apologized for the pilot who 'tried to kill James and you. I fired him the moment I had my feet on solid ground again. I also reported him.' Margery had offered Dave a ride in their plane. Now they were as thick as two stock agents. Dave drank steadily with Paul Delaney and Harvey Mannesman – they nodded wisely: if young men could still hold their liquor the world was yet safe for democracy – but he talked mostly to Margery.

Rhodes drifted in and out of the conversation. No matter how much they loved her, the musher was somehow apart – the one who would have to go *out there* again. *Out there* had nearly killed James Whitbury. She was glad he had survived. She wondered if he was vain; whether he was or not, she hoped frostbite would not mutilate him. Frontier had flown in the celebrated cold-weather specialist Dr Holly Terman to care for James and they would not have done that unless he was in serious condition. By the time Dave found out James was at Farewell, Farewell was blanked out by the storm.

'I thought only college boys prattled on about Thoreau,' Harvey Mannesman cut into the conversation between his daughter and Dave.

'Not at Louisiana Tech,' Dave said. 'We thought fertilizer-yield ratios, girls and football were pretty sophisticated.'

'You studied agriculture at Louisiana Tech?'

Dave nodded. 'I had a yen for the land. But every time I saved enough for a small piece, the price had risen. I could see I would be a salaried manager for the rest of my life so I came to where I could afford a few acres of my own.'

'Plenty of ranchers send their only daughters to the Tech,' Harvey said.

Dave looked Harvey square in the face. 'All of them seven feet tall,' he said. He was muscular but compact, several inches shorter than Rhodes and not much taller than Margery; such was his self-possession that his height was not evident until he referred to it himself.

Harvey chuckled. 'When you finish with James Whitbury, why don't you come look over my spread and see if I'm missing out on any of the latest techniques.'

Without answering Harvey, Dave gathered up their glasses. 'Would you like a proper drink?' he asked Rhodes, gesturing with his head at the storm outside. Rhodes had been drinking lime juice and soda because alcohol dehydrates and drives out body-heat, life-forces the racer must preserve. If the storm were to lock her in it would not matter but she was still on such a high from the race that she had no need of artificial stimulants. She said, 'No thanks,' and Dave went to the bar.

'Dammit Dad,' Margery said, 'I'm not ugly and I'm not

stupid. You can start laying out the dowry when he proposes. If you lean on him he'll tell us both to go to hell.'

'Sorry, my sweet,' Harvey said quietly. 'I'd do anything not to have you bring back those long-haired New York Marxists in their designer jeans and unwashed Porsches. I always wondered if I should count the spoons after they left.'

Margery was mollified but wary, knowing that Harvey spoke softly only as a prelude to lashing out. 'They didn't have the larceny of their convictions.'

Harvey smiled, acknowledging his daughter's wit, but briefly, to show he would not be deflected. 'But, until the ring is on your finger, button that lip you inherited from your mother.'

Rhodes looked at Margery, whose face tightened. Oh, my God, she thought, not now. She had long feared a volcanic breach between Margery and Harvey.

Paul Delaney said, mildly but in a voice that brooked no interruption, 'You know, Harvey, for over twenty years you have slandered your late wife. She was a dear, sweet girl, who never said a hard word to anyone. It's time you packed it in. Margery inherited her quick mouth from you and no one else.'

Harvey glared at Paul. Margery stared at him in amazement; even Rhodes could not help staring at her father. She had never heard him speak so harshly to anyone, least of all to Harvey, his lifelong friend. Not that it was untrue: one had only to know Margery and Harvey for a few years to identify the source of her inherited traits. And Harvey insulted his friends by his assumption that they should unquestioningly accept him at his own projection of a buffoon with more temper than intelligence.

Harvey decided he could not face down Paul Delaney.

He turned his glare on Rhodes. 'You got something to say?'

'I think you're right, Harvey,' Rhodes said sweetly. 'Only you're too late. If Dave was a haemophiliac, he wouldn't be discussing Thoreau with Margery after four days, would he?'

'What's this about a bleeder?' Harvey demanded of Margery.

'Nothing medical, Dad. Rhodes means, if my lip cuts him.'

Harvey was visibly relieved. 'At my age a man starts thinking of grandchildren,' he said.

Rhodes winked at her father. He had deflected, at least for now, the battle of the generations in the family nearest to them. She knew he had a chestful of military medals and of course that he was a good rancher, but this facet of him, incisive action firmly executed, she had never seen. She was flooded with an infinite sadness because one day she would have to part from him.

Harvey grinned at Paul. 'Let's hope at least one grand-child has more of Margery's mother than of me.'

Margery sighed, softly and briefly but Rhodes heard. She had never before known Margery to choose peace before friction.

Dave came with their drinks and distributed them. He looked at Margery. Rhodes could almost feel their minds mesh. She felt a vague stirring of envy and suppressed it.

Margery said, 'I was going to invite you to visit us but, if Dad wants to pay consulting fees for what he could have had free, that saves you airfares.'

'Me and my big mouth,' Harvey said.

'What do they say at the bar?' Rhodes asked. There was no need to specify the topic.

'Eep Anderson says –'

'I thought he left two hours ago.' Rhodes looked

towards the bar: the Indian was talking to his brothers and holding a short drink.

'He did. But he decided the storm would reach Ophir before he did and he'd rather wait it out in the bar close to home comforts than under ten feet of snow. That's his wife Puddin with the guitar. You're not thinking of going out into the blizzard, are you?'

'It could clear.'

Dave shook his head. 'You were ninth when you came in and no-one who arrived after you has left.'

'How ever do you know that?'

'The other mushers are watching you and Eep. Him because he's a regular front runner, you because you're a rookie running in the top ten. Eep and – '

They all looked up into the sudden silence. In the doorway stood James Whitbury. Risen from the dead. Silently, every person in the room rose.

The only sound was made by James stamping his boots and shaking his clothes, spraying snow. His few days' beard looked like a month's growth but he had showered and changed before coming to the tavern.

Rhodes looked at her watch. Since he could be assumed also to have fed and tended his dogs, he had been in town not less than two hours. If he had rested as well, he could have been here many hours. She had lost her lead over him; they were now level.

Someone started clapping in time to James's stomping boots. Others joined, then cheered and shouted and whistled. He had faced death on the Iditarod and come through and was here, visibly whole, lessening their own fear.

James was startled. He smiled shyly and blushed. Then he swept off his cap and bowed low, a cavalier gesture to hide his embarrassment. Someone put a glass in his hand. He raised the glass to the assembly and drank deeply.

190

That completed the adulation of the resurrected and the revellers resumed matters of moment at the top of their voices, as if a bell had been rung.

'You bastard!'

Her father glanced at Rhodes sharply but Dave Cohen, at whom her exclamation was addressed, did not turn to her. He was still looking at James, who strode through the touching hands towards them. Rhodes spun Dave around by his shoulder.

'You kept me here to let him catch up!'

'What?' Dave turned to James. 'How are your hands and feet?'

James held up his hands. 'Raw. But I'll survive. Skin's marvellous, just won't stop growing. Hello, Rhodes.'

'Congratulations on surviving, Mr Whitbury,' Paul Delaney said.

Rhodes would not let him run interference. 'I hold you responsible for your minion's petty tricks,' she said to James.

He shook his head as if to clear it. 'What are you talking about?'

'Your lackey tried to keep me here while you caught up.'

'Rhodes!'

She ignored her father.

'Nobody can go out in that blizzard,' James said, not hiding his irritation. 'Visibility's nil.'

'You came in through it!'

'When you're in that mood, cautious men will worship you from afar,' James snapped. He drew a breath to compose himself, nodded courteously to the assembled company and turned on his heel.

'You wrong him,' Dave Cohen said mildly. 'And me. I didn't know he was in McGrath until he walked through that door.' To Margery, he said, 'I'll see you later.' And to Harvey and Paul, 'Please excuse me.'

When he had left there was a long moment of silence. Rhodes felt the tangible embarrassment but she was damned if she would apologize. They were not out there on the trail trying to stay ahead of James Whitbury. She was.

'I think you should apologize to them, Rhodes,' her father said.

Perhaps he was right. She just did not know any more. The others had sat down but Rhodes still stood. She looked at her watch. Time. 'I'll see you in Nome.'

'The blizzard still blows,' her father said mildly. 'You're acting in anger.'

'No, I'm racing in the Iditarod. I'm not taking everyone's word it's impossible. I want to see for myself.' A small spasm of pain crossed her father's face. Rhodes realized that the parting had come sooner than either of them had expected. 'If it's really bad I'll turn back. I promise.'

'Of course.' Her father held her hand for a moment. Fear displaced pain in his eyes. 'You're a big girl now.'

Harvey Mannesman pursed his lips and shook his head, saying nothing.

She looked at Margery but Margery seemed unworried about the accusation Rhodes had levelled at Dave; she was smiling slightly, observing with her artist's detachment.

'I'll see you in Nome,' Rhodes said again and walked out, past James and Dave standing at the bar with a bottle of champagne between them.

Her team and sled dropped over the bank onto the frozen Kuskokwim. Rhodes kept her head down before the cutting wind, resolutely driving into the stinging snow. She was sad that now she might never see the overgrown

192

'old town' of McGrath, marked a mile away on the old course of the river by three rotten hulks of long-deserted riverboats: *Lana, Quickstep* and most of the upper structure of *Lavelle Young*; the hull of *Lavelle Young* had been turned into a barge and the pilot house helicoptered out to Fairbanks because in 1903 it had carried Captain E. T. Barnette on his way to founding that city.

Driving directly into the blizzard she simply had to keep her head down. As soon as she worked off the adrenalin of anger, she decided, she would return to McGrath and wait out the storm. None of the other competitors would come out in this blizzard. But she must be careful not to leave McGrath so far behind that she could not find her way back.

The wind changed direction and she raised her head to see if visibility was improved, if she could see Toots' ears. She could not. It took her some moments in that pure white night, in which all directions were the same direction, to realize the sled was travelling upwards. She shouted at Toots to stay on the ice, even if the overflow was uncomfortable. On the bank they would not only slow down but lose the river and the trail. Becoming lost in this blizzard could be fatal. The wind carried her words away and tried to fill her mouth with snow. Dogs and sled stopped. She ran alongside the sled and past the team dogs. Toots was already lying down and letting snow blow up on one side of her to form a windbreak. Sled dogs, when not under discipline for as much as a minute, will promptly lie down and not rise again until feeding time. They were in a lee, with snow blowing vortices. In one of these cones of silence and vision Rhodes saw a sign.

The cone stretched until its pointed end flattened against an obstacle. She recognized the blue steel and glass of the FAA tower. She was back in McGrath. Irrationally, she was glad that her father and friends had returned to the warm security of McGuire's; she could do without jokes about her lead dog being smarter than she.

'Oh Toots,' she said. 'How could you?'

The storm was too bad to travel anywhere. But Toots had forced her hand. The only discipline for sled dogs is the supremacy of the musher's will. Once the dogs realized she was not in control, her life would be hell. She could not leave the dogs with the idea that *they* could decide when to run and when to stop: soon they would be deciding to camp every five minutes even in fine weather.

Now I'll have to head into the storm or scratch from the race right here.

'You obstinately got yourself into this,' she told herself aloud. Even here in the lee of the building the wind swept the sound away before it reached her ears. 'Now mush or scratch. You haven't any other choice.'

She bent to put her face close to Toots' nose. Toots blinked – seeming to wink at her. Unreasonably, this cheered Rhodes. What must be done must be done, she thought, but there's no need to be grim about it. Still, she used her voice like she meant it.

'Mush!' she shouted as loudly as she could, her mouth an inch from Toots' ear. Her command dog jumped up and the other dogs followed her lead immediately. Toots cast Rhodes a resentful look; the other dogs looked guilty. Rhodes grabbed the gangline and ran from the relative peace in the lee of the buildings across the runway and into the blizzard, head down, trusting to her sense of direction to find the river. Her feet found the riverbank and slid out under her. She slithered down the bank on her bottom, Toots beside her, breathing hotly on her cheek. Near the bottom, before she could slide into the overflow and soak her clothes, she used the momentum of the incline to hurl herself onto her feet. Bending almost double to keep the wind off her face, she ran into it, knees pumping up and down like pistons.

She could not see her feet: only white snow, from which her knees appeared eerily as if jerked on elastic by some toymaker from the ice underworld. If she came to open water she would run right into it; she hoped desperately there would be none.

'Thanks but I showered at McGrath,' she formed words with her lips, trying to keep her resolution of doing what was necessary but with a light heart. It was not that easy.

As far as the confluence of the Kuskokwim with the Takotna River it was impossible to lose the trail. Every time she felt her feet angling up a bank she had only to turn back to the level howling snow on top of the river itself. That was comforting as a thought, even if physically wracking because the middle of the river offered no windbreaking trees and the banks were no protection against a blizzard swept head-on along the center of the river.

But then the trail would turn towards Takotna, the village, leaving the Takotna River to run cross-country around low hills and through scrub brush. She seemed to remember another sinuous river that the trail would cross many times. *That* was a recipe for becoming lost even in good visibility. In zero visibility it guaranteed she would be lost.

She decided that when she came to the confluence of the Kuskokwim and the Takotna she would turn around and return along the river to McGrath, having proved her will to the dogs.

The dogs gathered speed behind her as they gained

confidence. The overflow was less now and she would feel instantly if Toots ran up the bank. She stood to one side and let the team and sled pass her, then grabbed the drivebow and jumped onto the runners.

How she missed the confluence of the rivers and the turning of the trail, Rhodes would never know. Logically it was easy to explain: she had two feet of visibility and Toots had nothing to follow but instinct, no beaten trail or odor of previous teams, just a blanket of snow.

She first became uneasy an hour out of McGrath. She should long since have reached the joining of the rivers.

Damn! she thought, irritated before being frightened.

She glimpsed a flutter of surveyor's pink – Thank God! – and stopped her sled by digging in with the brake and shouting against the wind at the dogs. The hot pink had disappeared into the white embrace behind her. She took hold of the sled and dragged it back in what she hoped was a straight line. She dared not make a circle for fear of losing direction. At first the dogs resisted: sled dogs are not used to backing up. But Rhodes persisted and finally managed to start the sled moving backwards. The dogs no doubt were complaining loudly but their barking was torn away by the wind. She could not see them. It was as if she alone were present at the creation of the world, when everything was white and innocent and every action fraught with jeopardy.

She heaved the sled backwards – ten measured paces, twenty, thirty. Still no tape. She stopped to rest, praying her sled would not freeze to the ice under the loose layer of blown snow. She saw scrub brush around her knees. She was off the trail.

She resolutely ignored the implications.

Rested, she again put her back into pulling the sled and dog team backwards. It was slogging work. Another ten paces, twenty, thirty more. She gasped for breath. She could not afford to work any harder or she would start perspiring and contract frostbite. James had no skin on his hands – he was lucky not to have lost fingers . . . more. She was not vain but knew she would not want to live if she were less than complete. Crippled, maimed – even the words sounded revolting.

The hot pink was in the corner of her eye again. She reached out and the snow swirling over her parka and mitten formed a tunnel of vision. The hot pink was about six inches of lint, roughly torn at both edges.

Rhodes wanted to cry. She sat down in the snow.

Tying ribbons on her dolls after she became convinced her mother was really dead, that she would never see her again – the memory filled her mind to bursting; she felt hot tears flooding her eyes.

She stood up abruptly.

She would camp right here. If the blizzard did not last too long she might survive. Then she would search for more pink tape until she found the trail or until the rescue party found her. How far could a piece of pink tape have blown?

Keep calm! There is always hope.

Miles. Ribbons could blow miles in a storm.

She reached out to pick up the piece of ribbon. It would be a small consolation.

She threw her head back in laughter, mindless of the snow blowing into her mouth even with her back to the blizzard's main attack.

The pink ribbon was tied to the scrub. The *rest* of it had blown away. She was right on the trail!

'Hallelujah!' she shouted exultantly. *God, it's good to know I will live*.

Finding the remnant of ribbon did not mean she could continue but, if she stayed right here, it would be much easier for the rescuers to find her should the blizzard last a long time. And, if it should be over quickly, there would be no need for rescuers. She was not wet, was warmly dressed, with provisions in her sled, and the sled itself could provide a lee for her and the dogs even if her little tent and light tarps would not withstand the wind.

And she would be ahead . . .

Considering that you've been stupid enough to let your temper put you here, she told herself, you're not too badly off. You're only standing in a blizzard not too far from the dead center of Alaska. As if to confirm her optimism, the wind died for a moment and snow seemed to fall only in the area beyond the charmed circle of thirty feet around her. As she turned she saw Toots for the first time since they had left McGrath; Toots was lying down to present as small a target as possible to the wind but the cast of her head, supporting on each hair a small stalagmite of ice that turned the young dog gray, confirmed that she was awake and alert.

Into that charmed circle ambled a bear.

Rhodes stared at it, petrified. She knew that bears do not attack people unless provoked but, face to face with a bear standing over three feet high at the shoulder, she found she could not move a finger. Her mind, running at a tangent, even found time-out from fear to wonder that the bear was more brown than gray, even under the powdering of snow on its pelt. She had always thought 'grizzly' means 'gray'.

The bear looked casually at Rhodes. It licked its nose with a big red tongue and she saw most of its forty-two teeth: they looked just like those of a large dog – or a large wolf.

Rhodes shivered. The involuntary ripple through her muscles released her from the bond of fright. The bear would have poor eyesight but acute smell and hearing. Senses deadened by the blizzard, it could have found

198

them only by accident. She considered standing quite still until it went away again. Perhaps it had not seen her yet . . .

The bear seemed to nod its shaggy head politely at her. Then, with incredible acceleration, it ambled towards the dogs, two left legs first then two right legs together, like an elephant. In the moment before she acted Rhodes saw clearly the tips of the bear's two forward teats sticking through the pelt: it had two cubs that would be of opposite sex. Bears have one or two cubs, if two then always of opposite sex; only the forward two of the six teats give milk. It was obvious what had happened. The bear had cubbed in December in her cave and not eaten or drunk anything since, converting her bodyfat to feed her cubs. Now, prompted by her internal clock or hunger, she had come out of hibernation for food to replenish her strength. It was plain bad luck that she had stumbled on Rhodes. And the dogs.

Dogs do not share the immunity of people from attack by the world's largest carnivore. True, bears normally prefer not to attack a dog or dogs but in a crisis . . . Hunger after hibernation, hungry cubs waiting in the cave, a blizzard – all created a crisis for this bear. And she was in a foul temper from the cold of the blizzard so soon after the snug warmth of her cave. As she came upon the dogs she rose on her hind legs, intending to fall upon her choice and crush it with her weight as her large canines ripped out its jugular. An intelligent animal, she had learned a lesson from killing two young wolves – to her the same as dogs. The wolves had strayed from the pack on their honeymoon; one of the wolves had ripped her ear before being crushed by her weight. She would not have attacked the wolves except for desperation; now she was desperate again, and more experienced.

Rhodes heard her dogs reacting, some snarling, others

whining in fear. The bear rose above the dogs, claws extended, fangs bared. It roared, exposing gums exactly the color of the surveyor's tape marking the trail. The dogs strained, some aggressively towards the bear, others away from it.

Rhodes found herself running towards the bear.

'No!'

That was the wrong thing to do. If she threatened the bear it would attack her.

'*Hike!*'

She spun on her heel and grabbed the drivebow. One of her swing dogs had the bear by a paw just behind the claw. She saw the other claw slash downwards and rake the dog's belly open. Hot blood spurted over the snow. Frantically she shoved the sled to one side, trying to help her dogs turn it away from the bear.

'*No!* You can't fight it tied in harness!' The screams of the wounded dog drowned out her words.

Toots responded to the command but the other swing dog was inclined to fight the bear and the team dogs were trained to follow the swing dogs. Her sled was frozen to the ice and her dogs, oh God, her dogs . . .

The bear had the head of the swing dog in its jaws. Above all the commotion Rhodes heard the skull crunch. Blood and watery pink liquid and gray brains squirted out of the dog's ears. The bear seemed to be trying to lie down on the dying dog, to crush its ribcage by its own weight.

Rhodes knew there was nothing more she could do.

After Rhodes had been gone for a while – to rest, he thought – James carried a couple of bottles of champagne to the Delaney table.

'Sit down, Mr Whitbury,' Paul Delaney said. 'You're welcome.'

'James.'

Dave distributed fresh glasses. 'This is Margery,' Dave said.

'We've met. Memorably,' James said drily. 'Mr Mannesman.'

'Want to withdraw your bet, boy? Last chance.'

James grinned but did not answer; Harvey did not expect a response. He opened the champagne and poured. They all raised their glasses but no one seemed to have a toast until Paul Delaney stepped into the breach: 'The Iditarod.' They drank and James filled the glasses again. It was not an uncomfortable silence.

'Do your hands hurt?' Margery asked.

'Surprisingly my feet hurt more. I think hands heal faster, being exposed to air at least sometimes: feet, in socks all the time, stay raw longer.'

Encouraged by James's agreeable manner, Margery asked, 'Were you frightened you would lose your – ?'

'Listen, I was so scared, my knees knocked like castanets.'

'That speaks volumes for your good sense,' Paul Delaney said and Harvey Mannesman nodded in emphatic agreement.

James laughed. 'A lady I met at Farewell thought Iditarod heroes shouldn't let on they feel pain and fear like ordinary mortals. But, if you think about it, there would be no race if they didn't.'

Margery, sensing an intellectual argument, pounced. 'How's that?'

'There would be nothing to prove,' Dave said.

James said, 'Precisely. You can't be a hero unless what you do is difficult and dangerous.'

'More heroes are made involuntarily than by deliberately trying to prove things,' Paul Delaney said. 'In wars, for instance.'

'So proving something isn't conclusive,' Margery said.

'Back on the trail I met a man camping until the weather improves,' James said. 'He doesn't want the discomfort and risk of continuing in the blizzard. Would you call being a film stuntman a dangerous and difficult job?'

'Certainly,' Margery agreed.

'This fellow is a stuntman. He runs the Iditarod to escape his nattering wife and his foulmouthed children. He doesn't have to prove he's tough.'

'One can't have a conversation with people who insist on agreeing with one,' Margery said tartly. 'Why don't you go back to being abrasive and disagreeable.'

Harvey Mannesman chuckled. 'Other mushers, Joe Redington for example, don't have to prove how tough they are. I should say he, and others, run out of nostalgia for another time, before airplanes and helicopters put the mushers out of business.'

'The danger is the same, whatever the reason, whether sought or not,' James said.

'So you don't mind admitting you want to be a hero?' Margery asked politely.

James wondered if she was taking mental notes. 'This conversation started as a joke. Now it's turning serious. Being a hero is a public thing: a bit like sinking into a hot bath, pleasant while it lasts but you know it will quickly cool. Proving to *yourself* that you can do something, that's the lasting satisfaction.' He drained his glass. 'If you put me in your book, don't forget to make me handsome and clever and charming or I'll sue.'

Dave laughed aloud. Margery glared at him. Not a bit intimidated, Dave laughed even harder.

'Take a tip from an older man, James,' Paul Delaney said. 'Women hate having their wiles exposed.' He was warming to the boy. James was very different from the

202

abrasive metropolitan sophisticate Margery and Rhodes had made him out.

James nodded and rose without putting his hands on the table. 'I'll sleep some more; Rhodes has the right idea.'

'Oh, she's not sleeping, she's on the trail, running for Nome,' Margery said.

James laughed heartily. 'Hey, you're doing exactly what Rhodes accuses Dave and me of, playing tactics instead of racing.'

'No,' Dave said, 'Margery's right. Rhodes checked out an hour ago.'

'You're joking! With a whiteout for a hundred miles around?'

'She's a determined lady.'

James shook his head incredulously. 'I'll see you,' he said. On the way to the front door he stopped at the bar to send more champagne to their table.

'He's going to cuddle up until the storm blows itself away,' Harvey said. 'Smart fellow.'

No one mentioned Rhodes but they all thought of her.

Paul Delaney looked at his watch. 'Dawn. Or it would be, if we could see the sun.'

Rhodes kicked at the sled; it sprung loose. '*Hike!*' Her dogs ran, but raggedly, their rhythm broken not only by fear – and the unsettling odor of fresh blood – but by the weight of the dead swing dog being dragged along in harness.

The bear ambled along on one quarter, every now and again darting in to rip a mouthful of flesh from the dead dog. The head, fore- and hind-legs and tail were all gone, eaten. They dragged the dog's trunk with them still.

'Goddammit, you *can* outrun a bear!' Rhodes shouted

her rage and frustration at them. But not, it seemed, today.

Toots, nervous and frightened because she could see nothing in the storm, kept looking over her shoulder towards the bear: she could not see it through the white blizzard, could not see Rhodes to gain reassurance from her mistress. Her temptation, her natural inclination, was not to run but to turn and fight. Only superb training and years of discipline made her respond to Rhodes' frantic shaking of the drivebow and desperate shouts, sensed rather than heard.

Rhodes too was blinded, not only by the snow needling into her face but by a moving curtain of it all around her. She could see part of the sled but none of her dogs. Once, twice, she caught sight of the bear ambling along a few paces to her right. Once she saw it dart forward to bite the last leg from the carcass as the dead dog's trunk turned in midair after a bump. That was the worst of the ordeal, not being able to see. For all she knew the bear was eating her dogs one by one and, when it finished the dogs, would eat her. She leaned over the drivebow, clinging on with one hand, and undid the retaining net to pick up her father's pistol which, since the incident with the elk, she carried on top of her mandatory gear. But her gear had shifted in these wild maneuverings: her fingers, strive as she might over the drivebow, fell short of the pistol. Her firearm was out of reach when she needed it most. Stupid! If she survived this she would wear it at her waist, no matter how ludicrous she appeared.

If only she could somehow cut the dogs loose so that they could defend themselves by surrounding the bear.

If only she had not stubbornly come out into the storm against the best advice.

If only she could find a rock or tree to put her back

against so that she and her dogs together could face the bear.

If only it were midspring and the bear less aggressively hungry.

If only it did not have two cubs to care for.

If only Toots had not turned back to McGrath without command.

If.

She saw the bear again, only its head showing through the snow, blood on the fur around its mouth. It grinned at her with bloodied teeth.

'Go scavenge somewhere else,' she shouted. But this was an Alaskan grizzly, far removed from the tourist cabins and their dustbins that made the bears in the lower forty-eight seem such harmless, clowning beggars. This was no teddy bear. It was a meat-eating hunter seven or eight times her own weight.

She rummaged under the net again for a weapon. The sled tilted and overturned.

I'm flying through the air for ever such a long time. This is a dream. GOVERNMENT HEALTH WARNING. Dreams may be fatal.

Out of the fluffy flying snow she arrived at deeper fallen snow. She sank into it as if into the huge goosedown mattress her grandmother had slept on. No wonder the dogs had been running so slowly.

She rolled erect and looked at the axe near her hand. She must have grabbed instinctively at it just as the sled overturned. She took it in both mittens and gripped it fiercely. It was not a pistol but it was a weapon of sorts. She swept the axe-head through the blinding whiteness and encountered only yielding snow in all directions. She stood stock still and listened carefully but could hear no sound of dogs barking or whining or of the bear feeding. She heard only snow whispering fear into her soul and her

205

own labored breathing, hard and heavy in her ears. *I must not move hurriedly or at random*. In the whiteout, if she missed the sled by inches, she would be as dead as if it were miles. If she became disoriented and wandered away from the gear in her sled . . . Meanwhile, the bear eats my dogs, she thought with self-imposed calm.

She inhaled deeply and took three long strides forward. She swung the axe in a half-circle at the full stretch of her arm. Nothing. She turned slowly, deliberately. 'One hundred and eighty degrees exactly,' she told herself through frozen lips. Three steps back. Her footprints were almost filled, her body-impression erased. From her original position, but facing the other way, she turned leftwards ninety degrees. The sled had risen on the right-hand side and flung her off to the left: because she had turned around, she would now have to turn left towards it. For a moment, disoriented by the awesome white *nothing* closing in on all her senses, she doubted her own sanity. Should she not be facing the *other* way? No! This way! She burned to move, to *go*! – what could be happening to her dogs while she investigated her travelling padded cell? She calmed herself by force of will, long enough to compact a hole in the snow with the axe-handle. A marker to return to.

Three long strides straight ahead. It was so easy when one could *see*, find reference points and markers but, in that snowy blanket that had engulfed the dawn, she was white-blind. She stopped and swung the axe, head first. It nearly slipped from her fingers, freezing even inside her fur mittens. She gripped the axe-handle harder as she swung further.

The axe was positively jerked from her hand. She did not lose her grip, something had pulled it.

She stood quite still for a moment, hands perfectly still and positioned before her as she had arrested them

206

immediately after losing the axe. She gauged the direction it had followed. She hesitated. The next was the bravest step she ever took in her life. She bent to feel for the axe in the loose snow, keeping her feet motionless. Nothing. She straightened and took another step. She fell over the axe-handle sticking out of something unseen, held at an angle to the earth. At least she assumed it was an angle to the earth, all directions being the same inside that sphere of perfection into which only she and her axe-handle intruded reality. She looked up the handle but could not see the end. Without rising, she followed it hand over hand to the end. That was the handle end. Hand over hand the other way. What if the axe-head was stuck in one of her dogs? Her hands slowed to a crawl and stopped. She had swung it desperately, thinking only of hitting the sled, of finding the sled before she lost all sense of direction.

Wounding the bear, even threatening it . . . She really did not want to think of it. Bears are renowned for their volatile temper.

She forced her hands to clamber over each other to the head of the axe. It was stuck between two stanchions on her sled. She freed the axe, then crawled along the side of the sled, deciding by feel which way was forward. After what seemed an hour, she put her hand on a furry back above the level of her head. Huge fangs closed an inch from where she jerked her hand away. She screamed. For a moment she was face to face with the bear but no, the snapping muzzle belonged to one of her wheel dogs, a huge purebred malemute. She put her face close to his and he calmed enough to lick her. Working quickly she untied him from the gang- and tuglines; then, rising and leading him by his neckline, she forced her way forward through the storm from dog to dog, setting each dog free as she came to it but holding the necklines in her hand to

207

keep them from running into the blizzard to die of exposure. If the bear had gone, she would re-harness the dogs. If it was still there and attacked her, she would let the dogs take their chances with the blizzard rather than face certain death from the bear. She came to the swing dog whose mate had been killed by the bear. It strained towards her, whining in fear. Down one side the bear had gashed it red, exposing ribs but not tearing into the stomach. Mercifully the whiteout was so close she could not see the dead dog behind it. Nor the bear beyond . . . She untied the wounded swing dog and moved up to Toots. The lead dog's neck fur rose electrically; she did not look around when Rhodes undid her ties to the gang- and tuglines.

The bear was still there.

And Toots was no longer under discipline. She snapped near Rhodes' mitten, not at the hand but near enough to show her intent. She would fight the bear. Rhodes knew the other dogs would follow Toots. She could not drag them all along by main force. And there was no time for squeamishness with the bear eating the dogs still tied up on the far side of the gangline. She hated what she knew she must do next: she balled her fist and hit Toots as hard as she could on the nose. The dog was blinded and disoriented, all fight now out of it, and Rhodes was able to drag it away from the bear by its neckline, towards the back of the sled.

She did not want to go up the other side of the sled. But she had to.

It was far more difficult than on the first side. These dogs were nearer the bear. One startled dog bit into Rhodes's hand through the thick mitten and several started nervous fights with their fellows as she freed them. She hit one on the nose. It howled and skittered away and the others cowered before the fear-induced rage in her voice. None of the dogs except Toots and the malemutes wanted to approach that bear; perhaps they could smell it even through the snow, perhaps they simply *felt* its presence through the risen hackles on their backs.

Rhodes too *knew* the bear was still there. 'I'm more frightened than you, but there are more dogs in harness just there.'

At last, shivering so badly with fear that she wondered if her hands would operate the snaps and buckles, she came to the team dog immediately behind the swing dog killed by the bear. This dog was up and alive, though she could see only its tail and did not know if it was hurt. Leaning forward from as far away as she could, she worked quickly on the lines, trying to free the dog before the bear found out she was near. The dog knew she was there, straining backwards against her legs, but kept its head out of her sight into the snow curtain. Oh God, if only she could see where the damned bear was! Surely, if she could feel its presence, it could not be unaware of her!

Less fear makes more speed.

The dog would not stand still. Every time she gathered slack in the line to work with, pulling the carcass – and the bear! – closer, the cowering dog would back up against her. The other dogs made things no easier, pulling at the lines looped about her other wrist.

Her dog harness was not designed to be operated one-handed and the intense cold turned every snap and buckle into an instrument of torture to finger, hand and muscle. She gritted her teeth and endured: frustration vented as anger could delay her long enough for the bear to decide she was a threat and –

The lines jerked as the bear tore a chunk from the dead dog.

Rhodes's hand was trapped in the harness. She felt an

overwhelming temptation to push her head through the curtain of snow to see the bear. Not to suffer the uncertainty. To get it over and done with. She leaned forward, head following the receding limit of her vision; she saw the head of the still-tied dog appear, she –

Curiosity killed the cat.

She jerked her head back.

She tore her hand from the restraining loop. The last dog was loose. She started backing away but Toots and the two malemutes pulled the other way, towards the bear, barking and jumping up against their necklines.

The bear's acute hearing must have penetrated the deadfall of snow. Suddenly the bear, risen on hind legs to awesome height, appeared out of the snow, forepaws raised to attack. Rhodes could see the curving claws as the bear swiped at her. The footpad was black and coarse-grained, like cheap leather-cloth. The extended claws swiped half an inch from her nose and she fell backwards over one of the team dogs cowering behind her knees. That dog saved her life.

Rhodes rolled frantically in the snow, away from the bear, beneath a flurry of dogs, more dogs than she knew she had. She wondered if her back would break, leaving her helpless for the bear to eat.

She rolled into the runner of a sled and noted, without surprise, that it gleamed dull alloy. She rolled upright and ran towards the heads of the still-harnessed team that had just run over her. She had to pull her dogs away before they attacked the bear and were killed by it. And she had to warn James Whitbury to move himself and his dogs the hell away because there was a vicious bear only feet from them behind the curtain of snow.

Out of the persil-universe she cannoned into his back. He stood with his feet planted well apart and a monstrous revolver in his hand pointing directly to the sky. He held fast to fire two measured shots. She slid down his leg. The two sleds made a lee in which she saw the lower half of the bear, legs and teats and belly, as it ambled away, two right legs together, two left legs together, a strange way to run.

He bent to help her up. She hugged him.

'God, am I glad to see you,' she said, surprised at how mild her voice sounded. Now is my chance to become hysterical, she thought, but shrugged the inclination aside.

'Where's the bear?'

'Gone.'

Her arms were about to slide from his neck. He held her elbows to keep them around his neck. 'I like this,' he said.

'I thought you said no-one could survive the storm.'

'I came looking for you.'

She looked at him for a long time. Then she said, 'I believe you.' She was tempted to kiss him. 'I must gather my dogs.'

'Your sled is right behind you. Better tie on a safety-line.'

She was reluctant to leave his comforting presence but there was work to do. She took a sixty-foot coil of aircraft-quality braided nylon from her sled, tied one end to the sled and the other to her belt. If she failed to find her dogs in a radius of sixty feet, they were lost forever. She took the pistol in case she should run into the bear again, stepped over the runners – and fell over a dog. It was Toots. All her other dogs lay in the lee of the sled with their leader. 'Good dogs.' She gave them squaw candy from her pockets and fondled each dog affectionately. She felt drained but at least she had not been tied to the sled, like her dogs, while the bear darted in repeatedly to feed. She made her way to the front of the sled, then along the harness to where the bear had killed the swing

211

dog: nothing remained of the dog but a small discoloration on the snow, rust rather than red or pink; it disappeared in the still-falling snow even as she looked at it, leaving her wondering whether the strain had affected her mind. The dog's harness too was almost all gone, only frayed ends remaining where the bear had bitten through the steelcore cord. She shuddered. On her way back past the sled she picked up the first-aid kit and tended the swing dog laid open by the bear. She disinfected the wound, stitched and dressed it. She removed the dressing almost immediately: in the clean, almost sterile air of Alaska the wound would not become infected. The dog sat patiently while she worked, licking her hand when she finished. She inspected the others: one team dog had a toothmark with a small rip near the throat; no wonder it had struggled as she tried to unharness it. The bear had finished the swing dog and then attacked this one even as Rhodes, inches away, had worked to save it. And then, irritated at her interference, the bear had turned to attack her instead.

Rhodes shivered uncontrollably. She had to sit down, head upon her knees.

'What is it?' James bent over her.

She wondered how much time had passed. She put her arms around his neck and hugged him again. He held her tightly until she stopped sobbing. Then he said reluctantly, 'I hate to break this up but we have to rig a windbreak.' He disengaged himself gently.

She dried her face and attended to the second dog's wound, then fed the dogs. She helped James move the two sleds closer together and tie a lightweight tarp over them to make a triangular shelter for themselves and the dogs. Inside it they could speak in near-normal tones and hear each other. She was glad for the work; it kept her hands busy while her mind composed itself.

If James had not followed her . . .

'We're astride the trail,' he said.

'Really?' She was amazed. She had just run from the bear, not caring where she ran.

'Otherwise I wouldn't have found you.' He seemed to sense that she did not care to discuss it further and she was grateful. 'We could be here a long time. I don't want you to think you owe me . . . ' Embarrassed, he let the sentence trail away.

'It's all right. You don't have to convince me of your honorable intentions. The temperature will defeat any amorous maneuvers.' What a stupid, spiky thing to say.

But he seemed not to notice. 'We should eat before the adrenalin wanes and withdrawal symptoms start.'

In the early evening, after ravenously finishing a meal she had believed herself unable to face, Rhodes said, 'Soon we'll have to feed the dogs again.' She was pleasantly relaxed. She thought of the bear less and less though she would never forget it.

'Give it a few more minutes.' He reached out to twist their telescopic air pipe higher. Other light alloy pipes held up the nylon tarp against the weight of snow above them. 'We'll have to dig ourselves out when the snow stops.'

'I hope my father and Harvey and Margery are not too worried about me.'

'They'll hear when we reach Takotna. I hope it snows forever. Who knows when I'll next be around to save you and collect my just reward?'

She turned to face him. She said forcefully, 'I do wish you'd think before you speak. That was a hurtful thing to say.'

He looked down at the snow between his knees. 'I'm sorry. It's . . .'

213

She was sorry now that she had spoken. Impulsively she leaned over and pressed her cheek briefly against his. The stubble of his beard tickled and she giggled. He looked up at her, then back at the snow.

'Knowing why it happens doesn't make it easier to stop,' he said. 'My father was an international sportsman. I was an underweight wimp. I disappointed him. He had a temper one had to experience to believe, so I became defensive. I kept going at sports, weight training, everything, trying to prove something to him. He never noticed the effort: he expected it as his rightful due. Later, when I became a winner, it didn't matter so much, but the habit of being defensive was formed – What the hell are you laughing at?'

'Poor little James Whitbury, on the defensive. I've never heard such rubbish! You're the most aggressive man I've ever met.'

'You don't do too badly yourself,' he said mildly. 'I don't have to apologize to you.'

'We fight well together,' Rhodes said, adding without thinking, 'We'll make love well together.'

For a moment he was stunned. Then he laughed explosively. 'You're blushing! You spoke like me, without thinking!' He jumped up, grabbed her hand to pull her up, kissed her lightly on the lips as she rose, too quickly for her to turn away angrily, and said, 'Let's feed those dogs.'

As she worked, after recovering her composure, Rhodes thought, How gracious of him to give me time to cover my consternation.

In the night they lay in sleeping bags within handholding distance, listening to the blizzard whistling in the pipes they had stuck through the snow above them. James said, 'There's still the race –'

' – which I shall win,' Rhodes said with conviction.

'There's been talk of wolves.'

Rhodes had heard, but in her year in Alaska she had not seen a single wolf. She reached out to squeeze his hand.

'You're not frightened of wolves?' His tone of voice was incredulous.

'The widow Kotzwinger – she was my landlady while I trained for the race – tells tales of wolf-packs fifty strong. I ask you, James!'

He turned in his sleeping bag, peering at her through the creamy-gray gloom of the whiteout filtering through the lightweight nylon tarp. 'Researchers who specialize in wolves regularly tell incredible stories of howling with wolf-packs once a week, sight unseen, for years before catching even a fleeting glimpse of "their" wolves.'

'Perhaps that means wolf populations are larger than conservationists fear,' Rhodes said combatively.

James refused to take the bait. 'And fifty-strong wolf-packs are no figment of the widow Kotzwinger's imagination. Oh, I'll admit that anywhere but in Alaska a wolf-pack over twenty strong is unknown, but here there are several documented instances of wolf-packs of fifty-odd. Remember the size of that moose you had the run-in with? It would make mincemeat of fewer wolves.'

Rhodes shivered at the memory of the moose, 'Go on, give me nightmares.'

'On Isle Royale, in Lake Superior – '

'I've been there. No wolves on Isle Royale!'

'But there were. A troupe of wolves used to hang around the picnic tables waiting for scraps. Soon they didn't wait, they begged so aggressively that the rangers, fearing it was only a matter of time before the wolves ate a picnicker, put them down. But one wolf, called Big Jim, escaped and was last seen swimming strongly northwards, towards us.'

Rhodes shivered again. 'The widow Kotzwinger claims wolves prefer human flesh to any other. Surely you don't –'

'I don't see why not. If people have race memories, why shouldn't wolves have a genetic imprint of all the people they ate in earlier times when survivors of epidemics and plagues encouraged them as scavengers?'

When she did not answer, he said, 'Will you stay near me?'

'It *is* a race.'

'Many other racers travel near each other and camp together without forgetting they're in a race.'

'You really believe in those wolves, don't you?'

'Yes. I'd be much happier.'

'All right. Thank you.'

10
Musk Ox

When there was no more food towards the north and west the wolves conserved their remaining strength by retreating south of the 50° isotherm line; it was, in more than a symbolic sense, settlement on new territory. Those wolves unnerved by the loss of their old territory recovered their assurance and became fiercer and more daring than ever. With the added confidence of a fat summer, a huge pack, and the incentive of winter hunger gnawing at their bellies, the pack's attack on the musk oxen was more than ignorance overreaching itself.

Commonly wolves force their prey to identify themselves by chasing a herd of deer until one falls behind. They then rip its flanks and run it until, weakened by bleeding, it falls. If no deer lags the wolves give up the chase after a mile or two and repeat the process with another herd. On average they kill only once in every eight chases. This is the wolf's natural pattern; all other hunting forms are adaptations.

The musk ox under attack does not run. It stands and fights.

And, not only does the imperilled musk ox stand and fight, it backs up until it finds something, even a hump of ice, to protect its back. Thus positioned, its wickedly curved horns sweeping from side to side are impassable for wolves and dogs. On the open range even two wolves, working together intelligently, can bring down a *single* musk ox, especially a calf or old cow: one wolf will hold its attention at the front while the other darts in to shred its flanks; they can then wait for it to bleed to death.

But a single musk ox is an extreme rarity. Musk oxen live in herds which at first sign of danger form into one of several defensive formations, developed and honed in the mists of antiquity against attacks by wolves and powerful carnivorous cats. The Eskimo say the musk oxen 'form square' but actually the *karre* is an arrowhead or circular formation, with the most experienced bulls facing the threat and cows and immature calves behind or in the centre. Musk oxen can out-gallop wolves or dogs for several miles but then settle to a choppy lope and are overhauled within another few miles. If this herd had run at the approach of the wolves, perhaps the pack would have dropped out without casualties after a mile or two, but probably not – the wolves were too close to the brink of starvation. The musk oxen did not run. At first they ignored the approaching wolves; even when the wolves circled less than a hundred feet from the nearest calf, the musk oxen regarded them with contempt and continued cropping.

The alpha male darted in to the most exposed calf; before the wolf came within twenty feet the cow arrived, the calf huddled quivering under her belly, and three bulls stood between the cow and the wolf; their recurved horns, joined by a hard bone-boss across the forehead, slashed only inches from the retreating wolf.

Immediately the circular karre formed, adult males on the outside, hindquarters together but with space for the heavy shoulders and forelegs to move and for the horns on low-held heads to slash, with cows and calves behind them. From that moment the wolves' cause was lost. They should have retreated and found new prey. But here their genetic memory was overwhelmed by their desperate hunger. If they had been less ravenous they might have heeded the DNA signal that, once the karre was drawn, this was a laager to the end – a suicide pact of musk oxen.

Even if they killed every other musk ox, the last survivor would back up to the bodies of the fallen and keep the wolves from feeding until it too was killed. Even forty-seven wolves, as they were then, could not kill thirty-three musk oxen.

A wolf charged, testing. A musk ox stepped from the left-hand side of the phalanx of horns. With a single sweeping heave of its heavy head from left to right and up and over it ripped the wolf from anus to jawbone, casting the dying wolf over its shoulder into the center of the karre to be trampled by the cows and calves. Another wolf, seeing his opportunity, lunged at the exposed throat of the musk ox – and if successful would have ripped the musk ox from thick-skinned throat past the gristly chest muscles and diaphragm to genitals, for the wolf is a predator that is all jaw. But with balletic precision another musk ox stepped forward to cover his comrade: left to right, up and over, another wolf spilling entrails flew to its end under the hooves in the centre of the karre.

The first musk ox retreated, the line shifted to accommodate him and the second musk ox stepped back into the line. But already another was heaving forward, head low, horns sweeping into the wolves, catching two, while still another musk ox, standing forward to cover the blind side while the attacker returned to the line, destroyed yet another wolf aiming for the tantalizingly exposed jugular. Now the musk oxen pressed the attack, coming further forward to scythe the wolves. Their covering movements, even when attacking, had such military precision that the wolves, though gashing several bulls, did not achieve a single kill.

Eight wolves died on those horns before they admitted defeat. Another succumbed to its wounds the next day. The only food left to the wolves was man and his dogs.

The only men and dogs likely to cross the path of the wolf-pack at this season were the Iditarod racers.

Each racer was alone but the wolves were many and desperate for meat.

11
Port Safety

Rhodes did not worry about the wolves. She knew, as does everyone in Alaska, that Alaskan wolves belong to the species Gray Timber Wolf; though more likely to be cream or white than gray, they are seldom found on the tundra side of the hundred miles of thinning trees which in the Arctic uniquely mark the demarcation between boreal forest and the barren desolation of the 'marshy plain'. When the Bering Strait freezes over (less frequently than the mythmakers would have us believe) 'Siberian ice-wolves' have been seen at Nome and points north, or so it is said. The widow Kotzwinger had scoffed at the 'Siberian' origin of these wolves. They were, she said, real wolves but long since dead, a living myth from a time when Alaska had an abundance of wolves; occassionally the forest would be unable to support their numbers and some packs would be driven out of the trees onto the tundra. When Rhodes told her that Alexandre Dumas had described wolf-packs of between two and three thousand hunting on the treeless wastes of Siberia, the widow Kotzwinger laughed and demanded, 'What other lies does this French friend of yours tell?' Once or twice Rhodes wondered why wolves so fascinated James but did not mention them to him. She did not want to endanger her still fragile relationship with James by seeming to pry or by arguing with him from uncertain factual ground. The only other fact she knew for certain about wolves was that the French are inordinately afraid of them . . . hardly useful information.

Other things concerned them. Digging themselves out

was backbreaking work, snowshoeing into Takotna muscle-mincing. From there they were able to radio news of their survival – and learn that, now the storm was over and snow machines were clearing part of the trail, the rest of the field were closing on them, having hit the trail from McGrath while Rhodes and James were still digging themselves out. The trail Rhodes and James cut would make it easier for the followers to catch up, at least until Rhodes and James caught up with the track left by the leaders of the race. On the other hand, because of the storm, Rhodes and James were now only six hours behind the front-runners. The checker at Takotna was amazed to find two rookies running in the top ten. By unspoken consent they decided to do their utmost to stay ahead of the rest of the field. After less than an hour at Takotna James led them out on the trail again.

Despite having difficulty keeping her team on the trail while she broke in a new swing dog, Rhodes insisted on doing her share of trail-breaking. She had been worried about the wounded dog: it had appeared stiff and sore while they were snowed in but, as soon as it started running, it seemed all right, even eager. But her whole team remained uneasy after their experience with the bear. She herself was glad to have James nearby and when he decided to camp, she camped next to him. This was their long break. In the shorter breaks she had also stopped near him but, after cooking for the dogs, inspecting their feet and refitting booties, cooking for themselves and hurriedly finishing a cup of coffee, it was time to run again. Now, with more time, they sat by the fire with a second cup of coffee, their dogs curled up asleep with tails over noses and foot-pads close to their bodies, immune to the cold of the snow on which they lay.

'Next stop Iditarod,' Rhodes said sleepily. 'It means "far place". Actually it's *Haiditarod*, with an aitch, from the Ingalik Indian.' She yawned. 'I'm looking forward to seeing the place that gave the race its name.'

'What I'm looking forward to,' James said wearily, 'is a hundred and forty miles from Anvik to Kaltag, straight north on the frozen Yukon. A river of ice a mile wide with not a spot of snow on it. Two days of easy running.'

'Unh.'

'Are you listening?'

She was fast asleep. He spread her sleeping bag across her knees and set the alarm on his Rolex for four hours hence before sitting down to doze as best he could. The curse of the Iditarod, an old-timer had told him at the mushers' dinner, is that there is never enough time to sleep. And when you can, he had added, you don't want to.

Iditarod had boomed for less than five years while the gold lasted and then declined. A place of historical interest, it is over five hundred miles from the nearest road that could bring in tourists. The curious must go by dog sled or plane; those who fly in should bring a rope and helper to hold it while the plane is turned into the wind on the narrow river, the only place to land, plus an engine-oil heater that does not require electricity – the nearest power socket is over a hundred miles away.

'Tootsie's Place,' James said in front of a large dilapidated building. 'First massage parlor in Alaska.'

'You have a dirty mind. It was a boarding house.'

'With extra amenities,' he persisted. 'A lady called Black Bear lived here. She had tufts of hair on her body.'

'When was this?'

'About 1911. Bill Swift knows about her.'

'He wasn't born then either.'

'No, but he collects old newspaper archives about Alaska. She parted a good many miners from their tokes

223

of gold without . . . ah, providing the services she was famous for.'

'The first dog sled race was held here on New Year's day, 1911,' Rhodes said. 'But I suppose you're more interested in what happened in the 1914 race.'

'And what might that be?'

'Someone sawed part-way through all the stanchions on Mrs Swanson's sled to stop her winning.' Rhodes laughed, shook the drivebow and was off at full tilt past the two-and-a-half-storey remains of the Northern Commercial Company, heading for Shageluk and then Anvik on the Yukon.

After a couple of miles he pulled his toboggan level with hers. 'What happened?' he shouted urgently.

'Didn't Bill Swift tell you?'

'Come on, woman!'

'She won!'

Sitting around a fire at night, a moment out of time; they had been silent for a while. James lifted a lazy finger and pointed into the flames. 'Since time began, Man's worst enemy.'

'Man doesn't need fire,' Rhodes said languidly. 'The Eskimo didn't have fire until this century. They used the insulating qualities of snow, wore furs, ate an oil- and fat-rich diet to provide natural body-insulation. But that doesn't make fire an enemy.'

'By day,' James said, 'its smoke tells Man's enemies where to find him. At night it casts fearful shadows. All other species welcome darkness as a hiding place. Only men fear it as the unknown.'

It had been pale light when they stopped. Now it was fully dark and almost time to drive forward again into the vastness of Alaska.

'At least fire keeps the wolf from the door,' Rhodes said carelessly.

'That's a fallacy cherished by many people. But animals don't fear fire. Animals fear people, and with good reason. Generation after generation animals have learned that where there is fire there are people. The survivors are those who stayed away from people and, only by extension, from fire.'

The conversation stayed with Rhodes. There was a James she did not know, a thoughtful man inside the brisk, bright sportsman.

The hundred and forty miles of 'easy running' on the Yukon from Anvik to Kaltag became a miserable and dangerous three-day slog through steady forty- and fifty-mile winds gusting to sixty and seventy with the wind chill factor almost constantly on the wrong side of minus seventy. The smallest portion of skin exposed to it would soon start to prickle and then, unless warmed almost instantly, lose all feeling. They stopped every half hour to study each other's face for the giveaway dead white spots of incipient frostbite. The stops added to their misery but, when Rhodes demurred, James said, 'I don't think I could love you if your nose fell off because you wouldn't take reasonable care of it.' He was not exaggerating: a canteen of water Rhodes carried inside her parka, regularly sipping from it to combat the dehydration caused by the wind, froze solid in little more than an hour. He also liberally spread a thin odorless goo on her face from a big unlabelled tube. 'Norwegian North Sea trawlermen swear by this stuff.'

It was worse for the dogs. They ran directly into the wind without the protection of a sled in front of them to shield at least the lower part of the body. Unlike James and Rhodes they could not duck behind the sled for relief.

Rhodes' dogs were still demoralized after their encounter with the bear but even James' excellent command leader, General, needed constant encouragement. Delilah would just lie down and refuse to lead the team into the wind. When even General decided not to run, James took the gangline in his hand and ran for two hours in front of his team, leading them, diverting the wind a little with his own body. During that time they covered their fastest twenty-two miles during the three days they were on the Yukon's frozen surface. But he had to stop . . .

Rhodes saw James diving onto the ice. He did not fall – he *dived*. She was not hallucinating. She whoaed her dogs and ran forward to pull his dogs, who had overrun their prone master, from him. He lay on the ice on his back, grinning inanely at her.

She bent to put her mouth close to his ear, shouting against the wind, 'What are you playing at?'

He shook his head groggily. 'Not playing. Yellow Cab driving straight at me. Dived into the gutter to save myself.'

She helped him up. 'Stay on the runners.'

She tried leading from the front but after fifteen minutes saw a herd of wild mustangs galloping straight at her, lips drawn back from square grimacing teeth, foam flying along their heaving sides. When she recovered she was hugging Toots tightly and James was shaking her shoulder fiercely.

'This isn't a river,' she said through chattering teeth – from fear, she was beyond feeling cold, 'this is a desert with nowhere to hide.'

'What were you hiding from?'

'Horses.'

'Let's camp, Rhodes.'

'Schedule to keep,' she said stubbornly.

'Another half-hour.'

'Five or six miles ahead of . . .'

He picked her up, put her on her feet and steadied her, shaking his head doubtfully.

She hoped she did not look as bad as he did, chalk-white, stretched taut and wild. She turned deliberately and bent her body into that malignant wind. For the first time in her life she wanted a man to see her only at her best.

They advanced two miles in that half-hour, then turned towards the small lee of a bank where there was just enough space for the two teams. It was crowded but at least the edge of the wind was blunted; compared with the center of the windswept Yukon it was a haven of peace. Frozen hands made every snap a major operation of pain, frustration and fruitless anger. She hurt all over.

Rhodes' dogs, as dehydrated as she, refused water.

'Oh, damn!' she sobbed, anger and frustration suddenly intensified by the implications. All for nothing. She would *have* to scratch. She sat down on the snow in the lee and put her head on her knees to rest a moment and compose herself. When she looked up, it was to see James pouring water heated on his stove into a plastic bottle and screwing on a cap with a tube let into it. She shivered. 'No,' she said, 'I won't tube the dogs. That's revolting.'

'Wait and see,' he said shortly. 'Bring Toots.'

'James, if you stick that tube into my dog's throat – '

'Get off your high horse!'

Rhodes held Toots' head protectively to her. She knew many mushers forced dogs to take liquid by sliding a tube down their throats and pouring water straight into their stomachs. 'I'll try some meat-flavored broth,' she said without much hope.

'All I want to do is rest the tube on her tongue,' James said. 'Just try it.' He put the tube on Toots' tongue and squeezed the bottle. Toots rolled her head to rid herself of the tube but Rhodes could see a few drops of water coursing down the dog's throat.

'Hey, that's a good idea!' She picked up the tube, replaced it on the dog's tongue and James squeezed the bottle. This time Rhodes held the tube lightly inside the dog's mouth. Toots swallowed each time James squeezed the bottle. Giving all the dogs water in this way consumed more than two precious hours. Then they had to cook for the dogs, inspect their feet, retie their booties, cook for themselves and eat. Four hours left to sleep. They lay huddled in their sleeping bags, too tired to sleep but not talking either.

The rest of the journey to Kaltag was a blur for both of them, each kept going only by the will of the other. They took turns of fifteen minutes to lead their teams from the front, trying to cut the time available for the extra edge of cold there to foster hallucinations in their minds.

Rhodes would never know how they reached Kaltag. Those days forever would in her mind be a symbol of pain and exhaustion. Her scheduled meals totalled 5500 calories per day, 3500 more than while doing a full day's work on the ranch in Colorado. She made a point of eating every last scrap however tired and listless she felt; despite the sticks of butter she ate almost continuously as the equivalent of the fat she fed the dogs, she lost twelve pounds during those three days. Just south of Kaltag the wind blew her sled right over; she could not remember the incident when James mentioned it the next day.

She awoke on a couch in front of a double Yukon stove – two fifty-five-gallon drums stacked almost to the ceiling – in Larry Thompson's Kaltag home. Larry offered her a mug of coffee. After a moment she recognized him: the race pilot who had flown food to checkpoints for her and her dogs, as he had for other mushers.

'Eight mushers scratched on the Yukon,' he said in

greeting. 'Others are waiting out the wind wherever they can find shelter.'

'But not all?'

'A few hard men are still coming.'

She swung her legs off the couch with a sigh and found herself sitting hip to hip with James, whose face was hidden in a mug of coffee. In the open-plan white kitchen behind him women were preparing food.

'I could sleep another twenty-four hours,' James said into his mug. 'If only the others would have the good sense to stop and wait for the wind to die down.'

'You didn't,' the pilot said reasonably.

'Rhodes insisted,' James explained. 'What about the leaders?'

'Swenson and Peters are maybe four to five hours ahead of you. Susan left here three hours ago with Lindner right on her tail. A couple of other hotshots not long after that. They're all in a bunch. This far into the race, if one goes, the others can't take the chance of staying put.'

One of the women brought two plates of beaver stew to Rhodes and James. 'You two made a sweet picture, lying spoon-fashion on that couch.'

'It won't be easy to leave your warm house for that,' Rhodes said, gesturing at the unseen storm that forced them all to raise their voices. 'Thanks.'

'Bathroom's there and you can change in the bedroom. You looked done for last night. You're welcome to stay until the weather clears.'

Everyone in the room seemed to suspend breathing while they waited for her answer.

'Thank you but we have to go,' Rhodes said, trying to keep her deep reluctance from her voice.

She felt that only the innate good manners of these Alaskans restrained them from applauding her resolve;

she was encountering the phenomenon of running the Iditarod for every Alaskan.

'We're running a race, lady,' James said gruffly, playing to the gallery and enjoying it. 'And Swenson and Peters and Butcher are five hours ahead of us . . .'

Rhodes was relieved when their hosts, instead of being offended by the Bogart send-up, laughed merrily. One of the men clapped James on the back so hard he choked on his stew. 'Play it, Sam!' Rhodes thought, A real fan: he knows the right quotation.

Before they left Kaltag word arrived that the nearest runners behind them had cleared Eagle Slide and gained two hours while they slept at Larry Thompson's. They were still in the top ten but up to twentieth paid prize money. 'Until now,' James said grimly as they made ready to leave, 'it's been a camping trip. From here to Nome it's a real race and the devil take the hindmost. So let's watch our backs.'

'Yes sir! Just don't forget that we are in a race of our own.'

'I'm not. Hike!'

They struck out at 3.30 A.M. to cover the ninety-two miles to Unalakleet via the Kaltag Portage, Twenty-two-mile Cabin and Old Woman Cabin. On the Kaltag Portage they crossed from the Interior Alaska of the Athabascan Indians into the third cultural and climatic zone of Alaska, the Bering Sea coast of the Inupiat Eskimo. After Unalakleet the trail would curve around the saltwater Norton Sound all the way to Nome, with the Arctic Circle a psychological stone-throw-away.

Seventeen hours later, in Unalakleet, they fed and tended their dogs but did not cook for themselves. James said, 'The cheeseburgers at the Lodge are famous. I'll treat you.'

Rhodes wolfed three huge burgers and James managed

four, washed down with malteds, before the journalist invited himself to sit with them. 'You're travelling together, eh?'

'Stick to your knitting,' James said.

'Huh?'

'If you're a gossip-columnist, bugger off before I lose my temper. If you're a sports reporter, talk to us about the race.'

The journalist grinned and put his recorder and Pitman pad on the table. 'Actually I'm neither. Bill Swift of Frontier tells me your lightweight sleds will make it possible to replace a lot of snow machines with dogs. What I want to know is this: won't the dogs themselves be an unbalancing influence on the environment?'

Rhodes watched James's face light up.

'That's a good question. But, you know, Nature weighs every action on ruthlessly impartial scales. Earlier in this century misguided conservationists found that the Eskimo relied heavily on the caribou. They also knew that the only natural enemy of the caribou is the wolf. So they virtually exterminated the wolf in Alaska. As a result the caribou had no predator-control on their growth. Soon their numbers were too heavy for the lichen on the tundra and there was a famine. Even now the caribou has recovered only a sixth of their numbers before the conservationists wiped out the wolves. The tundra could take another sixty or seventy years to recover from the overgrazing.'

It was an impressive performance, judging by the journalist's face and the fact that he did not interrupt James. Rhodes had not thought of James as a conservationist before. First a talent for mimicry, now this.

'At about the same time as the conservationists were killing off the wolves,' James continued, 'the internal combustion engine took over from the dogs that pulled

231

the sleds. This was fortunate for the recovery of the caribou after the famine, because those dogs were fed mainly caribou. So, as part of the price for a breathing space for the caribou, we've had to put up with the environmental damage of the snow machines.'

James paused to finish his malted. The journalist, recognizing a properly structured argument, sat waiting. 'Now,' James said, 'the caribou herds have recovered to the stage where the few remaining wolves cannot cull them quickly enough to provide effective genetic control. If sled dogs were returned to Alaska in large numbers they could be fed the caribou that need to be culled to keep their numbers down to what the tundra can support. There is, for me, a beautiful balance in all this, a sort of inevitability that inclines me to believe in fate.'

The journalist checked his recorder and looked expectantly at James.

James nodded. 'Nature believes in genetics and provides, in the wolf, control such as a man with a rifle cannot achieve. Theoretically a moose can live to twenty years but in the wild his life expectancy, before the wolves eat him, is seven to nine years. If every moose lived to twenty years, he could contribute to the genetic pool only once. If Nature can manage three generations of moose in the same twenty years, then there are three inputs to the genetic pool. That means six times as many permutations of genetic inheritance is possible, so survival of the moose as a species is enhanced by a factor of six.'

The journalist looked around at the small crowd of locals who had gathered around their table while James spoke. Several nodded agreement. 'I'd like to quote all of that verbatim, if it's okay with you.'

James nodded. The journalist left. James indicated the spare seats. A couple of the men sat down. Others stood casually within earshot.

James has touched a chord here.

'Your sleds bring jobs for our people,' a middleaged man said.

'I hope so,' James said. 'It may take a while though.'

They nodded politely. Rhodes could not tell if their courtesy forbade questioning a guest too closely or if they were more interested in the next subject.

'You know about wolves?' the middleaged man asked. He seemed to be a civic leader.

James shook his head. 'Only theoretically. Not like you know them.'

Several of the men chuckled. Their leader rolled his gaze over them and they stopped.

'Old men know and some of us have seen the odd wolf, of course, even a small pack.'

'Seven wolves I once saw myself,' one of the other men offered.

'That's more than most men,' James said.

The leader said, 'But, this last year, we have heard many times of a pack half a hundred strong.'

Rhodes, watching James and remembering their conversation on the night of the bear, was still under the spell of his effortless exposition on the Alaskan wolf. She waited for him to raise an incredulous eyebrow or brusquely correct the man but James's face was attentive, even grave.

'I saw them myself,' the man said. 'About six weeks ago at my in-laws, hundred miles north from here. They were hungry.'

James asked, 'Why didn't they follow the caribou back to the forest?'

The other man shrugged. He could not know what motivated wolves. 'Many have seen them. This morning my cousin found eight dead wolves east of Port Safety.

233

They had been gored and trampled by musk oxen.' He paused expectantly.

'Forgive me,' James said, and Rhodes in that moment rejected any idea she had ever harbored that he was awkward in social converse, 'but you will have to explain that to me.'

'They are hungry,' the other man repeated.

'Wolves do not attack musk oxen unless they are very hungry?'

Heads nodded. 'That is so, Mr Whitbury,' the leader said. 'But not just very hungry. Desperately hungry.'

'I'm still missing something,' James said patiently.

The Eskimo nodded. 'They are desperate because they know better than to attack my people and they cannot kill a musk ox. There is nothing else for them to eat except the Iditarod racers.' He put his hands flat on the table, as if to rise.

'Hold on!' James said. 'Have you told the race officials?'

The other man smiled for the first time. 'You believe us because you know about wolves, Mr Whitbury. But how do we persuade anyone else of what we know only because we are Eskimo, because, as you tried to tell that reporter, the wolf was once our partner?' He rose.

They politely congratulated Rhodes and James on their high standing in the race and wished them luck to Nome, then left.

'What will you do?' Rhodes asked James.

'Tell the officials. You must try to sleep.'

'We're only three hundred miles from Nome: I'm not dropping out now for rumors of wolves skulking on the trail.'

In the depressing drizzle outside they parted. When he returned an hour later she was awake. 'Did they believe you?'

'No. They asked how long I have been in Alaska.'

* * *

234

Heading from Unalakleet to Shastoolik to Koyuk across the frozen Norton Sound, with only a barely noticeable line dividing the faintly green land-ice from the white sea-ice, Rhodes was thankful to have James with her: otherwise she would have become deadened by that featureless landscape, with not the slightest rise anywhere against the sere horizon. In college she had volunteered for an experiment in which she was locked in a pure white, featureless cube for as long as she could stand, then banged on the wall to be let out. Except that here there was no wall to bang, no one to let out the lone musher when the inattention attendant on boredom disoriented him; here boredom could kill. Sixty-two miles to Shastoolik, seventy-two miles further to Koyuk, the figures ran endlessly through her mind, alternating with images of her blind cross-bred pups.

The dogs became bored and disoriented and had to be led. At least that was something different, until it too became numbingly routine. She lost the trail momentarily and nearly panicked before she found it again, forgetting that James was with her and could help. The endless sameness aggravated their exhaustion. She scarcely noticed passing through old Shastoolik or the warm welcome of the people of the new village of Shastoolik. James pointed out to her that there were no blown-snow ridges in the old village, laid out in seemingly haphazard manner by the Eskimo; in contrast, the thoroughfares of the new village were hazardous with snow-ridges because the government surveyors had taken no account of prevailing wind direction. James talked to a group of Eskimo, then introduced one of them to Rhodes as 'the most famous of the justly famed seal-hunters of Shastoolik': the man told her about wolves that recently had tried several times to take one of the community's reindeer herd. She nodded politely. No, he had not seen the wolves himself but he had tracked them and there were 'many'. When he had gone, she shook her head at James. 'You're obsessed with those wolves.'

'If the Eskimo instinctively know about the wind, why not about wolves?'

'I don't blame you. Out there on the ice those mustangs again tried to trample me.'

'No, on the ice I have trouble with the Yellow Cab Company,' James said firmly. 'But we've come in from the cold now and evidence of wolves on the trail is mounting.'

'I'm not arguing about that. But you're asking me to believe those wolves will attack us because the Eskimo somehow know they are desperately hungry.'

He seemed about to argue, then thought better of it. Rhodes touched his arm to take some of the sting from her words; he had been hurt by the officials' evident belief that the Eskimo were playing a subtle joke on a new boy.

They were fourteen days into the race, the toughest Iditarod ever. Half of the starters had scratched already. Nome, so near and yet so far, seemed unattainable. James marvelled at Rhodes's fierce refusal to give up, to recognize the obvious, that they were physically and psychologically fully expended, bankrupt, that they put one foot in front of the other because it had become a habit ingrained by nine hundred miles on that terrible trail, because they were simply too whacked to think of something else to do.

Seventy-two miles to Koyuk, straight across the white ice of the Norton Sound.

Once, when they switched the lead, Rhodes asked James, 'What are you whistling?'

'*March of the Robots*, number one on the zombie hit parade.'

She managed a smile. Under appalling circumstances

he was trying to cheer her. 'There's never been a divorce in my family,' she said, and he nodded, as if he could see into her mind and discern the odd connection between finishing what one starts, good cheer and lasting marriages.

At Koyuk they slept in the armory. The rest perked them up a little, though they stayed only five hours before heading west along the coast of the Seward Peninsula. They were impelled forward by the knowledge that they lay seventh and eighth overall – the leading rookies – and were closing on the leaders with only a hundred and fifty miles to run to Nome. Pressing even harder, the serious racers behind them had reduced their breathing space to two hours. 'A one-place difference in Nome is worth at least a thousand dollars,' Rhodes told James when they heard this, 'and, higher up the placings, thousands of dollars.'

'Hundred-fifty miles is plenty of space to make mistakes,' the checker at Koyuk had said. 'Mushers have been lost for days on that bare ice. But you don't want to panic because your lead is only two hours. If you strain your dogs, they'll all come sweeping through.'

Back on the Norton Sound ice to Elim. Forty-eight miles in six hours; as fast, James thought, as they had run earlier in the race under better conditions. But the top contenders among those behind them had gained another hour. 'They're goddamn robots, they don't rest,' James said. Rhodes smiled but James wondered if she was not so fatigued that she had not understood him, smiling merely in response to his voice. For long stretches of time, perhaps hours, he lost himself, unaware of anything except staying on the runners or running in front of his team when necessary, one trudging foot in front of the other; suddenly they would arrive at a checkpoint and he would be alert, unable to fall asleep before it was time to run again. Every time they rested, the hard men closed, cutting their lead.

Golovin, twenty-eight miles across the ice of the Norton Sound, across Cape Darby through the Kwiktalik Mountains portage – blessed protection from the wind! – and down from the weary heights across McKinley Creek: there at last was Golovin, a few windbeaten HUD-gray buildings. Here, in 1925, Leonhard Seppala passed the diphtheria serum to Charlie Olson, who carried it as far as Bluff, within fifty-three miles of the dying children of Nome. The large white general store, Rhodes was pleased to notice, still carried the name Olson . . . The rest stop was over before she knew it. James thought Rhodes in too much of a hurry to leave; she thought he had given the signal. Across the hard-frozen Golovin Lagoon towards White Mountain, which they reached in just over eight and three-quarter hours out of Elim – ten minutes faster than the leaders of the Iditarod, said the checker. They were scheduled for a nine-hour break at White Mountain, including the mandatory one-hour vet-check stop. The vet said the swing dog wounded by the bear had recovered better from running than if he had been carried in the sled or left at a checkpoint. 'If you'd taken him off work the wound would've stiffened up and you would've had to put him down.'

'We'll camp a mile out,' Rhodes told James. 'I have some stinkfish buried there.' Toots' ears perked up at the word and Rhodes fondled the dog. 'It's our secret weapon.' James smiled at the reminder that the race between them was not over yet but Rhodes did not notice. She was back in Emmonak, nearly a year ago.

Twelve hours a day, six days a week, Rhodes gutted the king salmon the Eskimo caught in the teeming estuaries of the Yukon which at Emmonak emptied its brown silt

238

through many mouths into the Bering Sea. Every week she earned more than a thousand dollars and her keep. In this gray village of 300 souls there was nothing to spend the money on . . .

Emmonak. The leaden drizzle keeps everything muddy and there are no roads in or out. The only access is by plane or boat and few want to visit a hamlet three hundred miles out on the barren tundra, an eighteen-inch layer of insulating moss and lichen over permafrost that has not melted in millennia. Yet Emmonak has a grim beauty and plenty of daylight, even beyond the twelve working hours, to let it grow on the susceptible visitor. In this sub-arctic evening, light does not fade until an hour before midnight when the sun, behind the endless drizzle, sinks into the south-west. The hours of darkness are brief: the sun rises in the south-east at four in the morning, invisible behind the claustrophobic rain. Three hundred miles to the west, beyond the violent and forbidding Bering Sea, lies the tundra and permafrost of Siberia. That defines Emmonak. The rest is work.

Twelve hours a day, six days a week, her knife flashed its mesmeric rhythm, her eyes and mind tied inexorably to it because a moment's inattention could leave a finger severed by the razor-edged instrument. For the first time she understood why men cursed assembly lines: slash, glint, turn, glint, point, glint, lift, glint, turn, glint, sweep, glint – left hand to tail, pull, different glint on the reddish silver of the fish, another fish – slash, glint, turn, glint, point, glint, lift, glint, turn, glint, sweep, glint – left hand to tail, pull, different glint on the reddish silver of the fish, another fish . . . Automatic. The temptation was to daydream for a moment. She resisted it. On her first day the foreman had taken her to meet an old woman without a hand, just a stump. On the way back, he had told her how the woman in a careless moment at the gutting table

239

with a single stroke of Solingen steel had severed her own hand. The story had almost made Rhodes sick with its gruesome detail but she soon realized there was a point to it: concentration was everything.

On the seventh day she scrubbed the stink of fish from her, dried her hair, wrote to her father and Margery – and slept. Sometimes she made plans for the Iditarod, notes in a ringbound book. An hour after work each day she tended her pair of breeding malemutes and played with Blue; on Sundays they got two hours. She wrote to her father that had she not grown up on a ranch, accustomed to hard physical work, she would not have survived two days at Emmonak. Sometimes she was grateful for the long and strenuous days because they tired her mind as well as her body. She liked her Eskimo hosts but her life intercepted theirs at only two points: the gutting tables and a shared interest in sled dogs (and the Eskimo preferred four-wheel-drives to dogs and sled). English was their second language, making conversation slow and frustrating. She had always thought of herself, deprecatingly but not without humor, as a Colorado hick and content to be so. Now she was amazed to find a way of life beside which that of a Colorado ranchhand was almost cosmopolitan. It was unfair to demand of the Eskimo an intellectual stimulus of which only she felt need and that they were unaware existed. She worked harder to dull the keen edge of her mind on the fatigue of her body.

Her application did not pass unnoticed or unrewarded. One day the foreman stopped at her gutting table. 'That fish real rich in Riboflavin and Vitamin B complexes.' Rhodes sensed that he had rehearsed his words carefully. This was an important moment. The other workers stopped to listen. 'Good for dogs.'

'Giving me a well-paying job is big sponsorship already,' Rhodes replied. She had long since decided to carry no sponsorship stickers on the sled her father was handbuilding for her in Colorado with wood seasoned in Alaska. She did not want to offend by refusing the factory's sticker.

But that was not what he had in mind. 'Sure, any way we can help. You take as many fish as you can carry out. My brother-in-law, he already talk to Crazy Horse. Every time Crazy Horse fly by here, he give you lift to White Mountain with your fish. There you make stinkfish. It give dogs big boost for home run, Nome run, see?'

Rhodes joined the laughter at his apt phrase. Then she asked, 'Stinkfish?'

He raised his eyes to the heavens. 'You want to be Iditarod musher and you don't know stinkfish? Maybe you won't even make White Mountain.' All around them people laughed politely into their hands. Rhodes had a sense of having made not an embarrassing error but one that humanized her for them; from that moment the community seemed to adopt her as their own. 'But plant fish anyway. If you don't make White Mountain, I dig up your stinkfish for Granddad – very good for people without teeth.'

'Okay, Joe,' the woman at the next table offered, 'I tell her how you make stinkfish, no problem.'

Making stinkfish did prove to be no problem; nevertheless she could not have done it without the generosity of passing pilots flying the fish and other requirements from Emmonak across the Norton Sound to White Mountain on the Iditarod race route, only seventy-seven miles from the victory arch over Nome's fabled Front Street.

If ever I make it this far, Rhodes thought soberly as she swung the pickaxe to chip out another small piece of the permafrost. She had been told to dig to four feet through the permafrost and she intended following her instructions despite the blisters the pickaxe-handle had rubbed on her palms. There was a time when Harvey Mannesman had tried to take up golf, she remembered, and she and Margery had laughed when he came home with blisters on his *thumbs* from holding the club wrongly; it was ludicrous for an outdoorswoman like her to have such soft hands. After digging the hole the rest of the job was easy. In the bottom of the hole she arranged a layer of long grass the pilot had flown in from Anchorage because up here nothing grew except the lichen Cladonia that the Eskimo call 'reindeer moss'. On the grass she laid the headless and gutted fish, over that another thick layer of grass, then some boards, a mound a couple of feet high of the permafrost 'dirt' she had painfully dug out . . . and that was it. The grass, the boards, the mound on top, all for the sole purpose of keeping out the flies; if the flies reached her fish, the foreman warned her, all she would reap for her hard work would be a seething mess of corruption.

As one of her going-away presents when she left Emmonak in mid-Fall to train at the widow Kotzwinger's, her fellow workers gave her a big box of locally made stinkfish with which to train her dogs; it was the gift she appreciated most, knowing how much backache had gone into its making.

But she *had* made it to White Mountain, eight months later. Her stinkfish was just ripe when she dug it out. Silently, she apologized to the foreman's grandfather who now would not be getting it. The dogs jumped up, yapping, and she flung them pieces. She ate some herself.

'What a smell,' James exclaimed as she approached him with a portion of stinkfish on her plate. 'Don't come near me!'

She kept her hand out with the offered salmon. 'It's delicious.'

'Now I know,' he said, taking the plate and sniffing it, 'why Eskimo women are inviolate.' She watched as he took a tentative bite. 'Once over the smell, it does taste good,' he admitted.

'I'm sorry I haven't enough for your dogs as well.'

'I'm feeding them only beaver on this last stretch. Want some? I have more than enough.'

'No thanks. Stinkfish with fat is better.'

'We'll see tomorrow in Front Street in Nome.'

'Yes, we'll see tomorrow,' Rhodes agreed. For a while, co-operating with him so that they could both stay alive and ahead of the hard men cutting into their lead, she had almost forgotten their own race. 'Hey, do you know why Eskimo children were first given school meals in Alaska, oh, back in the 'twenties or 'thirties?'

'You have an insatiable curiosity. Tell me.'

'Because the white teachers couldn't stand the smell of the stinkfish the kids ate at home, so they persuaded the Education Board to give them a free breakfast at school.'

'Remind me to tell Bill Swift; such items fascinate him. Listen, in New York you could sell all of this fish you could produce. It really tastes good.' He had cleared his plate.

Rhodes shook her head. 'It's not like garlic, an odor that evaporates in twenty-four hours. You will stink for a week.' She almost added, I have marked you mine, but too much was unspoken between them. After the Iditarod, out of the pressure-cooker struggle for survival against terrain, weather, raptors and competitors, they would have to start afresh. Their love was too new and bore too heavy a burden of past misunderstandings to allow for large assumptions. It was something yet to be confirmed and strengthened. Wisdom I had not a fortnight hence, she thought, wondering vaguely if it was a quotation from somewhere.

Even in their sleeping bags they wore their down pants over thick worsted trousers (which themselves had nylon windbreaks on the fronts) and huddled together for extra warmth. For once, it was easy to sleep, though after four hours both were awake.

'This is a nine-hour break,' James said sternly.

'My feet itch. They want to know which of us will be first down Front Street.'

'I too have ants in my pants.'

'It's only seventy-six miles.'

'Then let's go!'

If they had kept to their schedule it would have been another musher rather than Rhodes and James that the wolves waited for as, neck and neck, they raced out of Port Safety.

The wind still blew strong enough to cause discomfort, though not the instant pain they had encountered on the Yukon. Out of White Mountain the trail ran through ten miles of hard-frozen muskeg across which James set a medium pace. Rhodes was content to keep him in sight without pushing to pass. He led her up into the three-hundred-foot hills and down across the creeks between them, out onto the Topkok River. At Topkok Head they came onto the sea-ice again and James hung back, which Rhodes took as a signal that they were still cooperating. She passed him and led on, now and again looking back to see his team a couple of hundred yards behind, shadowing her through the night.

She considered letting him win to protect his male ego but immediately dismissed the idea. He was no chauvinist; besides, if he ever found out, the deception would destroy him, and them. She had always been able to lose grace-fully after giving her best shot but she liked winning and James would know instinctively if she held back. There was also Harvey's ten thousand dollars riding on the outcome – Harvey would pay the money with a grin if James honestly beat her but she could never again look him in the face if she threw the race.

She would have to time the final sprint into Nome just right because her dogs, thanks to the bear, were in worse shape than his. They had picked up noticeably – she had observed James too noticing – when she fed them the stinkfish, but not enough: they needed time to rest and recover their strength. The Topkok Valley funnelled the thick wind-angled snow straight into her face. They should have waited until morning – but she could not have slept again. Better to finish it now. She looked in the direction of the town of Bluff, hidden a few miles away by the crests of the terrain and the snow; she thought of Charlie Olson handing over the diphtheria serum to Gunnar Kaasen who would race the fur-wrapped parcel those last few miles into Nome, and of Leonhard Seppala following slowly to let his dogs recover from their heroic exertions. Just before Port Safety, she found a lee in which to feed and rest her dogs. James and his dogs shared the lee with them but they did not speak much in their last break for nourishment or rest until they drove down Front Street in Nome. Rhodes could hardly believe she had made it this far.

After a little over two hours James rose and looked down at her for a moment. 'Afterwards,' he said, then seemed at a loss for anything else to say. 'Afterwards,' he said again, shook the drivebow of his toboggan – and went. 'Afterwards,' Rhodes said softly. She went too. There was nothing left to say before the winning post.

They checked in at the Safety Roadhouse at 7.51 A.M. on the sixteenth day of the race. 'Twenty-two miles to Nome,' said the checker. 'There's six mushers spread between twenty minutes and an hour ahead of you.'

'And behind us?' James asked and Rhodes nodded. Their dogs were not fast enough to catch the front-runners so they could not hope to gain places unless one of these greatly experienced mushers made an irretrievable error. But they were rookies: they were not supposed to be in the top ten – and they would not be if the rightful claimants to those prizes caught up with them.

The checker understood perfectly. 'Bloody Bobby Franks is about eight minutes behind you on the trail down there. He's running like he's got a turpentine rag up his ass.'

James looked at Rhodes. She was beginning to believe with him that some of their competitors never slept. 'He has big dogs,' Rhodes said.

The checker, who had cast a professional eye over their dogs, took the grain of her remark immediately. 'Bobby always goes easy in the early part of the race, saving his dogs, then finishes hard. It's his style.'

Rhodes and James looked at each other and grinned. 'Let's see if we can keep our lead,' James said.

To lighten her sled Rhodes flung everything but the mandatory snowshoes, axe, sleeping bag, booties and post parcel onto the pile of gear discarded by the front-runners. She weighed the pistol and holster in her hand (she had felt so foolish wearing it at her waist that she strapped it to the sled near to hand), decided it was unnecessary weight – *What can happen in twenty-two miles?* – and gave it to the checker to hang on a peg next to the weapons of the front-runners. She studied the wounded dog, considering dropping it because a dog team runs only as fast as the slowest dog in it; she decided not to, because it was trying so hard, a reason she knew to be unsatisfactory and sentimental: she just could not bring herself to drop it after what it had been through with her. James too flung everything out of his sled except the mandatory gear and gave his revolver to the checker for safekeeping. He stuck a finger into one of the cracks on his sled. 'A hairline crack,' he pronounced hopefully. 'Just last until Nome,' he told his toboggan, patting it fondly. The checker hung bib numbers around their necks and checked them out of Port Safety, Rhodes at 7.58 A.M. and James a minute later at 7.59 A.M.

Rhodes set a pace of nine miles an hour, as fast as she dare without her dogs keeling over on her. Norman Vaughan, the Colonel, had told her, 'No matter how you save your dogs all the way to Safety, from there to Nome you must run like you expect every dog to drop dead underneath the arch on Front Street. To Safety you run to satisfy your ego, from Safety to Nome you run for the money.' But her father had another saying: 'To win, first you must finish.' James ran his team right on her heels, pressing, but she resisted the temptation to look back. Two miles out of Port Safety she passed a sign stuck in the ice. *Nome 20 miles*.

Less than a minute beyond the sign she came upon the wolf-pack descended from Big Jim.

She knew the wolves were there even before she saw them lope over the little rise, hardly more than a frozen wave; they ran silently, sleek heads down, not straining, confident they would soon feed.

She looked around and saw James shout a curse or instruction – she could not hear which – over the urgent, terrified barking and whimpering of their dogs. Her own had not recovered from having a teammate killed and eaten right next to them and they were tired, almost as fatigued as their mistress, at the end of twelve hundred miles across Alaska in vicious weather. But, driven by fear, they took off as if they were sprinting in Colorado after a fortnight's rest. Rhodes, still caught up in the race that had become second nature to her, sighed at the realization that now they would consume all their reserves, leaving none for the sprint down Front Street.

In the next moment she adjusted to her new circumstances. *Don't be stupid, Rhodes Delaney!* Yet she still hesitated a moment before shaking the drivebow for even more speed.

A wolf ran past her right knee and she screamed. She raised her boot from the runner to kick at it, then realized it was black and white and in harness. Delilah, James's fast leader. James was driving his team between her and the wolves. For the briefest moment fear, the fatigue of that long trail and lost sleep combined to put a ludicrous thought into her mind: James comes to say, *I told you so*. But he was bent over his toboggan, searching for his firearm, she thought.

'You chucked it out at Safety!' she shouted at him.

He uncovered his short-handled axe and looked doubtfully at it. 'I know that! Yours?'

She shook her head. It was at Safety with his. Weight. Defence. Damn!

Already the wolf-pack was less than a hundred paces from them directly to their right, running on a converging course to intercept them in less than a quarter-mile, less than a minute at their present speed.

James tore his eyes from the wolves and brought his axe from his toboggan. He hefted it in his hand: short-handled, lightweight alloy. It would not be much help against fifty hungry wolves. He threw it back into the basket. What now?

'Hey!' James shouted at Rhodes. Her face was strained and that hurt him; anyone so beautiful should never have to be fearful. Or eaten by wolves ... The thought shocked him as a bucket of cold water thrown into his face would not.

'Hey yourself.'

He was glad to see the little smile on her lips. 'Sorry. My mind . . .' They were so close together, they could almost make normal conversation. The whole business was unreal, happening to someone else. *But I don't want to die!* 'Slow down but keep beside me.'

'What?!'

'Slow down but keep on that side of me. We won't make it to Nome at this rate. We can't outrun them.'

Rhodes looked doubtful but touched the brake with her boot. Toots, looking over her shoulder at her mistress, stumbled and fell. Rhodes drew a sharp, painful breath of freezing air, and let go the brake. In that moment of grace Toots was up and running before the other dogs could overrun her and tangle the harness, immobilizing dogs and sled and musher. The potential disaster averted, Rhodes felt a shiver of foreboding run its icy fingers down her backbone, vertebra by vertebra, a sadist prolonging the pleasure of cruelty. She was damp with the perspiration of fear – not exertion, she had done nothing yet. The same fear burned calories she could ill afford after a fortnight of almost superhuman exertion in sub-zero temperatures. But there was nothing she could do about it. If she contracted frostbite and her ears or nose fell off . . .

If that happens the wolves can have me.

No! It was a stupid thing to think. Defeatist. Perhaps as little as fifteen or sixteen miles down the trail lay Nome, final checkpoint of the Iditarod Trail Sled Dog Race, people and safety and a future. Before then there would be snow machines with people reaching out to meet the mushers and lead them into town.

'James! As fast as you can!'

James looked thoughtfully at the wolves who, on any momentary glance, seemed to progress at the same speed as their quarry and on parallel course but were nonetheless both gaining and closing. He gave his frightened dogs their head and let them match the speed of Rhodes's team. He hoped that when the crunch came, as inexorably it would, the dogs would not be dead beat in their traces. Oh Christ, what a choice!

Almost unnoticed they had returned to the frozen Norton Sound. There was nowhere to hide on the Bering Sea.

The wolves picked up pace to close faster on the two dog teams and their mushers. They were now less than twenty-five paces away.

On one side Siberia, on the other wolves . . .

'Haw, haw, haw!' Rhodes shouted to turn her team left, away from the wolves, towards Siberia. 'Haw, haw!' she heard James shout over the hullaballoo of terrified dogs. But dog teams need space to turn, while a wolf-pack wheels in the length of each individual free-running wolf. *Oh my God, I've cut it too fine for James to turn as well*.

Even then, in that hazardous split second, James had to admire the wolves' superb nerve and supreme timing.

And Rhodes, another superior athlete, felt an overwhelming sadness that now she would never finish the contest, would never reach Nome. *But I will!*

It struck her that this had been a race not against James but against Alaska, represented by its wolves.

We're aimed directly at the heart of Siberia.

'Gee, gee, gee!' Rhodes shouted frantically to turn her dogs back towards Nome. And 'Gee, gee, gee!' as Toots turned reluctantly and the team followed sluggishly, their reflex discipline almost totally eroded by terror of the wolves.

'Gee, gee, gee!' James shouted hoarsely. He dragged his foot offcenter to steer his toboggan to one side, slowing his dogs to give Rhodes room to maneuver as she heaved with scrabbling feet on the mirror-ice at the side of her sled to turn it more tightly.

The wolves were no longer closing, they were *there*, snapping close enough to their prey for the odor of flesh to pervade their nostrils, for the pinpricks of hunger to stab their tongues and cramp their stomachs, near enough to frustrate and enrage them. Rhodes, seeing the saliva fleck from gaping wolf-jaws, suddenly believed that they were *desperately* hungry.

The wolves overshot and the still-turning dog teams ran into their midst.

'YAAAARGH!' James shouted as Delilah plowed into the wolf-pack. An Eighth Dan had once told him Judoka shout not as a ritual but to demoralize and terrify opponents. Anything is worth trying, he thought desperately. Out of the corner of his eye, he saw Rhodes jump back onto the runners, her team almost parallel to his, Toots running straight into the wolf-pack, trying to hold back but running too fast, being too disciplined about sudden stops, having learned too well the painful lessons of being overrun by the heavy team and wheel dogs and the unyielding sled.

Rhodes saw dogs and wolves and sled and man and woman converging on an arrow-point. *How many angels on the head of a pin?* Toots struck a wolf with her shoulder and the wolf, not yet fullgrown, flew away. Strange how her mind calmly fed her images of jeopardy – the wolf-pack turning slowly, ever so slowly to cut off their escape once more – an illusion of perspective at the apex, soon to accelerate blindingly on the roundabout.

It never once occurred to either of us to turn back towards the security of Port Safety and let Bloody Bobby Franks beat us.

'Straight through them and towards Nome!' she shouted

at James. 'Hike!' She shook the drivebow and pumped with her foot. There was a chance it could work: for the moment the wolves were intent on positioning themselves for the attack which –

'No, don't snap at them, you stupid dog!'

Toots snapped at the tail of a wolf at the point where the two arrowheads met, merged and would almost immediately become a tangled bloody mess. Without thinking, Rhodes ran along the side of her sled and grabbed the gangline and ran on, right into the wolf-pack.

Don't stop, don't look down at their gray backs, don't look back. For God's sake, don't look back and show fear!

Six feet to her right, James ran in front of his dogs, gangline in hand. Incredibly there were three wolves between them, two cream and one flecked gray. Fortunately these wolves were still looking for their pack-fellows.

That blessed state could not last long.

Already the wolf at whose tail Toots had nipped was turning towards them, head and body, setting itself up to launch –

Motion caught the corner of her eye. She was past the distraction and turned reflexively to look. The gray wolf between the two cream ones also was turning, face pointed at her, slant eyes already appraising her and testing her. Desperately she tried not to show fear, tried to project *another* conscious thought from her mind: *The face of the wolf is much fuller in the cheeks than that of the Alsatian.* But immediately her fear supplied the reason – *Because the temporal and maseter muscles, the flesh-tearing, bone-crushing engines, are so much more developed all the better to bite you with* – and, before she could tear her eyes away, the hollow in her stomach had flung a bridge to the hollow in the wolf's stomach.

Almost instantly all the other wolves' eyes turned hungrily on her.

In that moment, second perhaps – she knew not how long she stood rooted – her dogs and sled slid by her, the drivebow fell under her hand and –

James saw her hesitate, turned in the act of jumping onto his own runners and shouted desperately, 'Come on!'

– she jumped for the runners.

They broke out of the far side of the wolf-pack. Rhodes shook the drivebow for more speed but her dogs had nothing more to give. She did not have to look around to see the wolves were right behind her, she *knew*.

The wolves, knowing fear precedes submission, now readied for the kill. Noses down, ears flattened, slanted eyes fixed on their quarry, the wolves focussed all their frustration and hunger on the woman, the man and their dogs running terrified before them. They remembered eating another man who had come on a sled, and before him the one in the forest at the alloy-gleaming plane . . .

Rhodes felt breath burning her throat, not the scald of cold but the flowing lava of fear aggravating exhaustion. But the run for their lives had only begun. Their futile earlier turn of speed would now have to be paid for. In her heart and mind she knew they would not survive. They were too near the edge of collapse, too far gone in exhaustion, too sapped of will by two weeks of cold and exertion on the Iditarod. They had no reserves.

But we will run until the dogs drop dead and we drop dead. That won't be long now.

She had never expected to welcome death.

Except that the wolves would eat her alive, tearing her flesh and swallowing chunks of it while she breathed and bled and screamed and –

She could no longer resist the pressure of anxiety. She

253

looked over her shoulder. The wolves had gained but were not straining: their tongues still lolled easily in their obscene pink mouths. They were running their prey over the brink of exhaustion, the way a puma chases mustangs over a cliff to kill them easily. They would become so tired they could not resist when the wolves sliced them with those teeth so prominently displayed. The wolves could lie in a circle at a safe distance and wait for them to bleed to death.

A girl at college had attempted suicide by cutting her wrists while lying in a hot bath; she had reported afterwards that it is by no means as painless to bleed to death as many people believe . . . Rhodes, who had a block about people's names, could remember the girl's name – Maryjane Luxton, twenty, from Dallas, Texas; she had left college shortly afterwards to marry a mortician from Palo Alto.

'Being run over by mustangs is a far better thing!' Rhodes shouted at the wolves and flung out her hand in a sweeping gesture. One part of her fevered mind was rehearsing with her high school drama group.

A wolf snapped at the blood on her mitten. Blood? Where had it come from? A drop of blood splattered her face. *A wolf has bitten one of my dogs*. She looked numbly at her bare hand and, beyond it, the wolf hastily gulping her mitten before the other wolves could take it from him.

Don't touch your face and get blood on your hand.

'Don't touch your face!' James shouted.

But her hand was already feeling for more blood on her face – blood for the wolves to follow! She stared in horror at the blood transferred from her face to her hand.

When she looked up, James was dragging his foot to slow his dogs so that he could fall behind to shield her.

'No! Go, James, save yourself!'

She twisted around on the runners and lashed out with her boot at the wolf still swallowing her mitten. She caught it squarely in the teeth, felt them snap. Blood spurted from the wolf's lips. It gagged on the mitten. She kicked again. The wolf dropped away from her. Instantly the rest of the pack fell on it, a mass of ripping fur and blood.

A moment's respite, she thought without relief, turning away in revulsion. *If they show one of their own kind so little mercy, how much can James and I expect?*

When she looked back there remained on the snow not even a speck of blood. The wolves were twenty paces behind her, gaining fast; several still chewed lumps of the vanquished wolf. James was still slowing.

'Go, James, please! Go!' Her breath sawed in her throat and she slumped over the drivebow of her sled.

James stood on the brake of his toboggan.

'What are you doing? Damn you, you don't have to prove anything to me.' Her anger brought her upright.

'Stop!' he shouted. 'Turn. Show them you're not frightened.'

But I am, more frightened than I have ever been in my life. More frightened than I was underneath the ice on that river, more frightened than when the bear attacked me.

But she too stood on the brake of her sled, with such force that the wheel dogs sat down on the ice and slid for a few yards on their hind quarters before regaining their feet. The dogs looked over their shoulders, first at the wolves fanned out behind the two sleds, then at her, perhaps wondering if she had gone mad.

Not madness, an act of faith in James's judgement; he knew more about wolves than she did and obviously believed that if they kept running they would die.

She scrabbled in the basket for her axe.

A wolf snapped at her heel.

She jerked, slid off the brake. The sled surged forward and the wolf's jaws crunched six inches behind her heel. She swivelled her body from the hip, screaming at the wolf, not words, pure distilled anger, swinging her axe, hitting air as the wolf danced away grimacing. She turned on the runners, changing feet. The wolves had fallen back before the scything axe but now they closed on her again.

Were they warier now she faced them and demonstrably meant to fight?

Her sled was running ahead of James's. She felt behind her with her foot and found the brake, stepping on it too hard, almost losing balance, milling her arms to regain equilibrium as the brake bit. Conjunction of suddenly slowing sled and the way she overbalanced brought the wolves within snapping distance: one closed its jaws on the loose nylon in the armpit of her parka.

Rhodes screamed. She dared not let go with that hand because it was the only one on the drivebow of her sled – in her other hand she held the axe. If she let go she would fall face-first onto the ice under the ravening wolves. That thought, *face-first*, gave her strength.

The ninety-pound wolf swinging from her parka had its paws clear off the ice. Pain seared her. She was convinced her muscles would tear.

James shouted something but she could not make out his words; a red haze blanketed her ears as well as her eyes.

She had no strength to swing the axe into the wolf clenched onto her. Soon the other wolves would bite her elsewhere, not only her clothes but into her flesh.

She relaxed her fingers, allowed the axe to slide through her hand. Oh, so slow! Her fear was so great that her mind tuned out, mercifully detaching itself from her body. She sat in a comfortable seat, watching her ordeal on film.

(With odor capsules: she could smell the rancid carrion on the breath of the wolf and on its pelt.)

When she held the axe just under its head, she shoved the shaft into the wolf's mouth where it clenched the thick fold of her parka. Then she levered. The wolf growled, the parka tore. She heard these sounds, somehow comforting, over all the cacophony of terrified dogs and of James's shouting. The wolf let go as suddenly as it had grabbed her. Taken by surprise, she continued levering the handle of the axe; it tilted crazily and, with all her unbalanced weight behind it, slid down the wolf's mouth and throat. The wolf mewled like a hurt baby. She failed to open her hand in time to let go the axe and followed the wolf down, propelled face-first onto the ice by the abrupt stop her sled now executed; she had kept her foot on the brake until she was pulled from it by the falling wolf.

Please God, let it be quick!

Yet, even as she prayed, the spark of life struggled fiercely for survival; without any conscious prompting, she rolled and rolled again, her feet scything out to tumble a wolf which crossed her course right then and –

Open wolf jaws inches from her face, the wolf's lips mottled gray and black, its mouth inside as pink as its tongue, foam flecking the back of its arched throat and ribbed palate. *It has been running as hard as I have.*

Blood and brains squirted from the wolf's ears before she heard the crunch of bone and saw oozing matter forced out where Nature had provided no orifice. The jaws still snapped shut, though the wolf was dead on its feet. They would have snapped shut on Rhodes's face were it not for James's hand on her collar dragging her clear as he vigorously chopped with his short-handled axe at the wolf's head.

She scrambled groggily to her feet against the leverage

of his hand and he dragged her between the sleds. They stood between the two dog teams, chests heaving. Even over the pounding in her head Rhodes could hear the dogs panting their exhaustion and fear.

For a moment they were safe while the wolves ate the pack-brother into whose gut she had shoved the axe-handle, impaling it, and the other one that James had killed. But soon the wolves would come again.

For a pack of nearly fifty wolves, eating two full-grown wolves took less than sixty seconds, including inevitable fights over choice portions. That minute wasn't long enough for James and Rhodes, or their dogs, to recover.

Rhodes wanted to run in terror but knew she lacked the strength. Nor could her dogs run: they were not even straining to flee – the towline lay slack on the ice. Several of the dogs were lying down, with wolves only forty feet away! She wished she could think of something to say to James but she had no breath for speaking, she could only cling tightly to him.

The wolves approached again, circling, calling to each other, eerily like the distant sound of children talking among themselves, communicating without specific enunciation. Some had blood on the fur around their mouths . . . Some snarled at their prey.

Only a few of the dogs managed a snarl in reply, notably the big wheel and lead dogs. The others whimpered and cringed or lay resignedly awaiting their fate.

A wolf darted towards Delilah.

James pushed Rhodes away and bent over his swing dogs to wield his axe but the handle was too short and the wolf too fast. It escaped unscathed. Another wolf darted towards Rhodes's team, straight at the dog the bear had gashed and whose wound had opened to spray Rhodes with blood (none of her dogs, she now knew, had yet been bitten by a wolf); the blood had clotted and closed the wound again but the odor of it hung in the air, evident even to Rhodes. Where she found the energy, Rhodes would never know. She jumped across her team and stood squarely in the wolf's way, facing it empty-handed. The wolf slithered to a stop just short of her, offered her a whimsical grin, turned and walked casually away, tail twitching.

James cursed.

'What?'

'They're testing us.'

Rhodes had no breath for reply. She darted quick glances here and there, not daring to take her eyes off the wolves for more than a second at a time. Without a weapon she felt naked and vulnerable even though for now the wolves kept their distance, some even lying down and grooming themselves. Others watched Rhodes and James with wary eyes but several – *those who have breakfasted best on their late comrades* – curled up with tails covering their noses and all four paws pressed tightly to their bodies, luxuriant fur protecting them from heat-loss to the sub-zero temperature of the air and snow in which they lay. *They are in no hurry to feed.* Rhodes wondered what would happen if they tried to drive their dogs through the encircling wolves. But she knew already; the wolves would attack. Now she and James had their backs to the sleds, forming a compact front that offered the wolves no opportunity to take them from behind but –

Her eye fell on a wolf chewing the blood-stained handle of her axe, not twelve feet from her, with a relish she found –

'My daddy carved that handle with his own hands!' Before she could stop to think, instinctual outrage propelled her towards the wolf and her boot swung to catch it on the neck behind the ear. The wolf rose over her axe, unwilling to give up the juicy, bloody morsel. It bared its fangs and growled from deep in its throat.

'Rhodes!'

Too late to be cautioned. Too late to let discretion be her best friend. She had taken those few steps and now could not turn her back. Or even walk away backwards. At the slightest sign of weakness the wolf would be on her, tearing her throat.

I should have thought of that before I kicked it. She was a pillar of ice. Her stomach contracted to a baseball, hard and vicious, curving through her from the outfield. Then, suddenly, it relaxed and Rhodes Delaney sighed – *If I delay too long, James will try to help and perish with me* – and stepped forward boldly to die. When the wolf hesitated a mere split-second, she picked up the axe from under its nose.

She had never wanted anything more than she did then to turn and run. But her weight carried her forward, almost onto the wolf.

The wolf, snarling still and unafraid, took a single step backwards prior to launching its attack on her throat. In that microsecond of advantage, while the wolf secured a better angle, she swung the axe with a force she had never known before, cutting its spinal cord, slicing through jugular and muscle so that momentarily it appeared as if the wolf were bending its head in submission. Then the head lolled sideways, almost severed. Blood spurted onto her legs as the wolf's heart beat its last but she stood quite still over her trophy, daring the pack to claim it.

They came, but not too close. She swung the axe again to sever the head, bent, picked it up. Overarm she hurled it at the wolves, who shied away. The head rolled thirty feet beyond them. Every wolf's head turned to follow it, then as one the pack fell upon the single small head. When the melee cleared, two more wolves had been wounded and eaten and a third slunk on the edges of the pack, wounded but not badly enough for the brutal euthanasia of its fellows.

Rhodes did not watch, instead dragging the wolf she had killed by its tail towards her dogs. She wielded her axe to cut the wolf roughly in two while James watched her and the wolves in equal amazement. Rhodes threw one half of the wolf to James's team and the other half to her own team.

'Have a snack,' she said aloud. Her breath had almost recovered its even tenor.

'Feeling better?' James asked. *This is not a woman to be crossed lightly.*

'Much, thank you.'

'That was stupid.'

'I know. I couldn't – '

'And very brave.'

' – let them eat the axe-handle my daddy carved for me. I'm sorry, my darling. I just didn't think.' She walked around the dogs to stand between the teams with him.

'It was exactly the right thing to do.' He hugged her tight. All around them, their dogs tore at the flesh of the dead wolf. Over her shoulder he could see the remaining wolves in a tight circle, noses together, tails waving. *Body language. A conference.*

'I wish I knew what they're saying,' she said.

He decided not to ask how she knew the wolves were conferring when she had her face against his shoulder. 'They're considering whether they're hungry enough to sacrifice some of their number to eat us.'

The wolves broke their circle and reformed it facing outwards. First one started howling, then another and another until all were howling, a very large sound for so few throats, the orchestrated grandeur of nature. Impelled by a force she had never experienced before, eerie and chill, Rhodes flung her head back and defiantly howled back at the wolves. The call to the chase sped the same thrill down lupine and human spines –

– *as the hunting horn down canine, vulpine and red-jacketed vertebrae.*

She had always despised her peers' social-climbing ambition to join the Hunt but now she had greater empathy with hunters and hunted alike. She was not ashamed of venting the impulse to howl with the wolves: on the contrary, she was exhilarated by it and, less rationally, liberated from the stigma of her vengeful killing of the wolf her dogs were even now eating.

The circle broke and, without warning, a wolf launched itself against Rhodes' unprotected back. James had held her throughout, knowing exactly what moved her; now he swung her to one side and down. Before he could follow her to the ice, the wolf hit him squarely on his chest and flung him through the air to land bone-jarringly flat on his back on the ice, sliding out into the open, away from his toboggan, his dogs and Rhodes.

Rhodes, rising to face the wolves, saw them part around the two sleds to stream towards James, closing ranks beyond the sled and the dogs. She turned with them, with the flow, and then she was running towards James: as she ran she saw only too clearly, vignettes in slow motion, the inevitability of disaster, a nightmare spiralling inwards to consume itself in horror.

Rhodes fell over the wolf she was passing. While still in the air, she saw the wolves check, then run on towards James' prone body. But there were more wolves behind her, ever more wolves. She rolled and, still with the momentum of her fall, regained her feet to run on amid the omegas, passing them to catch the betas and the alpha until –

Lycanthropy
I comprehend, for without transformation,
Men become wolves on any slight occasion

I never could stomach Byron.

Beyond James, the wolf who had brought him down slid along the ice and scrambled to its feet but she was nearer to James and the wolf no longer counted, indeed seemed to flinch at the snarl she directed at it.

– until she arrived ahead of every single wolf, to stand spreadlegged over James, to defy the wolves, to be eaten with him if need be, to –

The wolves flowed around them, individual wolves within her range – she could have reached out and petted them, scratched their ears like dogs punished for a misdemeanor but now back in favor – yet none snapped at her and she knew it was over even as the pack, once past them, again turned towards her and James.

James turned between Rhodes' legs and pushed himself to his feet, his hands on the ice betraying fatigue.

'Here comes the Eighth Cavalry.' He pointed, ignoring the wolves still swirling around, as the wolves ignored them. Snow machines raced towards them. A light plane circled overhead and a helicopter thrashed along above the ice, overtaking the snow machines. 'Those houses are the fish camps of Fort Davis. We're two miles from Nome.'

Incredulously Rhodes looked the other way. Yes, there was Cape Nome, *behind* them.

The last of the wolves streamed in bifurcated flow past the two mushers who no longer feared them, parting ten feet from the man and the woman, running around their dogs, joining again ten feet behind the sleds. The humans were no threat but not food either. The wolves would return to their original territory where, even if they did

263

not all reach it, they felt safe as Nature's servants. The forest was their home and they longed to be there.

Rhodes fondled Toots' ears reassuringly. 'I feel as if I understand these wolves.'

'They're returning to their forest,' James said with conviction.

They have tested us. That is the way of the wolves. In their own territory, they know each and every animal through testing it several times a year: when the animal weakens, they kill and eat it. To them, I am simply another animal to test and, eventually, to kill and eat. Weirdly – and she knew it was weird – she was comforted by her knowledge and acceptance of her foretold and inevitable place in the food-chain of life.

Rhodes pointed to a thick black horizontal line, with a small vertical bright orange bar stopping its rear end, approaching them from the skyline. 'Bloody Bobby Franks.'

'The people in the snow machines will want explanations.'

After what they had just gone through she did not want to race even two miles against him – but a thing completely done is a thing well done.

'They can wait. So can Bobby,' she said.

He grinned at her. 'Yes, let's finish the job. See you under the arch. Hike!'

'Under the arch. Marchez!'

12
Nome

It was like descending a mountain handcuffed to a rolling rock. Her body still shook from the confrontation with the wolves, the fear of her final bravado stupidity catching up with her, adrenalin only now coursing to the extremities of her system. It had all happened so quickly. Her breath rasped even as she called 'Marchez!' Dutifully her dogs broke into a ragged run but the rankest novice could have seen how near the verge of collapse they were, dogs and musher both. James and his dogs, running parallel to her, twenty paces to her right, were no better. After two weeks on the trail running had become a habit. Somewhere vaguely at the back of her fraying mind she was grateful for the established routine of driving relentlessly towards Nome: for the moment it would keep them from having to talk to people, from explanations. After she passed under the victory arch in Front Street – if she reached Nome, if she did not fall off the runners first – she knew that for a day or a week she would be disoriented: having striven singlemindedly that far, and suddenly arriving, she then would have no purpose. But there would be people to help her over the hump into reality, people she loved: her father, Margery and Harvey. And James.

People shouted at her from a snow machine. She shook her head. The question was repeated. 'Is that hand in your pocket hurt?'

'Wolf ate my mitten.'

'Here, catch!'

A mitten curved through the air. She removed her hand from her pocket just in time to field it; she had almost let

265

go of the drivebow with her other hand. Look Ma, no hands. Look Ma, no sled. I fell off less than a mile from the victory arch at the end of twelve hundred miles and lacked the guts to limber my body erect and finish the race.

James nodded his head rhythmically over the drivebow, passing into moments of unconsciousness. The decision to run just two more miles demanded, relative to his remaining energy, almost as much as crossing Alaska or fighting off the wolves. Every time the Yellow Cab on runners came too close, pulled by a team of desperately hungry wolves, he would waken. He wondered if he should stop and change leaders: General would be more dependable through the streets of Nome and the boisterous crowd that would spill out of bars and shops and houses. But Rhodes ran right beside him and he would lose precious minutes, never to be recovered. Toots would be perfectly at ease with people and vehicles: Rhodes in Colorado famously used her team like other people use a car, to run into town for post and groceries . . .

'Hey, if you fall asleep, you'll fall off,' he shouted at her.

Her head jerked up.

Both teams stood still. People shouted questions at them from a snow machine. Rhodes and James shook their heads. Then their heads hung again. 'Bloody Bobby Franks is catching up fast!' a voice shouted. They did not look around. They were too exhausted even to swivel their eyes towards where the trail turned off the frozen ice of the Bering Sea into the intensely desired and long-dreamed-of Nirvana of every dog-sled racer in the world, Nome. At the western end of Front Street, in front of City Hall, stands the arch built by Red Olson from a huge spruce sawn down the middle and carved with the words *End of Iditarod Sled Dog Race 1049 Miles Anchorage to*

Nome: it marks the exact place where in 1925 Gunnar Kaasen delivered the fur-wrapped parcel of diphtheria serum. And there the Mayor of Nome now waited for them to hand over their symbolic cachets carried from Anchorage to Nome by dog sled.

Toots lifted her leg against the snow machine. Rhodes heard the hiss of hot liquid on the ice. For a long moment she stared at the dog and the dog stared back at her. The act of nonchalance infuriated her.

'This is a race! Hike! Hike!' And, before the startled James could react, she gained thirty yards on him.

'Dammit, she's right! The race isn't over. Hike! Go, go, go!'

They ran down Front Street's four lanes but Rhodes in her mind saw the narrow old street with its falsefronted frontier buildings, lined by serious-faced townspeople wondering desperately whether the serum was in time to save their children.

The lights of a police car flashed as it led her in; she could not remember when it had appeared but it was part of the grand Iditarod welcome. The men in the car beamed at her and pointed to her right. She turned her head to see Delilah level with her and gradually gaining. Rhodes shook the drivebow of her sled but her dogs had nothing more to give. The race was now in the hands of men long dead, of Charlie Olson and Gunnar Kaasen and Leonhard Seppala. Merely shaking the drivebow wearied her. She did not want to shout: this was a hallowed moment, as if she were an architect who had built a cathedral. She did not hear the crowd lining the street, the fire siren announcing their arrival, the Dr Schultz Last Frontier Band (Official Iditarod Band) striking out from the door of the Bering Sea Saloon.

James too was in a daze, partly in amazement that he had made it this far. But exhaustion also informed his incredulity that he had jumped badly, twisted a ski on landing, and was now rolling downhill at a gathering pace. Yet, clearly, he saw Delilah reach Rhodes's heels, then his swing dogs level with her, then the team dogs . . .

Past the police car with its flashing lights he could see the chute of snow-fencing through which they would race towards the arch. He shook the drivebow but his dogs had nothing in reserve. Then James remembered . . . A little smile grew about his lips, all the jubilation that exhaustion would allow. Yes, Rhodes was right. It *was* a race. He reached into his sled to –

Rhodes saw James directly beside her, levelpegging.

They entered the chute side by side. The police car had turned off unnoticed. Before them stood the victory arch, the platform and the waiting Mayor.

Rhodes saw her father in the crowd. He smiled gently, encouragingly. Harvey shouted at her, words lost in the crowd noise. Before them Margery jumped up and down excitedly without letting go of Dave's hand. Rhodes saw James –

– pull the whip out and –

Rhodes smiled delightedly across the few feet separating them. Yes, still a race!

– smiled at Rhodes and raised the whip and cracked it high over the heads of his dogs and felt the jerk through his arms as the startled dogs pulled with their very last ounce of strength and Delilah edged ahead of Toots –

First dog's nose across the finish line wins!

That was when Rhodes raised her voice to shout one single hoarse word over the heads of her dogs –

'*Stinkfish!*'

– and her dogs, conditioned throughout their training by receiving this special delicacy for one final effort above and beyond the courage of sawing breath and aching lungs and burning muscles, found in their love for her a single last spurt of power. They lurched forward almost on the line.

James jumped from the runners to smack the arch with the palm of his hand, and so did Rhodes. Their crazy momentum carried them forward to fall on their faces in the snow, facing their dog teams which had turned because there was nowhere else to go; they were at the end of the line.

An amplified voice boomed at them. It was lost as the balls of fur jumped on them and, catching the excitement of the finish, started wagging tails in their faces and trying to lick them at the same time. James found her and clasped her to him as they rolled together in the snow.

Rhodes was content to roll and roll. 'Stinkfish!' James chuckled into her ear. They laughed and laughed to celebrate the delicious secret of all the years they would share.

Acknowledgements

A novel such as this is never written without a great deal of help. In particular I should like to thank Alaska Administration Commissioner Lisa Rudd for introductions I would not otherwise have known I needed; and Alaska State Historical Library Librarian Phyllis DeMuth for pointing me to people, other libraries and institutes of specialist knowledge internationally, and for copying for me taped interviews with Joe and Vi Redington and with John Poling. These interviews were originally conducted by the Iditarod National Historic Trail Office Project of the US Bureau of Land Management, whom I also thank for their foresight. The British Broadcasting Corporation's 1979 program on the race served to renew my awe of Alaska and its people and was the direct impeller of this novel. Though this book was written before the appearance of Tim Jones's *The Last Great Race* (published by Madrona, Seattle), now that it is available Mr Jones must surely earn the esteem of anyone who wants to know about the spirit of Alaska and its people; I found it invaluable for checking race-facts, names of people and places, and as an arbiter of variant spellings. Irish Helicopters freely supplied information on survival procedures under adverse climatic conditions; the modest desire for anonymity of the prince of researchers at the Scott Polar Research Institute Library in Cambridge makes me none the less delighted for xeroxes of as-yet unpublished draft papers exactly covering my requirements. Then there was the tolerance at being called away from their dinners or their work or even sleep when I mixed international time zones, exhibited by nearly two dozen experts, researchers and consultants on wolves, conservation, Siberia, the Black Death, sub-zero temperature medicine, endurance psychology and diverse other specialities; their patience, under pressure for unequivocal plain-language answers to questions they have spent a lifetime defining, is here rewarded by anonymity to protect their hardwon reputations against slips or irresistible flights of a novelist's fancy – my gratitude to them is matched only by my reluctance to forego the pleasure of dropping so many eminent names. It goes without saying that errors of commission or omission should be laid solely at my door.

A few notable Alaskans are mentioned by name and many of the real-world heroes of the Iditarod Trail Sled Dog Race are shown passing through on their way to the Iditarod Hall of Fame at Knik. I trust they will forgive the presumption of taking their names in the interest of heightened reality.

A writer's physical tools are normally not important but this book would have been more difficult to write without my battery-operated Epson PX-8 portable computer; it works in places electricity has not reached, continues to operate after typewriters have frozen solid, and is the only laptop wordprocessor that survives the tender attentions of airline luggage handlers. I am most grateful to Gerald van de Poll and the service department of Europlex in Dublin for cheerfully and promptly servicing my hard-used electronics, and to Jerry Sweeney of Chip Electronic Services in Cork for wielding his artistic soldering iron in emergencies.

Much thanks to my wife Rosalind for reading the final version of the manuscript and to our son Charles for the odd spot of quiet at crucial moments.

Finally, a very special word of thanks to my friend Stuart Jay who, on this as on other novels of mine, generously sacrificed his sleep for the persuasive power of my ideas, the propriety of my syntax and the greater glory of my prose; may none of his novels take a decade to write and may all be best-sellers.

André Jute
Alaska & Co. Cork, Eire, 1979–1989